P9-CNI-215

TO MATT WITH LOVE

MOON
& SUN
I

Chapter 1
Before the Offering

The sun slid down toward the tops of the trees. I only watched for an instant, for though everyone in Hillrush had been working since before sunrise, we were not yet finished. We raced the sun, and at that moment it seemed it would beat us all.

My best friend, Catri, lugged the last wandering lamb from her family's flock into the barn, and her oldest brother trudged in, carrying his cot and blankets and a long knife and a bow and arrows. Catri told him, "Mama said she'd bring your drink and dinner before the offering." And then she turned to me. "Any chores you have left, Genna?"

I said, "Nothing that has to be done by daylight. I have spinning and knitting tonight, but I've done the milking and the wash and brought in the clothes."

Catri's mother raced past us in one direction, chasing her three youngest children into the house. She would not attend the offering; her husband would offer for her and for himself and for his oldest son, while she kept the children safe.

Hargard the priest ran in the other direction, past the Justice Tree and toward the prayer house, his green tunic and baggy breeches flapping behind him. He glanced over his shoulder at the sun, muttered, "Oh, Spirit and little gods preserve us," and picked up his pace.

Catri and I looked at each other, suddenly uncertain. I said, "Uncle Banris wanted to make an offering for us this year."

"You told me," Catri said.

I had. I'd forgotten. So many things were going wrong. Papa had been missing for two years and was surely dead, and we struggled on with that. But recently Mama had gotten sick with the *saku*, which caused the sort of confusion and wandering that had taken Papa from us, and lately, she never remembered to eat. I overheard the yervi who'd come to treat her sickness tell Uncle Banris that she probably would not live to see the next season's offering. Uncle Banris, meanwhile, hung over Mama like a blue-cloaked version of

Death, badgering her to marry him so her children would not be orphaned.

And poor Mama, so lost and confused most of the time, kept telling Banris that she could not marry him while Papa was still alive.

She had asked me, as the oldest of her seven children, to give our gifts to the nightlings that night in her stead.

We had little enough to give. With Mama so sick, with Papa dead — or mad and starving and wandering through the wilds, which meant dead — my brother Danrith and I were the working members of our family. Danrith was twelve and I was fourteen, so we were near enough to being adults that our work was acceptable for offerings. But we were not as quick about our work or as skilled as our parents had been.

Catri said, "Papa told me I could offer for myself tonight."

I brightened. I was afraid to do my first offering. I'd been sure I'd be there alone, the youngest, the only one offering for the first time. But if Catri was going . . .

"Papa said he thought I'd be able to help you, and you'd be able to help me."

I would have hugged her father right then, had he not

been helping the other men carry the village's heaviest bounty to the Treaty Stone.

"I have two bolts of fine winter wool," I told her. "The last of Mama's weaving and the best of mine. And we're giving a copy of the village daybook that Danrith transcribed, plus two bag-cheeses that I made."

A silence followed. Catri elbowed me, and I realized that I'd been frozen in place, staring at the setting sun. She pulled her family's crop wagon behind her. I saw one finished dress in it, made to a design the nightlings provided. "My offering," she said.

I looked at the dress in awe. The cloth had not come from the village but from the nightlings themselves. It was beautiful, shimmery stuff, finer than the finest silks I'd ever seen. Catri had made the cloth into a simple dress, but the plain cut of the material only showed off her gorgeous stitching and the careful way she'd pieced colors together so that they flowed into and out of one another. It was the most beautiful dress I'd ever seen.

We dragged the wagon past the Millard house, and past Old Gentimy, widowed as long as I'd been alive, who was lugging last fall's potatoes out of her root cellar to her wheelbarrow to take to the Treaty Stone. She's old and alone and poor. She can offer potatoes, and no one will punish her.

Hargard the priest had slipped around us somehow, and was walking from window to window at our house, closing the shutters and painting a circle of vinegar and pine pitch on each one, muttering the blessing against the dark as he did so. I could hear Danrith on the other side, bolting each shutter into place as the priest finished.

I hurried in.

"Not much time left," Dan told me.

"I'm getting our offering now," I said and ran into the kitchen, where I'd set everything aside earlier. The cloth and the cheeses were there. Dan's book was not.

My heart leapt like a startled lamb, and I checked the table and under the table and in the folds of my two bolts of cloth. Nothing.

The missing book would be Dan's fault, I knew. Or at least I hoped. So I gathered up everything on the table and on my way past him said, "Bring the daybook out to Catri's wagon, and hurry. She and I are going together, and the sun is close to the horizon."

He had the grace to look chagrined. "I forgot to put it back. I added extra," he said and ran up the stairs to the room that had been Papa's study, and that Uncle Banris had taken over, even though our house is not his house.

He ran down the stairs with it in his hand, a small

leather-bound book filled with Dan's careful writing. Columns of numbers — the counts of our herds and people, the produce the village sold, the items it bought — all gathered and brought to our house by the villagers, for Danrith kept Hillrush's counting just as Papa had trained him. He couldn't do the justice as Papa had, of course. Uncle Banris did that.

But Dan kept all the sums and trades, and understood the picture they painted, too.

After the offering, the nightlings would have a copy of those numbers. Why they would want them, I could not imagine. Papa, though, had included a copy of Hillrush's daybook in the first spring offering each year. So Danrith did the same.

With all our offering in the wagon, Catri and I ran to the edge of town, the wagon behind us banging and rattling over the ruts in the road. A bonfire burned in the firepit at the north edge of the Treaty Stone. The sun had not yet set, but the bonfire would tell the nightlings the offering waited. Once dark came, they would arrive and take it all away.

Hargard had finished blessing the village's windows and doors, though he had probably trusted many of the houses to his assistants. There are fifty-four dwellings in the village, after all. More than three hundred people live in Hillrush, and they all count on the blessings, for the nightlings could slip through unblessed windows and doors and take away children or adults. Hargard stood in the center of the Treaty Stone, waiting for Uncle Banris to arrive so that he could bless us and our offerings, and ask Spirit and the little gods for our protection through the night.

Lately, it seemed neither Spirit nor little gods had much interest in keeping us and ours safe. After almost every offering, someone had gone missing — sometimes several people — always boys and girls, or young men and women just arrived at adulthood.

But though we seemed to have lost the favor of our Spirit, still we prayed.

The village adults arrived as we did, dragging or carrying offerings, gathering around the low, flat circle of the Treaty Stone, waiting.

Catri and I stood back a bit, but those older and taller than us scooted us toward the center, toward the edge of the stone itself. The words of our treaty with the nightlings were carved into it. The treaty is long, and tedious to read, and the site carries the feeling of a curse about it, so none of us lingers there.

Uncle Banris arrived, dressed in his finest clothing, and pushed his way through everyone to walk into the center of the stone, beside Hargard. Papa had once done that, I thought, though I had never seen it. And I could not imagine Papa ever having been so rude, or so overbearing. Banris raised his hand and said, "The moon is full, and tonight will stand in the sky as witness to this remembrance of the peace we made with those who haunt the darkness. We, too, stand witness, that we keep within our bounds as the nightlings keep within theirs. That we bear no weapons against one another or against the creatures of night. That we give thanks for the mercy we are shown, and that we remember to show mercy in our turn."

No one said anything. They would have cheered for Papa, I thought, because everyone loved him. And his words would have been better.

Banris started to say something else, but one of the old farmers at the back said, "Would you talk till the sun sets, you fool? Let the priest speak his piece, and let us pitch our treasures and flee. We'll give thanks for nightling mercy when our bellies are less empty."

Catri and I heard cheers for that.

Hargard looked awkward and uncomfortable as he stepped forward. "Spirit with us, guard and guide us. Little gods, light the paths of our feet. See us safely home by dark and safely here by next light."

Then he stepped off the Treaty Stone.

Mother Beechalt, who lived across the street from my house and who was friends with Catri's parents and who had been friends with mine, said, "Go, girls, put your things in first and hurry home."

The nightlings take children and young men and women in preference over all others. Everyone understood, and they made way for us. I placed our household offerings on the center of the treaty, where Uncle Banris had just stood. A few women nodded approval at my cheeses and murmured good words about the cloth. The men muttered gratitude that Jhontar's boy Danrith had kept up the accounting of our village. Girls older than we whispered envy at Catri's beautiful dress.

We did not stay to see what else went on the pile, though. The sun sat fat and orange on the horizon, and the valley below us already lay in darkness. The nightlings would be there, perhaps looking up toward us. They would be coming up the hill soon.

We held hands and ran back to the path that would take Catri to her home and me to mine.

We hugged each other. "Be safe," she whispered to me.

"You, too." And then I laughed. "We can sneak out at first light to see what they brought for us in return."

Nightling offerings are usually trinkets — beads or shiny bits of glass made to look like gemstones, fancy colored feathers. Never food, never cloth, never anything practical. But that is the way the treaty goes. We give what we have. They give what they have.

"Our first offering," Catri said. "I thought it would be . . . different. That it would feel more important."

I shrugged. "Meet me here first thing in the morning and we'll go back to the stone. Maybe it will feel more important then."

I did not tell her that Danrith and I had another adventure planned for Offering Night — one that made putting the offering on the Treaty Stone seem like nothing by comparison.

Chapter 2
The Forest by Night

Outside, something scratched at the shutters Hargard had blessed, but I pretended not to hear it. "True dark is here," I told my brother Danrith. "The yervi is attending Mama; the younglings are all in bed. Uncle Banris must have locked himself inside the cellar again — I've heard nothing of him since twilight."

"We can't go yet," Dan told me. "I hear nightlings outside the window. And whispering."

"No you don't."

"I do, though, Genna," he said. I heard the pleading in his voice. "They're saying, 'Come. Hurry, children. There is but little time.' *Nightlings.* And on Offering Night."

I gave him a stare I hoped would still his flapping tongue. "Since we must go out, and since we plan to hurry, both we and your nightlings will get what they want."

He clutched at my sweater, knit by Mama for me when she was still well, imbued with her love and a handful of spells. I pulled away from him, and he whispered, "We can't just give ourselves to them."

I turned on him, instantly and unreasonably angry. I heard what he heard; I knew he was telling the truth. But it didn't matter. "Stop it!" I whispered, not wanting to warn Uncle Banris that we were anywhere but in bed. "We have this one chance to save Mama — this one night, Danrith Caersson of High House, and barely enough time to sneak out and get what we need and slip back inside before Uncle Banris catches us. We don't have time for omens and portents and creatures. Nor for waiting nightlings who've come to spirit us away."

I grabbed his shoulders and stared into his eyes — at the same level as mine, though he is two years younger than me — and said, "By next season's offering, she'll be dead, Dan. It's now or not at all."

He stood before me, quiet, with huge, frightened eyes. After a long moment, he nodded. "I'm taking Papa's sword," he said.

"You can't. Just by being outdoors tonight, we risk breaking the treaty. If you carry a weapon, we might as well declare war."

My brother looked at me out of the corner of one eye and said, "Let it go, Gennadara Yihannisdattar of High House, if you want to be naming true names. The nightlings are not our only danger. The ghost said I'd need it." He pulled Papa's sword from behind the shelf of Papa's common-law books, where it did not belong.

So he had been planning on saddling us with it all along.

I would have fought him over the bringing of the sword, but first, the noise might have caught the attention of Uncle Banris, and since Papa disappeared, Banris had turned strange and frightening. We did not want his attention. And second, we had no time to argue.

So I turned my back on Dan and gathered pails, spikes, taps, and a mallet, and told him, "Get the white staff and the twine." And then I unbarred the heavy oak door and stepped out into darkness and silence.

The full moon had not yet risen over the treetops, luckily for us. Light slipped between cracks in the shutters of our house and the other houses in the village. Barns, too, were shut up and locked for the night, all the animals tucked safely away with someone inside to make sure the doors stayed closed. No villagers moved outside their houses, nor would they until the sun touched the horizon in the morning. This was Offering Night, when nightlings had full right to enter the village, and when anything left out might disappear by dawn.

Including Dan and me. But we didn't have any other choice.

So we walked to the forest by moonlight, my brother and I, into the heart of the nightlings' domain.

"You should have told the servants to take the pails and gather the sap by daylight," Danrith said as we crept through the maze of trees. "I can hear things moving out here."

"You think they would listen to me? They listened to Papa before he disappeared. But with Mama so sick, the servants don't bring anything back anymore." I sounded frustrated, I realized. "They take everything they gather for their own families, and say the trees weren't generous. And Mama will die if we don't get the sap. Or wander away some night like Papa did, and die where we'll never find her."

In the spring, in the hardwood forest to the west of Hillrush, the sap begins to rise. And in the ancient, deep-rooted taandu trees, magic rises with it, rich and strong and vital. Mama, who is the village yihanni still, even though she is so ill, uses the taandu sap to weave protections against the nightlings for the whole village, and spins out blessings over new babies, and wardings around children on their true name days, and childgifting for couples newly married, and a hundred other things. The village healers, the yerva, make medicines with it to keep people and livestock and crops healthy. Our papa's longtime best friend, who has always been Uncle Banris to us and who took Papa's place as caer of Hillrush when Papa caught the *saku*, deals with the other villages and the capital as well as with the nightlings who haunt the world after sunset. He sets up trades when we have more taandu sap — or any other thing — than we need, or when we haven't enough, and offers justice in the village, as Papa once did — though Papa was beloved and Uncle has become despised.

Among other things, we trade in taandu sap, since Hillrush sits next to the Nightling Forest, and since the sap is so important to the humans of Aeiring. Once a year, for three short months, every adult well enough to walk and carry pails goes into the forest to tap the taandu trees; our villagers harvest the sap, which will be the village's magic until the next year. We harvest by day, because of rule, covenant, and promise, and all the villagers are out of the forest and into marked human spaces before last light. It's as well, truly. In daylight the sap runs clear, and in daylight the forest is mostly safe — though not safe enough for children. Which was why we were sneaking out at night — no adult would let us travel in the forest by day.

Not even Mama or the yerva enter the forest by night.

"They're whispering again," Dan insisted.

The wooden pails banged against my left leg, and the mallet and taps in them rattled. I held my spike, which I would use to make holes in the tree's bark, tighter. The dirt road that led into the forest glowed in the moonlight. Shadows moved across it, seemingly unconnected to anything in the real world. The chill in the air raised gooseflesh on my arms, and the soft, irregular rustling and clacking of grasses and branches made it seem we were not alone. But we could not go back to the house without at least two full buckets of sap that I could boil down to make into a healing syrup for Mama. We couldn't. So I lied.

"I don't hear anything," I told Dan.

He was twelve, old enough to apprentice in a man's work — and he was apprentice caer, though Uncle had not bothered to continue to teach him since Papa went missing. But Danrith hated the darkness much more than I; he slept on the floor near the hearth at night, not for the warmth but for the light. "Genna, you need not pretend. I'll not run home and leave you here alone. But I'm going to draw the sword."

"You can't." I turned to glare at him. "If you walk in the forest with blade drawn and unprovoked, you'll declare war."

"And if I don't, and if the nightlings have already declared war, we'll die, and if we die, that will be the end of Mama, too. And then who will care for Ebecka and Lil, and Morith and the twins? We have to live through this," he said. His voice sounded sullen.

"You *must* keep the promise. We travel under nightling mercy right now. If they attack us, draw the sword. That's forgivable. But you won't have to. They, too, have much to lose by breaking covenant. They'll lose Offering Night, for one thing. When we get to the first untapped tree, we'll stand back to back, and I'll hold my spike tightly, and you will keep your hand on the sword hilt. And we'll stand like that until the moon begins to set and we have to leave. We'll be safe enough."

He gave me a narrow-eyed look I didn't like at all. But I was oldest, and as long as I was the oldest person around him, my word was rule. He would obey me, and he would abide by rule and covenant — at least long enough to get us well into trouble. In his eyes, though, I saw that rule, covenant, and promise would fall by the wayside the instant he thought us in danger, and the village would find itself at war next morning and never know why.

We live uneasily side by side with the nightlings. They hold the heart of the forest and the southern meadows, and graze their beasts by moonlight there and even in the full dark. We hold all of the village and fields of Hillrush and the meadows to the north and the edges of the forests.

The promise is that our peoples will not cross into each other's territories with weapons bared, that we will act as neighbors, and that we will not travel at all through the heart of each other's domains uninvited.

So we live by rule, which is simple:

Mankind is Sunkind,
And rules by the light;
Sun's rise to sun's set,
No less and no more.
Nightlings are Moonkind,
And rule in the night;
Sun's set to sun's rise,
Or there will be war.

And we adhere to covenant, which is the treaty hammered out by Sunkind and Moonkind, by dayfolk and nightlings, after the bloodiest war the world had ever seen. And we keep our promise, which is our peace. But we live nervously.

THE FOREST BY NIGHT

Since Papa disappeared, Dan had sworn he heard nightlings whispering outside our windows after dark. Uncle Banris says Dan is a liar, and that nothing he says is to be heeded. But though he is twice as bothersome as most younger brothers, I've found him honest in all other ways. Dan stays by fire and light and sleeps lying atop an old sword he took from Papa's chest after . . . well, after. And when he sleeps, he talks in a stranger's voice.

He and I moved under the canopy trees, into the deeper dark of the forest, but were careful not to leave the road. Because the trees had not yet leafed out, moonlight still reached us, but the shadows grew livelier and more numerous.

Dan started looking around. "Not yet," I told him. "We have to find a big, old tree. Otherwise, we won't get enough sap tonight to do any good. We won't get a second chance to just walk out of the village."

"It's not going to do any good anyway," Dan said. "When we take our two buckets of sap to the yerva, she'll see that it's dark instead of clear, and she will know what we've done. And she won't touch it."

This was true. Night sap is tainted by moon magic. Humans never use it or trade for it. I've heard it's poison to us, though Mama thought it was dangerous in some other fashion. But night sap was all we could get, because both of us were still too young to be permitted into the forest by day. But we weren't going to a yervi, something I hadn't yet told Dan. "I'll boil the sap down to syrup for her myself," I said. "And I'll spell it." I had determined that my mother was going to live no matter what I had to do to make it so. I was certain my intent would protect Mama from the dangers of night taandu sap — intent, after all, is what guides the effects of day sap. Mama would live, I swore, to keep my sibs and me safe. Papa had gone where he could not look out for Mama, and Uncle Banris frightened me. When he called me to bring him something, I did not like the look in his eyes as he regarded me. Mama still had clear times, and a way of appearing silently from around corners that kept Uncle Banris careful around me and my sibs, but if Mama died not only would I lose her, but I would have to flee our home and our village, and take my younger brothers and sisters with me. I would not trust their safety to Banris's care without Mama around.

Dan and I pushed deeper into the forest, away from the young trees at the edge, until the forest cut off any view of the meadow behind us. And now I clearly heard voices, whispers from the trees above us and from the forest to either side of us. I clenched my spike so tightly my hand hurt, and my fingers felt like they would never straighten again once I let go.

Dan said nothing now, and neither did I, but we looked at each other, and could see our own fear reflected in each other's eyes.

Dan nodded to a massive old taandu tree just ahead, and we picked up our pace. He planted our white pole in the road, hammering it into the dirt with the mallet. The white pole serves two purposes: It marks the road for those who must step into the true forest, and it reminds the nightlings of covenant and promise. We are your neighbors, it says. Under duress, we have your word for our safety.

Dan began to unreel the twine we tied to the white staff. Then we stepped off the road onto the pillowed, sweet-scented loam of the true forest. The sound of our footsteps faded to our own ears, and the voices grew louder. We did not look for the nightlings; we knew from stories that we would never see them unless they chose to be seen. We knew, though, that they watched us.

At the tree, we put down our buckets, and I held the spike steady with both hands. Dan hammered it in, making a hole big enough to fit one of our taps.

"This is harder than I thought it would be," he said.

"It goes in the depth of a finger," I told him.

"It may. But the tree is made of iron, I swear."

We kept at it, and I saw the last of the black disappear, and the white line on the spike go flush with the bark.

"Stop. This one is ready."

We loosened it with the bucket peg attached to the bucket for just that purpose, and even so, it still needed both of us pulling with our full weight to free the spike. Dan put the tap in, and we hooked our first bucket over the hook at the end.

"One more," I said.

The tree fought the next spike just as hard, and we stood damp with sweat when sap finally started to flow into our other bucket.

We looked at the moon. It had not yet reached its midpoint in the sky; we had a lot of darkness still before us. "Back to back," Dan said. "And touching, so that nothing comes between us."

We leaned against the tree so that we were guarded on one side. Our backs touched, as did the backs of our heads. I could hear Dan's breathing, as quick and nervous as my own, and I could only wish to see the moon race across the sky. Dawn could not arrive fast enough for me.

Above us and around us, the voices grew shrill. Words we did not understand, cadences alien to our ears, emotions that echoed of anger and fear — but who among the nightlings would fear us? Who would be angry with us? They didn't know us. We weren't anyone. We weren't even adults.

Then the forest fell silent. All the voices stopped, and with them, the breeze through the trees and the mutterings of the birds and the calls of hunting animals. All the night froze, and neither Dan nor I dared remark on it. We were so frightened, I could hear neither his breathing nor my own. Beside us, from both taps, dark sap dripped into wooden buckets with a hollow echoing *plink, plink* that seemed in the terrifying stillness to be as loud as the ringing of bells.

We waited, knees trembling and mouths dry, crowding close to each other like cornered lambs trapped away from their mothers.

"Don't draw the sword," I whispered to Dan, so low I feared he might not hear me. "Not yet."

"I won't," he said. "Unless they come after us."

A pause, and the forest seemed to breathe in. And then, a musical voice above us. "I will not come after you. I wish only to speak with you, but with my own safety guaranteed."

We could never mistake that voice for human. Not ever. Notes layered over notes, low tones and high in the same syllable, as if the speaker had several voices that chimed in harmony. A lute player strikes one string and many vibrate in sympathy — a nightling speaks, and music happens. I love to sing, though I have a crow's voice, but hearing the nightling speak, I thought I would never sing another note.

"So long as you don't attack us, we will guarantee your safety," I said.

"Then I will come down and speak with you. Should you harm me, you'll die before you draw a second breath, and we'll overrun your village and slaughter everyone in it before the sun rises."

"We know rule, covenant, and promise," Dan said, and I could hear an edge of anger in his voice.

A silence. Then the nightling dropped to the ground beside us, a few steps away from the tree and just beyond our reach. In the darkness, I could see only the pale, delicate oval of a girl's face, a silhouette slender to the point of fragility, and the centers of two dark eyes, pupils huge and luminous and reflective as a cat's. She had neither wings nor talons nor fangs, though I had heard nightlings could have all three. And yet the nightling, even in silhouette, could never be mistaken for human. "Your uncle, Caer Banris, broke both covenant and promise. And this is why your people die."

I turned and shook my head. "He's not our blood uncle — he was our father's friend. And now he is the caer. But he keeps rule, covenant, and promise."

The nightling uncovered a tiny crystal that hung about her neck, and pale light surrounded her. She had skin the soft yellow of a farm duck's chick, and hair the bright gold of buttercups. It stood out from her head like dandelion puffs just before the wind blows them away. She stood a head shorter than me, and wore a boy's breeches and jerkin and high, wrap-laced boots — but I could no more have mistaken her for a boy than I could have mistaken my beautiful mother for one.

I felt, oddly, that I knew her, which was nonsense, of course, for nightlings and humans were forbidden to meet. But still, the feeling persisted.

She said, "Banris of Greathaven, now caer of Hillrush, went to the kai-lord before the sap-run three years ago, requesting the magic of immortality and power. These are our magics to give, but we do not share them with your kind, so our kai-lord told him to go back to his village and live the life he had earned. But this Banris said that if the kai-lord could make him caer, and then master of all

Aeiring, he would give the kai-lord two hundred sixty vials of daylight taandu essence each year — sixty-five at each season's trade — and his pick of ten servants from among your people at Allsummerday, and one ten-square bolt of purple silk each year in exchange for these secrets, and swore the lives of the villagers as forfeit should he not keep his word."

I looked at her, trying to make sense of what she said. "But the kai-lord told him no, of course."

"The kai-lord loves to bargain, especially when he is sure to get the better of the deal. He cannot get pure daylight taandu essence except from humans. The buckets cannot be placed until the sun has risen, and must be drawn in before it sets — and his nightling slaves cannot leave Arrienda until the sun falls below the horizon, and must be back inside the gates before the smallest edge creeps over the horizon. So he treasures daylight taandu essence. Nightlings have no means to make purple dyes, either, so our silks are never purple. And none of your kind serve with the nightlings by choice, yet the kai-lord and his court have as much use for slaves as any."

"Your kai-lord told him yes," Dan whispered.

"He did."

"Three years ago . . ." I thought backward. By Lastday three years ago, Papa had caught the *saku*, the plague that struck our village that year, and that now sickened Mama near to death, and he had grown more and more confused, seeing things that were not there, crying in alarm at monsters and ghosts and unspeakable happenings, eating little, speaking nonsense — until one night while the moon was full and the rest of the house slept, he crept out the front door of the house against rule, covenant, and promise. We never saw him again. I knew in my heart that he was dead.

Three years ago, taandu sap had run slowly.

Two years ago, it had been even scarcer.

I said, "The sap barely ran at all last year. And what's more, Uncle Banris knew it would be bad before the first day of the run started. Warm weather plagued us all winter, and the spring came unevenly. Two hundred sixty vials — that would have been half the village's magic on a good year. Neither last year nor the year before were good years. Nor had Banris the approval of the village elders to give a single taandu vial away, or to sell a single one of the villagers into bondage." I grew angry, and my voice grew louder. "I don't know a thing about purple silk; I've never seen it, but perhaps Banris the Caer has, or knows where it might be found."

"He knows. He delivered sap, servants, and silk in the first year, and servants and silk in the second, but he fell behind on his payment of taandu sap."

I tried to comprehend that my uncle had sold people we knew to the nightlings. "Then punish *him*," I said.

She smiled, a tiny, knowing expression, and said, "We would. For he betrayed your father, who was *our* friend. The new caer, well, he thinks he's a friend of the kai-lord. And the kai-lord . . . he's just waiting for the most profitable time to destroy Banris. That will certainly come, but only after the kai-lord has sucked the last embers of life out of your village."

Something struck me then. "Wait. *You* knew our father? You?"

A faint breeze blew through the trees and rattled their branches, and I shivered. She looked around warily, and her voice dropped. "He was helping us. We're slaves of the kai-lord. My parents used me as a messenger because no one pays attention to children, so when they could get me out of the gates, I and others like me came to your house by night. Your mother would gift us with spells and medicine, and your father would teach us the ways of war and diplomacy. Because of him, we found out we were once free. Because of him, we are fighting to become free again."

I tried to imagine my beloved father as a defier of the laws, as a covenant-breaker, one of those men against whom Uncle Banris raged with such fury and such venom. But I could not see Papa as evil, no matter what he had done.

The nightling read the confusion on my face, I suppose, for she said, "There is no evil in freeing slaves. Slaves are not rightful property. Slaves are captives against their will, and those who help such captives speak light into darkness and order into chaos."

I considered that. It *felt* true. And I could imagine those words in Papa's voice. In fact, as I thought about it, I could almost believe I was hearing him say them.

I returned to the subject of the kai-lord and Banris.

"What is Banris's punishment?" I asked. "For acting beyond the rights of a caer and for failing to keep his bargain with the kai-lord?"

"Who knows?" The nightling shrugged. "Your caer has the secret of immortality now, though he has not fully paid for it. The kai-lord might have use for such an ally. For now, he punishes your villagers in the caer's stead, for the deal made with a caer is made as well for all of his people. By rule, covenant, and promise."

"By rule, covenant, and promise," I agreed. And then the other thing that she said brought itself to the front of my mind, and I stood there staring at her, feeling my stomach turning, feeling the world beginning to spin beneath my feet. "Uncle Banris has the secret of immortality?"

"Yes."

"He will live forever?"

"If the kai-lord does not destroy him for his failure to pay, and if the caer makes the necessary sacrifices. If he lives, Banris will one day rule over all your people as the maraesh of Aeiring. The kai-lord gave him exactly what he requested."

"He's immortal," Dan whispered.

"Well . . . no. Not yet," the nightling said. "He may have taken most of the steps in the spell, but he has not yet completed the final two."

Something about her voice as she said that sent a chill through my blood, and I said, "What are the final two steps?"

"Because Caer Banris is childless and cannot sire children, and because he is without a wife, he must marry a woman who has children whom the marriage will legally bind to him as his own offspring. When he has done that, he must offer blood and breath of his children to the Nameless One."

Dan and I turned and stared at each other, and I thought of Banris's cold eyes watching me as I went about my duties. "Blood and breath of his children," I said, and at the same time Dan said, "He has to marry Mama and kill one of us to become immortal?"

"No," the nightling said. "He has to kill all of you."

I slipped my hand into Dan's, and he squeezed hard. We still breathed. But we breathed because my mother yet lived, I thought, and still had some sense of where she was. I knew he had asked her for her bond and troth in marriage, claiming that he wanted to care for his best friend's children if anything happened to her. And I knew she had refused him, swearing that she believed Papa still lived, and that she had seen him.

Everyone else believed Papa was dead — Dan vehemently so — but Mama, in her confusion, would not. And now I was grateful that she did not. As long as she remained strong enough, she would refuse Uncle Banris. If she died unwed to him, she would be free of Banris, and we would be free of the threat, for we would be our father's children alone, not bound to the man who desired our lives — or more truly, our deaths.

But Mama was dying, and not slowly. Her will grew weaker every day, and Uncle Banris now stayed in our home to oversee Mama's care, and ours, and each day he begged her to marry him so that we would not be orphaned at her death. One day she would be too weak to refuse him, and Hargard the priest or one of his apprentices would, out of nothing but kindness, perform bond and troth because he would think he would be helping us.

Nor were Danrith and I the only children. At home five more of us waited, the youngest — the twins — only two years old. The caer watched us all, planning his eternity, and he waited.

"Each night since we realized Banris had no wish to honor rule, covenant, and promise — at least each night we could slip away — we have come to your house to speak with you," the nightling said.

I looked at Dan. "They *were* outside the window."

"We were," the nightling agreed.

We stood in silence for a moment, with only the dripping of the sap into our two buckets to give the night a voice. Then the nightling added, "No sap you take back can save your mother or any of the others who have fallen under the kai-lord's curse. They can be saved only if you bargain with the kai-lord to set them free."

Dan said, "Us? We're children. The kai-lord would never speak to us. No bargain we made would be legally binding."

"The kai-lord makes his own rules," the nightling said. "And he would bargain with you if you offered him something no one else could give him."

I asked her, "What would we own that a kai-lord would covet?"

And my brother said, "What must we do?"

The nightling nodded. "You both have your mother's ways and your father's. He was a good caer. If we did not have the kai-lord we have, your father would still be with us, and all would be well." She looked sidelong at the two of us. She didn't move, and doubt surrounded her like the light she'd wrapped around herself, but at the same time she looked vaguely hopeful. "Come with me. Leave your buckets — you will not need them and they cannot help you. You must speak this night with the kai-lord."

I did not wish to go deeper into the forest. I did not like the idea of standing to beg a favor before the most feared of all the creatures in our world. But some things you must do when you are the oldest child, with brothers and sisters who need you and a mother who dies by a traitor's treachery — the same treachery that stole our father from us. I did not want to go into the forest.

But I went, and Dan dropped the spool of string that would have led us back to the road, and went with me.

The moon lay fat and tired along the ridge to the west by the time we reached the nightlings' home, which our guide named Arrienda. A great door of carved marble stood before us, set deep into the side of the hill so that daylight might never reach all the way to it. On either side of the doorway, enormous stone stags danced, and astride the larger one on the right was carved a nightling man, his hair a mane that whipped like a pennant behind him. He held the moon in one upraised hand, and his stone eyes were fierce as they stared into mine.

The nightling girl who had led us to this place rapped once upon the stone with a slender metal rod; the door rang like a chime.

We waited, and in a moment it split down the center, and a tall nightling dressed in flowing black, and with face hooded and hands gloved, stood before us. The girl slipped through the door and whispered in his ear for a moment. The hooded nightling nodded, then turned to us.

"Your sword," he said to Dan. "Else you may not enter."

We looked at each other. "I told you not to bring it," I said.

He glowered at me but handed it to the guard. "I want it back when we leave."

The guard said nothing. He merely took the sword and beckoned us inside. The nightling waited, and Dan and I took deep breaths at the same time and stepped through the stone arch.

Neither of us forgot that we stood where we did on the sufferance of the nightlings, nor that our presence in the heart of their domain could be a breach of covenant should they decide to forget that they had invited us.

Yet I could feel no evil in the place. Evil born of magic gives the very air a sour taste, like milk spoiling nearby. The air in the nightlings' barrow smelled sweet; it carried a light promise of flowers in the meadow, of green growing things, of the spray from a waterfall.

The floor was solid stone like ours, but shared nothing except its origins with our homely reed-covered pavers. Made of blackest marble and polished so smoothly that we could see the full reflection of the nightling who led us inward, as if he walked across the undisturbed surface of a lake, it marked this place in which we found ourselves as another world entirely from the one we knew.

The floor dropped and curved to the right, so that we walked down a long spiral. I caught sight of nearly concealed holes in the walls to either side of us, and knew that eyes watched our progress, and that, likely as not, weapons tracked us. Should we do anything wrong, we would die between two blinks of an eye.

We reached a grand cavern after long walking; in our progress downward we had passed dozens of passageways that led off from the spiral we traversed. I thought many nightlings might live in this one barrow — and then I got a good look at the cavern, and realized our little village had to sit within reach of one of the greatest and most powerful cities in all the world. And it was with the master of this city that vile Banris had made his bargain. I could only wonder where he had found the courage. Or the courage to cheat him.

We continued to follow the nightling who had led us into this place, but we followed wordlessly. Creatures winged and taloned that had never flown in daylight flitted and soared through the tall arched corridors, chasing fishes of the air and other creatures that I could have only thought at home in water. Squat, wide-mouthed monsters in every imaginable color, and dressed in velvets and brocades of the most beautiful workmanship, spoke in bell voices to men and women tall as willows and twice as graceful, who furled and unfurled huge, delicate butterfly wings behind them. Nightlings with skin green or gold, pale lilac, vivid orange, snow white, ebony black, yellow or pink or richest royal blue moved through those same corridors, talking and laughing, followed always, always by black-cloaked, black-hooded silent attendants.

Nor were the exotic creatures and the even more fantastic nightlings the only wonders. Gardens grew along the way, trees curving and swaying, their leaves of gold and copper and ruby red; sweet-scented bushes brushed us as we passed; and flowers in every imaginable color glowed from beds planted by a master gardener with a genius for beauty.

Some faint music called us forward, almost impossible to hear, yet enchanting nonetheless.

I know the quiet beauty of apple blossoms in spring. I love the sweet awkwardness of newborn kids and lambs, the comfort of a cushioned rocking chair, the serenity of a shake roof on a rainy night, and of sturdy stone walls and a fire on the hearth come winter. These are good things, but simple.

The beauty and magic of Arrienda were extravagant, shocking, breathtaking . . . exhausting. My mind could not take in everything, and I wished I could sneak away for a short while and hide my eyes.

I wondered if humans had ever even imagined the possibilities I saw as finished works. I thought that if I stayed in this place for one lifetime — or a dozen — I would never cease to wonder at the miracles that spread out before me.

But I could not let myself be seduced by beauty.

The nightling finally guided us off the main thoroughfare and beneath another arch, this one leading into a square dominated by a splashing fountain. Beside the fountain stood a tall, fierce nightling, pale-skinned and pale-haired as the girl who had brought us to the city. Unlike the lavishly dressed nightlings who passed through the corridors, this man wore clothing of a simple cut, unadorned by embroidery, gemstones, or other ornament. It was of deepest purple silk. He played a long, spiral-shaped wooden flute, and the music he made was deep and dark and hypnotic. As he played, the water in the fountain formed the shapes of dancers, and swirled and swooped with every note.

"Kai-lord," the black-robed guide called out, and the master of the city put down the flute he'd been playing and turned to greet us.

"Whose are these?" he asked, looking Dan and me up and down as if *we* were property.

Our guide said, "I do not know their names. But they are the children the covenant-breaker seeks to bind into death with his spell. They were wandering in our forest after dark, but they carried the white staff, and they minded their manners."

The kai-lord looked both of us over, then said, "They are the children of Caer Jhontar of High House and the yihanni Seldihara?"

"Yes, kai-lord."

He returned his attention to us. "Your lives are forfeit under Caer Banris's contract with me."

I nodded, miserable. I do not think I have ever been so afraid. Still, I found the courage to stare into his eyes and say, "Yet since the caer must kill us to complete the spell you gave him, we would lose nothing and gain much if you killed us, since killing our brothers and sisters would become pointless with us dead, but not by Banris's hand."

He watched Dan and me, and for a long, uncomfortable time he did not speak, so that I thought perhaps he was deciding he should do just that.

Then he chuckled. When he spoke, his words surprised me. "So you found out about his treachery, did you? I wondered how long that would take." He smiled at my brother and me, his eyes, for the moment, warm and kind. "My name is Letrin Trikantis, which in your tongue means He Who Holds the Moonroads," he said. "I am kai-lord of all you have seen, and much that you have not. Welcome to my domain. Your courage and your honoring of covenant and promise speak well of you. Perhaps we can make a better deal than I made with Caer Banris. Tell me your names."

Names and the telling of names are sacred between my people and the nightlings, and though no one ever thought their children would one day exchange names with a kai-lord, every child in our village past the age of speech was taught how it was done.

I said, "I am Gennadara Yihannisdattar of High House, daughter of Jhontar, who was the Caer of Hillrush and son of the caer before him, and grandson of the caer before him; and of Seldihara of Far Harbor, the yihanni; and I am first in the line of their children. Our people have traded with your people since before covenant."

"They have indeed," the kai-lord said.

"And I am Danrith Caersson of High House," my brother said. "My lineage is the same, save that I am second-born."

The kai-lord nodded to our guide. "They are well mannered." And he turned his attention back to us. "Caer Banris hides in your cellar at this moment, protected from me by spells woven there by your mother and your father. I cannot see what he does in there. Can you tell me?"

Dan and I shook our heads. "He won't let anyone in there. He says he works on the business of the village, and that with the sickness spreading, he has to have privacy at night."

The kai-lord laughed, but it was not the way happy men laugh. "The sickness, which you call the *saku,* is a curse he brought upon your village. Did you know that?"

We shook our heads.

"Let me show you something," he said, and turned and waved a hand at the water fountain behind him. The water rose up and formed itself into figures — one was Banris and the other was Papa, but Papa as he had been when he was well. The water took on the colors and textures of them, so that I would have sworn my living father sat before me on the bench beneath the Justice Tree, talking to his friend as I had seen him do countless times before.

Papa said, "It was a long, hard day today, but we accomplished much." He leaned against the enormous trunk of the Justice Tree and closed his eyes, and I felt my throat tighten. I missed him so much. Beside me, I heard Dan sniff.

Banris said, "Imagine the day when you won't have to plow a field with an ox or thresh wheat or repair snowshoes before you dispense justice." He smiled and spread his arms wide. "You'll sit in grand chambers holding the staff and seal, dressed in court robes embroidered with gold, and you'll settle the cases of the rich and powerful instead of a petty dispute over the ownership of three ducks and a wandering cow. They speak well of your justice throughout the Highlands, Jhon. Someday the call will come, and —"

My father opened his eyes and grinned at Banris. "Stop! Could you see me dressed in court foppery? Could you see me dispensing my brand of justice among the corrupt, rich fools of Greathaven? They and their hired lawspeaks would drive me mad inside of a day, and by the time I'd jailed three or four of them for bribery, they'd have hired assassins waiting for me around every corner. Besides, I like my ox. He's a good lad. And weaving strapping through a snowshoe frame is as soothing to a man as knitting seems to be to a woman. I like this life."

"You only think that," Banris said, "because you've never known any other. The opportunity for a judge of the courts, or even a judge of the maraesh's High Court, would be boundless. No one would care that you profited from a gift or two here or there. In the city, things are different. *You'd* be different. But you'll be fine. When the call comes —"

"The call came," my father said, and he was no longer smiling. "At the end of Fox Month, just after winter offering, two retainers of the maraesh rode into Hillrush and offered me chambers in the Middle Court of West

Greathaven, with a promise in writing from the maraesh himself that if I were all he had heard, I'd have a seat on the High Court in five years."

"That's wonderful," Banris said. "Great judges wait whole lifetimes for an offer such as that. So when do we leave? I suppose you'll have to wait for a replacement, though this village is dying off by leaps and gallops, and in a few more years, none will live here at all, and the Nightling Forest will overgrow the whole thing." And under his breath he added, "And good riddance."

I had never seen Banris so happy.

"I refused the position," Papa said. "Greathaven is no place for me. No place for Seldi, or for the children. This has been my family's home for more than a century. My friends are here. My roots are here."

Banris looked like an ox hit by a felling stone. His eyes went blank and his mouth gaped. And then he shook himself, and suddenly I could see his anger. "I'm your friend," he said. "I've been your best friend since we were children. Since my family came here. You *knew* I wanted to go back to the city. You knew I hated it here — I've always hated it here. And you knew my only way of finding a place in society there was as your assistant, your associate, your friend."

My father sighed. "You were a boy who deserved a better father."

"What do you mean by that?"

"You deserved a father who did not get himself banned from Greathaven society. Such a father would have had the moral courage to resist the pressures of the rich and decadent, and he would have passed that courage on to you."

"He was a corrupt old fool," Banris said. "I didn't need him."

"All children need their fathers, just as much as they need their mothers. Sometimes, though, children need their fathers to be better men than they're capable of being. Your father's weaknesses and corruption marked you."

"They did nothing of the sort," Banris snapped.

"Yet you suggested that had I accepted the maraesh's appointment, taking gifts would be excusable. That tempering justice for those who could buy my favor, while keeping it unadorned and unsoftened for those who could not, would be acceptable." Papa leaned forward and rested his elbows on his knees. "For you, my dearest friend, as much as for my wife and children, I refused the appointment. Here, where temptations are few, you are capable of being a good man. There . . ." He looked earnestly at Banris. "There, where everything you yearn for is temptation, I fear you would fall into your father's footsteps."

Banris stood, his fists clenched at his sides, his face red with fury. "You made such a decision for me? You made this decision without even asking me? How dare you?"

My father stood to face his friend and said softly, "I made that decision because the maraesh's men came seeking me, and because if I took you to Greathaven with my wife and my family, you would be trading on my name. My name, which unlike your father's name — and your own — still has its honor intact. When the maraesh's men come seeking your services, the decision to go or stay will be yours, and you may make it without consulting me, I assure you."

When he said that, I saw something dangerous flash across Banris's face.

But then the kai-lord released the magic that had put my father and his friend before us. The spell broke, the water that had been Papa for those few moments splashed back into the fountain, and Dan and I both reached for the place where he had been before we could stop ourselves.

The kai-lord said, "That was the moment when Banris decided he would have by trickery everything that your father had earned by honesty and hard work. He came to me two nights later, offering me a bargain. A contract."

"You could have told him no," I said.

"As I could still tell you no," he agreed. "To win a contract with me, you must first offer me something that I both greatly desire and that I cannot obtain on my own. I'm the Kai-Lord Letrin of Arrienda," he added. "Immortal, the master of magic and unquestioned ruler of the greatest kaidom in the world. How many things of that nature do you think exist? And more than that, you must offer me this thing on terms I find favorable. Banris offered me a great bargain."

Kai-Lord Letrin sat on the edge of the fountain so that he was only a little bit taller than Dan or I. "Would you rather make good on Banris's contract?" Letrin asked.

I trembled as I spoke. Nevertheless, I said my piece. "By his word, Caer Banris bought our father's death and the deaths of others in our village, and he seeks the deaths of my mother, my brothers and sisters, and me, whether he kept his oath or broke it. I would do nothing to save him; I would not lift one finger to prevent his shame. But if I can save my mother's life and protect my brothers and sisters from the evil he would do them all, and spare the rest of my village, I will do everything within my power to make good on his word." I looked to Dan, and he nodded.

"I stand beside my sister," he said.

I added, "I must tell you, I know of no source for purple silk, or even for purple dye. I know of no way to gather enough sap for two hundred sixty vials of essence save to have our entire village gather it, and I cannot think they would take my word for it that they must. And we are all freemen in my village; I cannot offer anyone but myself as servant to the nightlings, though myself I offer freely."

He laughed softly. "So you will swear to make good on a traitor's oath, though you have neither the knowledge nor the skills nor the power to carry through on your promise."

Dan and I both nodded.

"Knowing that if you failed, you would die first, and all the rest would still die?"

We nodded again.

"I don't like Caer Banris very much. It seems he's rather . . . clever . . . with clauses. Perhaps," he said softly, and suddenly I could see no trace of amusement in his eyes, "you and I can make a different deal, firstborn."

Chapter 3
Dinner in Arrienda

All I remember of Letrin in that moment is his eyes. They seemed to me deep as the oceans of fable, as if, should I dare to step toward him, I would fall into them and meet my death by drowning. Those eyes, cold as iciest winter, sent a chill through me that I can neither explain nor fully recall. Dan's hand slid into mine again, and we locked our fingers together.

"A different deal," Kai-Lord Letrin said with a slow, careful smile. "Surely you do not wish to make good on a deal that will result in your deaths and those of your siblings at the end of it. For even if you save the village, the caer will not spare you. He cares not for your mother or for your brothers and sisters or for you or for anything but that he become an immortal with the world in his hand. But you . . ." And he looked at Dan, and then at me, and tipped his head slowly to one side. His smile grew a little broader.

He stood before I could think of words to say, or even before Dan could — and that is a trick — and said, "You will be my guests at dinner tonight. We will feast you, for so few of your people brave Arrienda." He swept a hand out and around, encompassing the great city in which we stood, the wondrous realm over which he ruled. "And while you prepare for the feast, you must think of what, exactly, you want." His smile gone, he said, "In the meantime I will be thinking of what I want. And once we have eaten and drunk and sung together, we will sit down, just the three of us, and we will see if we can come to an agreement."

Then he was gone. I cannot say how he left us — only that one instant he stood before us and the next he did not. Behind us, the black-robed nightling who had led us to him cleared his throat and said to the nightling girl — who had been, I just realized, nowhere near us while we talked to the kai-lord — "Take them. You know what to do."

Things were going on around us that I did not understand. I was frightened as much of the nightling girl and her calm "I know what to do" as I was of Letrin and his unnerving smile.

"Come with me," the nightling girl said to us. "I will find you both clothes appropriate for a feast."

She said nothing else, but led us into a maze of corridors, softly lit from some source I could not find. We walked and walked, and the silence began to weigh on me. So, more to hear a voice than for any other reason, I said, "Kai-Lord Letrin frightens me."

"You should be frightened," our guide said, in the quietest of whispers. "He does not mean you well, nor any of your kind."

And then she fell silent again. Dan and I looked at each other. I could see his fear in his eyes. I hoped that I looked more reassuring than he did.

"Then why will he offer us a way to save our people?"

"Patience," she said. And we held our tongues and followed her even deeper into the twilight world below the surface.

We came at last to a door of wood, free of any feature save, in the very center, a smooth hole carved away and patiently rounded, in place of the latch and handle I would have expected. Our guide hooked her fingers into the hole and pulled lightly, and the door swung open without sound. I stared at it; I could see neither hinges nor locks, and could not figure its workings, nor could I understand why I thought it so lovely when it was so plain.

When we stepped through the doorway, lights sprang up around us of their own accord, though no hand lit a lamp — nor were there any lamps to light. In the room, rows upon rows of garments spread away into the distance, and all of them seemed to me a rainbow caught and captured in silk and velvet, lace and gauze and barathea, that most beautiful of pebbled silk-and-twills.

In all my life I had never seen such colors; dyes are tricky things, and in our village we do well with blues and yellows and browns and greens and madder red. But even these were dull, dark colors by comparison. Before me I saw crimson, warm amber, and the green of spring leaves, the clear yellow of buttercups, the bright pale blue of the autumn sky. I gasped, and beside me Dan murmured, "An acre of purple silk would be lost in here."

Our guide turned to us. "Quickly, tell me what you want. What you will ask him for."

"Our mother's life," I said without even needing to think about it. "Our father's, if he still breathes. The lives of our brothers and sisters, and the people in our village. And their freedom. These were not things that were the new caer's to offer."

Dan nodded. "And for protection from Caer Banris, for each of us."

"No immortality? No riches of the seven kingdoms? No flying chariots or crowns and thrones?"

Dan said, "No," and I said, "Of course not."

She looked at us for a long moment, studying us carefully. Then the nightling said, "I believe you. Very well. If you do exactly as I say, I will make sure you have a fair chance to make your bargain."

Dan and I both nodded.

"First, drink only from the cups I bring you, and should anyone else refill them, do not drink from them again. Eat only from the plates that come from my hand, and if you are offered a bite of anything not from me, refuse it, no matter what the person who offers it to you says."

I started to say something, but the nightling put a finger to her lips. She stopped far down the row in which we had been walking and said, "There it is." She pulled down a dress for me, a gown of palest blue samite — rich, heavy silk woven through with threads of gold and silver that gleamed in the pale light, and blue slippers that seemed far too tiny and delicate for my feet. For Dan, she gathered up tunic and breeches of black velvet, and velvet-edged boots with workings of silver. Then she turned to me and said, "Wear your hair in a single braid down your back, and if the kai-lord says anything that upsets you, pull the tip of the braid around to your mouth and brush it against your lips."

I frowned, puzzled, and she said, "If we get through this night unscathed, I will explain everything to you. Along with the things you have asked for those you love, however, you must ask for two other things. You must ask that your own lives be spared. And you must ask for the ruby key."

Dan looked at me. "Will you remember everything?"

"Yes."

He said, "If our guide has something to write with, I'd like to write everything down on my hand. And if you forget anything, you can look to me, and nod, and I'll show you."

"Do that," the nightling girl said. "It may save your lives. Others who have bargained with the kai-lord would have done well to have brought one of you with them."

"Perhaps we should ask for Uncle Banris's death," Dan said, his voice angry.

"That would be a mistake. Never ask for anything that would hurt someone else. You cannot know how the new caer came to the place where he is right now, nor what path you may have to travel on your own. You did well with your requests. Think only of what will help, both you and those you love, and never desire that which will harm." She sighed.

"Now let me warn you of the chores that the kai-lord will ask of you."

I felt dread in my belly at her words.

"When you ask him for the ruby key, he will know that one of us helps you, and he will try to find out which of us has so betrayed him. You will not know me to see me, and you do not know my name. This is by design, for I wish to survive this night, just as I wish to see the kai-lord come to the end he has earned."

"The kai-lord? He is frightening. But he did not seem to me to be . . . evil. Not as Banris is evil. You wish to see him dead?" I asked.

"I and all my family, all my friends, and all my friends' families, are his slaves, owned by him, used by him, and disposed of by him as he chooses when he tires of us for any reason. He is the fully finished monster your Caer Banris wishes to become," she said. "You will see that monster yet this night. When the kai-lord finds that you cannot give me to him, he will grow angry. Stand your ground — he has feasted you and has promised you a deal, and by his own rules and code, he must then give you a deal. But he will try to cheat you. If you have done as I told you, you will be able to see his cheats for what they are. Each time he tries to cheat, you must tell him what he wants cannot be done and demand another exchange. At last he must offer you something that is possible, even if very difficult. But he will offer this and at the same time suggest that since you are such shrewd bargainers, perhaps you would like to ask for one thing more. Under no circumstances must you try to change the terms you first set."

She turned away, leaned for a moment against the dresses, and said, "This is so very hard. I do not think that you can prevail against him — the guilty and the evil do well in the kai-lord's bargains, but the innocent he devours like new bread." She touched my hand, and her fingers were cool. "Be strong," she told me. She turned to Dan. "Be strong."

Then she said, "Dress quickly. I will find something with which you can write down your end of the bargain."

"When he offers us the task that is only very difficult, what should we do?"

"Accept it, even if you know that you cannot carry it out. Even if he wants a mile of purple silk, agree to this."

"But then we will be as badly off as before."

"No," she said. "Because if you remember to ask for the ruby key, and if you do as I have told you, I will join you. And that which you cannot do, I and all my brethren who have suffered longer than you can imagine, can do. If you will help us, we will help you."

Dan and I changed quickly into the glorious clothing our guide had given us. I put on the dress with some misgivings; we had passed many that seemed to me very like it, and yet the nightling had seemed to be hunting for just that dress. Why? Why the clothing Dan wore? What was the ruby key that the nightlings made it the terms of their service?

I did not wish to stand before the kai-lord of the nightlings to make a bargain; my hands trembled so that I could not tie the lacings on my bodice. Our guide at last saw my distress and did the lacings for me. "Calm yourself," she said. "Fear serves only him."

I nodded, and smoothed the wondrous skirt, and undid my hair from its bindings. The nightling handed me a comb of heavy silver and a hair tie.

I combed my hair and braided it into a single braid that hung all the way down my back.

"No," the nightling said. "It's much too long. Wait a moment." She left us, darting between two rows of clothing.

I stared at my brother. "What if she doesn't come back? We'll never find our way out of this place."

"We will," Dan said. "Just as we will make our deal tonight with the kai-lord. You and I will do what we must." His words were certain; his voice cracked, though, shattering his illusion of confidence. Still, he wanted to comfort me, and for that he was a good brother. I hugged him and said, "We will. You and I together — we'll save her. We'll save all of them."

"All of them who deserve to be saved," he said.

I nodded. We would speak no more of Banris, but he was in both our minds.

Then the nightling returned, carrying scissors. She did not ask me; she simply darted around behind me and lopped off a forearm's length of braid. "Now you'll do," she said.

I did not protest, though I wanted to. What I did, I did to save my mother, my brothers and sisters, my village. I did not think a bit of hair would be the last thing I would have to sacrifice.

She handed it to Dan. "Don't lose it," she said. "And by no means let it fall into the kai-lord's hands."

My brother held the stump of hair with an expression between dismay and disgust.

"Give it to me," I said, and snatched it from his hands, and shoved it down the front of my dress. "I'll burn it the first chance I get." I appreciated him, but he was such a boy sometimes.

She waited while I pulled on the slippers. They fit perfectly, but I know not what magic made them do so. And when I was done, I looked at Dan. He looked the part of a youngling prince or even a king.

The nightling girl studied us. "I will be with you, and I will serve you. Remember what I told you at all costs. When the time comes for you to make your deal, you will not see me, but I will be there."

And she handed Dan a stick of what looked like charcoal rolled in paper, with the point sharpened. "It's a moonstick," she said. "A tiny magic. Write what you will — you will see it fade, then disappear. But when you need it, you will be able to see it."

Dan wrote carefully:

Save Mama, and Papa if he still lives.
Save our brothers and sisters.
Save the villagers and their freedom.
Protection for all of us from Banris the Caer.
Our own lives spared.
The ruby key.

We stood for a moment, staring at his hand. The dark letters turned silvery, and then melted into his skin and were gone.

"Now, to make them reappear, you must want to see them again," our guide said. "Desire it with everything you have in you."

Dan frowned, and after a moment, the letters curled like smoke across his skin and I could read them. When he quit staring at them, they again faded away.

Our guide said, "You are ready — at least, you are as ready as I can make you. It's time to go. The banquet awaits."

Walking into the banquet was like walking into a field of flowers on a summer evening, with the air full of lightning bugs and the promise of a perfect night. The hall smelled of perfumes so faint and delicate they almost weren't there, but breathing them in sent shivers down my spine. The music seemed only music in part, for in it I could hear not only strings and the sweet rush of wood flutes, but also the songs of birds and the chirping of frogs and insects.

"Oh," Dan whispered.

"I can't believe it," I agreed.

An enormous table anchored the feast, surrounded by nightlings in every imaginable shape and form and size dressed as beautifully as flowers could ever hope to be. They moved in and out, talking with one another, laughing softly, with voices that seemed to me to be just another part of the music. I felt heavy and lumpish and graceless, a pretender in a fine dress.

Dan and I followed our guide to the head of the table. She whispered, "The two of you will sit in these seats, but you must not sit until after the kai-lord has taken his throne."

She need not have said anything — Dan and I had been well trained by Mama and Papa. A child's place is to stand until the last adult is sitting. We would have to guess with the nightlings, because many of them looked so much younger than the two of us but seemed to be regarded by all around them as adults. I decided I would just sit when the last of our hosts sat, and let Dan take his seat half a beat behind me.

We took our places, standing behind our chairs but not speaking to anyone. We watched everything, and stared at the table, which held plates so delicate and beautiful they seemed spun of bubbles, and flatware of gold, which came in forms I did not recognize. Knives and spoons I have seen and used all my life, but I had no experience with either the two-pronged thing that looked like a broken pitchfork, nor the sinuous handle with the ring on one end.

Then the kai-lord appeared through a door, and with great fanfare. The volume of the music increased, and everyone ceased speaking and watched him as he crossed the mirrorlike floor. Kai-Lord Letrin took his place at the head of the table, and everyone else moved to their seats.

"Where are my two guests?" he asked, and Dan and I nodded to him.

He stared at me, at my hair and the dress I wore, and he grew pale. He looked to Dan next, and I could see confusion in the kai-lord's eyes. He took his seat, and all the nightlings sat after him, and Dan and I last of all. And all the while he stared at the two of us, saying nothing, his fine eyebrows knitted together and his lower lip caught between his teeth as if he were a child asked a question he could not answer.

No sooner had Dan taken his seat than the trays came in, carried between nightlings as if they were tremendously heavy. As each reached the long table and the nightlings lifted the covers, scents filled the air that set my stomach to growling. I had eaten nothing the night before, and I had to guess we were now well into morning. I lacked sleep, and I felt hungrier than I ever had, and every uncovered delicacy looked finer and smelled more wonderful than the one before.

I heard Dan groan.

Beneath the table, I caught his wrist and squeezed it. He'd had nothing, either, and usually ate twice as much as I, twice as often.

The servants began dishing out the food. Dan and I waited, and when it seemed everyone would eat but us, and just as I was thinking that surely no harm would come from just tasting the roasted and stuffed goose before me, a hand put down a plate in front of me, and another in front of Dan. The plates held plenty of food, but only beans and bitter greens. I glanced up and found that our guide had presented them. Servants moved along the table filling gold goblets with dark ruby wine, and one filled Dan's glass and mine, and moved on. But after an instant, our guide reappeared, and neatly exchanged our goblets with some that looked just like them, but that had been filled with water.

So. Water and boiled beans and bitter greens, when all around us nightlings devoured the finest feast I had ever seen in my life.

But we had been warned. Dan and I ate our greens and beans with the little pitchforks, as we saw others doing, and drank our water, and when we emptied our plates, our guide replaced them with others, with food no more palatable than that which we had just finished.

I confess, I had a hard time remembering that I ate my dreary meal for my mother's survival and the safety of everyone I knew and loved, or that I drank water instead of wine for the same reason. No one can know who has not taken food with the nightlings how their feasts bewitch the senses.

Then, as I ate, the kai-lord turned to me, and with a smile said, "Here. You've had none of the stag, and it is tender and succulent — the finest I believe I have ever had." He held out one of the little pitchforks with a bite of meat dripping gravy, so close the rich aroma curled straight into my brain. Stag is the food of kai-lords or maraeshes, forbidden to common folk, and I wanted that bite as I think I have never wanted anything else in my life.

I started to open my mouth, but Dan pinched me hard on the back of my arm, and I only managed not to shriek with the strongest of wills. I said, "My thanks, Kai-Lord Letrin, but I eat no meat."

He shook his head as if I amused him and did not pull the fork back. "You did not get those sweet curves, nor those round cheeks, from a diet of bitter greens. Here. Just a taste, and I promise you if you don't like it, I will offer nothing else."

I tried to remember what I was to do, and again Dan came to my rescue. He gave my braid a yank, and I recalled what our guide had told me. I caught the tip of it between my fingers, and pressed the little curl of hair below the ribbon against my lips. I shook my head and said nothing . . . and to my amazement, the kai-lord shivered and drew back the proffered bite as if I suddenly terrified him.

He stared into my eyes, again frowning, and then looked from me to Dan. He seemed in that moment suddenly very old and frail, though an instant before he had seemed younger than Papa had been, and hale and strong and in his prime.

He offered neither Dan nor me another thing during the whole of the meal, nor did he say another word to either of us. I caught him staring at us when he thought us unaware, and he seemed so sad as he watched us that I thought my heart would break.

We came at last to the end of the feast, to the end of the singing and dancing, to the end of wonders spread before me and forbidden to me, and I thought the worst was over.

Then the room cleared of all the guests, though servants still cleaned, and the kai-lord said, "Then come, both of you, and sit with me, and let us see what I can do for you, and what you can do for me."

He smiled, and his smile seemed to me warm and friendly, but his eyes once again looked as cold and dark as those of any snake. He led us to a recessed circle in the floor near a tall, wide hearth in which a cozy fire blazed. In the circle, cushions lined the perimeter and a great soft carpet filled the rest from edge to edge. It seemed a comforting, friendly place.

I sat to the right of the kai-lord. Dan took a place on his left, facing me, his hands in front of him in such a way that I could see the palm on which he had written our requests, but Kai-Lord Letrin could not. I tucked my skirts around me and swung the heavy braid over my shoulder so it dangled in easy reach of my right hand; I wanted to have the tip of it close by should I need to make the odd gesture our guide had suggested.

Kai-Lord Letrin turned to face me. "You are the eldest, and so speak for the two of you; is this correct?"

"It is," I said. I folded my hands in my lap and tried to look and feel old enough to be speaking directly to a kai-lord; to be someone who, after being feasted, could calmly take the fate of her people in her hands. But I didn't feel that way inside at all. I was terrified that I would make an awful mistake, that I would do something wrong, and that my mother and my brothers and sisters and friends in the village would all die because I was a fool.

"All the world lies before the two of you at your age," Kai-Lord Letrin said. "And I can give you any part of it you desire. My magic has limits, but they are the limits of your imagination, of your desire, and of your passion. Dare to dream grand things. Dare to reach out and ask for wonders, for wonders are mine to give."

I waited, saying nothing, and he smiled a little. "You could be a princess in a distant land, or a queen. You could have gold and jewels, sailing ships and trade routes, spices and silks and servants to meet your every whim. You could have a prince worthy of you, handsome and strong and passionate. And your brother could have things equally wonderful for himself."

Or we could live forever, I thought, and be rulers of the world. If we could pay the price, and if we were willing to.

"Anything you ask of me, you will have it. I promise that. But once you have asked what you will of me, then I will ask what I will of you — and I will have that."

I knew the rules. This was exactly what my nameless benefactor had said would happen. So I waited.

"You're patient. You know already what you want, do you?"

I nodded.

"Then tell me, and it shall be yours."

I drew breath slowly, trying to find calm. And the more I tried to get myself under control, the more control eluded me. But Dan sat across from me, and on his palm I saw the words I needed. I read them, and with my voice trembling, I said, "I want to save Mama and my papa if there is still breath in him — wherever he may be — and my brothers and sisters and all the villagers from the curse the new caer has brought upon them, and besides their safety, I want to win their freedom from his bargain. I want protection for all of us from Banris the Caer. And Dan's and my lives spared." I paused, and carefully added, "And I want the ruby key."

Until I said those words, he'd smiled and nodded. But the instant I asked for the ruby key, he leapt to his feet and leaned over me and roared in my face, "Who set you to this, you insufferable sneak? Who of my own people is the traitor who tries to snare me in this trap?"

He grabbed my face with both of his hands and dragged me forward and stared into my eyes, and I could feel him digging around in my mind, as I might rummage through a trunk to find a misplaced trinket. My skin stung, I got dizzy, and just for a moment I seemed to be floating through a dozen different places all at once.

My brother shouted something that I could not hear clearly, for the kai-lord's hands covered my ears. Dan then tried to drag the kai-lord away from me, and when that didn't work, he kicked the kai-lord in the back. I heard arrows being nocked and bowstrings being drawn in hiding places all around us. But Kai-Lord Letrin shouted, "Stand down!" to the walls. Then he turned, catching Dan across the face with an elbow, and from the corner of my eye I saw Dan go sprawling.

He turned back to me and wrapped his fingers around my throat. "You will tell me what I wish to know!" the kai-lord shouted at me. "Or you will never leave this place."

CHAPTER 4
TRICKS AND BARGAINS

I thought the kai-lord would kill me right there. I went limp, and the kai-lord stopped immediately. He took his hands from my throat and put me down with shaking hands and backed away, and I saw in his eyes again that odd fear I'd seen before.

Like he'd seen a ghost.

Like I was the ghost.

And he settled himself on the cushions, and took a deep breath while he stared down at his hands. He looked over at Dan. "My apologies," he said, and looked back at me. "My apologies to both of you. I fear I have failed greatly as a good host. I fear . . . many things, and betrayal most of all. I will give you what you have asked for — you already had my word on that. But tell me, please, who had you ask for the ruby key."

"I cannot tell you," I said, "because I do not know."

He stared into my eyes. "You tell the truth. Completely — and yet you must know something."

He turned to Dan. "You — what can you tell me? Who set you to this task?"

Dan shook his head. "I know nothing more than my sister about this."

And then, in our host's eyes, I saw a return of slyness, and the faint quick flash of a clever smile across his lips, hidden fast as it appeared. He said, "Never mind. Let it be. I know my own well enough, and I'll find the traitor among the many. Now, accept my apologies, I beg you, and let us discuss what you can do for me to earn the boons you have asked."

"I forgive you," I said.

Dan nodded. "I, too."

"You're good children. Very much your mother's children and your father's, poor lost soul."

We hear that a lot, Dan and I.

"Now," the kai-lord said, "in exchange for the favors you have asked of me, I ask something simple — something that children could do. I want a meeting with Maraesh Janeck of Aeiring. You need only convince him to talk with me once."

The maraesh rules over all the human places in Aeiring. He is human and rules from Greathaven, which is closer to Hillrush than some places. But our guide had said the first things the kai-lord would ask for would be impossible things, and if we agreed to them, we would find ourselves in his debt and in default. "What you ask cannot be done," I said, not knowing why. I could only hope and trust that our guide had given me good instructions.

I knew in an instant that she had, for Kai-Lord Letrin's pale face flushed dark, and his lips became a thin, hard line. I caught my braid between my fingers and tugged and twisted at it, nervous, and the kai-lord's eyes started watching it as if it were a snake and he a hatchling's mother.

I determined that one day I would discover the meaning of all of this — ruby key, braid, dress, and nervous fidgets. In the meantime, though, I waited.

"Yes — impossible. You are only children. So something simpler." He looked from Dan to me and back to Dan. "Bring me the black stone Banris keeps in his possession."

Black stone? I knew nothing of such a stone, but it did not seem an impossible thing.

Danrith narrowed his eyes and spoke before I could. "That black stone is his heart." The kai-lord jumped and turned to stare at my brother. No harder than I stared, certainly. What did he mean that the black stone was Banris's heart? The kai-lord wore the same shocked expression he'd worn when I played with my braid.

"How do you know that?" Letrin grabbed my brother's shoulder and stared into his eyes — and then he let go of Dan and moved back. "You're only half a boy," he whispered.

"And half of me knew you as a greedy, plotting youth, Letrin." Dan's mouth moved, but the voice that came out of it was the voice that spoke when he slept, fighting endless losing battles and mourning an unending stream of warriors and wizards and women and children.

"You travel with the dead, girl," Letrin said to me. "You'll find such creatures make dangerous company."

Now he leaned back and studied me with an expression I did not like at all. He smiled a bit. "If you will not bring me Banris's heart, then cook for me a stew that will satisfy me."

I laughed at that, for everyone knows nothing cooked by humans could ever satisfy one of the nightlings. "You must give me something possible, as what I have asked of you is possible."

He nodded. "You're a bright child. And, yes, what you asked of me is simple. An easy thing, a nothing. Surely you could give me something more challenging. I'll do what you have asked, but you have asked for nothing for yourselves." He turned to Dan, who now bore a red and swelling knot below his right eye where Letrin had struck him. "You must want something of me, ghost-bearer. To rid you of your haunt, perhaps?"

I could tell from the expression on Dan's face that he wanted to see the kai-lord keel over dead. But he said, "My sister spoke for both of us. We want nothing more than what we have already asked of you."

Letrin turned to me. "Something . . . just a little something. A chance for me to make things up to you both for my shameful behavior."

"Nothing," I said, "but what we have asked of you. If you do that, you will have done all that we need or desire."

Now he became very still. It was Banris's sort of stillness — the stillness of a man who has bargained to murder children for his own immortality. He sat without movement, without blinking, seemingly without breathing, for a time so long I wanted to shift in my seat or say something or look to Dan.

But again, dealing with Banris had trained us for this. Those who sit still and make no noise suffer less than those who call attention to themselves.

"You will," he said to me at last, and his lovely voice had turned to gravel, "find for me a child named Doyati, and you will bring this child to me. Tell me not that this task is impossible, for I know it is not. And all the gods in the sky above and those beneath the ground help you if you fail in this task, for my wrath will consume you and everything you know and love. You want what you have asked for. Well enough. I *will have* what I have asked for, or you will live only long enough to wish with everything in you that you had never been born."

I had seen that face and heard that voice echoed in my own home, and I knew those relentless, remorseless eyes. As long as I saw Kai-Lord Letrin as just another version of Uncle Banris, I felt strong enough to deal with him.

"Very well," I said.

"You have from this moment to dark of moon to find the child."

I figured that as quickly as I could. Fifteen days. It seemed like very little time, but the nightling girl had said the nightlings would help us. Perhaps it would be enough.

The kai-lord held out a hand, and a scroll appeared in it from thin air, accompanied by a little flash of light. He placed the scroll on the table before us and spread it out.

I read it, and so did Danrith. It looked to me like exactly what Dan and I had asked for, and exactly what the kai-lord had asked for, written in plain terms that made up a simple, straightforward agreement, but I looked to my brother, who'd had some training in contracts with Papa.

Dan said, "It has no small letters and no trick words. Go ahead, Genna."

I took the onyx pen the kai-lord proffered, and on the line he indicated, signed my true name.

The kai-lord signed his true name. Then he took the contract, said, "I'll keep this until your return," stood, and vanished into nothingness before either Dan or I could insist on a copy for ourselves, a point I liked not at all.

He left the two of us and a host of servants alone in the room. Neither Dan nor I had any idea what we might need to do next.

Then a tall nightling approached us. He wore plain clothing, and I thought he must be a slave, but he sounded just like the black-robed guard who had let us in and brought us to the kai-lord. "You will follow me out now."

We didn't dare ask what had happened to the nightling girl. Or our own clothes. Or even how we might begin the task to which Kai-Lord Letrin had set us. Or how we were supposed to approach the kai-lord when we had accomplished his task. We meekly followed, because we did not know what else to do.

Back up the spiral we went, with the feeling all the while of eyes watching, of weapons trained on us should we do something wrong; on we went, I in a dress worth more than the house my parents lived in, Dan in clothes too fine for any event we might have in our village, ever.

Up took longer than down, and worked us harder, and felt scarier. We had thought when we came to the forest by moonlight that when we returned home, we would be able to offer Mama some help. Instead, we could offer nothing — not even an explanation. We would not be going home. No child named Doyati lived in our town. Doyati was no human name.

So where would we go to find this child?

"Out," this tall, silent guide said when we came at last to the vestibule that would take us back to the world above the ground. And then, in the softest of whispers, so soft I would have thought he said nothing save for the kiss of his breath on my cheek as he said it, "We've kept your sword for you. It will wait in good hands. Luck to you both."

And then we were outside the great stone doors, standing in shadows, with a task that was not impossible but that might as well have been, and two weeks to accomplish it lest we be the cause of the deaths of everyone we loved — and perhaps of Caer Banris, too, but I looked at that as a possible benefit.

"So what do we do now?" Dan asked me.

"I wish I knew. I guess the first thing we need to do is get out of the forest — but we can't go back home. Not dressed like this, not when we've been gone all night on Offering Night. If Uncle Banris has been looking for an excuse to kill us, this would be one he couldn't resist."

"Then which way?"

"How many ways are there? If we try to find our way back to the road, we can walk away from home." I rucked up my skirt and tucked the folds into the dress's lovely belt, and stared ruefully at the beautiful slippers, made for the glasslike perfection of the polished marble floors in Kai-Lord Letrin's city but not for the must and mess of a forest floor or for muddy roads.

Dan said, "Well. Let's go, then. I wish I still had my sword."

"If you'd had it when we met with the kai-lord, you would have run him through with it."

"And a good thing for all of us if I had. And they could have given it back to me as we left."

I said, "Maybe they were being watched, Dan. Maybe they couldn't have. And I'm not going back to ask for it. Something tells me we were lucky to get out of those gates the first time. I don't want to try my luck a second time."

He considered that for a moment, then nodded without comment. He yawned, and I yawned, and I pointed us in a direction at random.

We started walking, sighting on the sun that was already halfway up the sky. I yawned again, and my eyes tried to close on me, though I fought to keep them open. "Where are we going to sleep?" I asked Dan. "What are we going to eat? We have no money, no weapons, no food, no idea where we have to go, no idea how we're to get there. We haven't even decent traveling clothes! We dare not go home, but that's the *only* direction we can safely rule out."

We were traveling toward what I judged to be west, directly away from where I guessed our village to be. We plodded, and my head quickly grew heavy and my eyelids drooped. I yearned for my bed, though it was nothing fancy — a cot strung with rope topped with a cob mattress. As I plodded along, that cob mattress grew softer and softer in my imagination, and more welcoming.

We moved past taandu trees so large a man could have hollowed one out and built a whole house inside it, and lived there with wife and children and servants. We did not stop, but kept moving, hoping that we would come across the road, for the forest felt trackless and directionless to both of us. We knew our way around fields and hills, but like most humans, we stayed well clear of the hearts of forests.

We plodded while the sun stood at the arch of the sky, and plodded while it began its descent. The forest did not thin, and did not offer any markers, so we began to feel that no matter how far we traveled, we had not moved at all. I yearned for something that would tell us we did not wander in circles. Beside me, Dan stumbled and barely caught himself before he fell. I stopped to lean against a tree and looked down at my legs and saw them bleeding. I could not feel them; I was so tired that as I looked at them, they did not even seem to belong to me.

And my stomach hurt from hunger. The beans and bitter greens we'd eaten had not been meant to fill us, and they hadn't. I was thirsty — I would gladly have taken the kai-lord's wine right then and not worried a bit about what else was in it. And for all the world, I would have slept on a rock if I could have found one. But Dan and I knew that the heart of the forest held no welcome for us, and that we dared not sleep until we got ourselves away from it.

Then, as the shadows grew long and the sun dropped far enough that we could see only the glow of it from behind the hills, I heard a voice that at first I thought could be only wishful thinking. It said, "You've gone far enough."

I turned, thinking I dreamed while I walked. And the nightling girl who had been our guide and ally in the kai-lord's city stood behind us, carrying kit-bags and looking not even a little weary. "I'll be traveling with you. You're off his land, and he does not know I'm gone. We'll travel together as best we can — and we'll change directions tomorrow, for you're going the wrong way. But tonight, the two of you must sleep."

I could only wonder how she'd caught up with us.

"My name is Yarri," the nightling girl said. "You can know it now, for no matter whether you know it or not, I dare not return to Arrienda until the kai-lord is dead. If it takes forever, then I'll never go home again."

"Why can't you go home? We won't tell anyone your name."

"I can't take that chance. If the kai-lord ever learns my name, he'll kill my entire family, and everyone who was ever my friend, and everyone I spoke to even occasionally. He knows there is a plot against him, and he shows no mercy to those who have any part in it. Not even children."

So Yarri, too, had everything to lose. This was a sobering thought for me.

Changed back into our own clothes, which Yarri had brought us, we sat in a tent she had carried with her, a square of fabric that had fit into the palm of her hand before she unfolded it, but that pitched, created a shelter with room in it for the three of us and a handful of friends. In the darkness, its silky walls, lit by a tiny flameless light she hung from the arching supports, seemed cozy and strangely sturdy. I knew the walls were thinner than the silk of the dress I'd worn, but they kept out the darkness and the wind. And the tent floor, pitched over soft, loamy ground, made the place seem almost palatial.

She was making a meal for us, using a ball of light she'd rolled in her hands to heat a clever folding metal pot. I yearned to touch that pot and see how its many leaves worked together, but I was even more hungry than I was curious, and more tired than I was hungry. So I studied the pot from a distance and was amazed.

Pouring tiny bags of powders and dried leaves into the boiling water, she said, "I knew the two of you when you were small." A tiny smile crept to the corners of her mouth, curling them up. "Only children dare carry messages for the rebellion. Since we are nothing but the children of slaves, and destined to be slaves ourselves when we are of age, we come and go ignored by nearly everyone." The smile stretched to a grin. "Of course it's always best to look busy, as if sent on an errand by an adult."

I laughed. "I know that trick. Always carry a hoe or a weed digger or a curry brush and hoof pick, and never, ever look happy when adults are looking your way."

Dan said, "I make this face when I'm reading," and furrowed his brow and pushed out his lower lip, "so that everyone will think Uncle Banris or Mama set me the task rather than that I chose it myself."

I giggled, for I recognized the face he made, having seen it so often.

Yarri covered her face with her hands. Her laughter was the sound of bells and falling rain. "You made that same face when you were a baby," she said. "Usually when you smelled just terrible."

It hit me again. We had known her. She had worked with and respected our father, had liked our mother, had watched the two of us toddle around as small children. She was, by her reckoning, still a child, and looked to me to be about Dan's age, but I could not help but wonder how old she was by our reckoning.

So I asked her, "How long have you been a child? How long will you remain a child?"

She shrugged. "Our time is not your time. We operate in your time when we're in the sunworld, though it does not sink its hooks into us as deeply as it does into your people. In our cities, time is what we make it." She sighed. "But we're living in your time now, and it races. The three of us must eat, and you must sleep for a short while."

Dan and I looked at each other. "Then we won't have a full night to sleep?"

"A few hours only. My skin burns in sunlight, so we will have to travel during nightling hours. But you'll rest well. The broth I've made will return your energy to you as you sleep, and when I wake you, I have a tea with me that will give you energy when you drink it."

"Could we just drink it now and be on our way?"

"No. With no sleep, you're more likely to begin seeing phantoms than you are to make any real progress."

Dan muttered, "I see them already. Or one of them."

Yarri ignored him. "I'll stay on watch while you sleep. I'll give you no more than the time it takes the moon to move from its first station to the second. When I wake you, the tea will be waiting, and you'll be able to start out. We have a long way to go, I fear, and getting there is only half the challenge."

"It seems an impossible task, when the boy could be anywhere in the world."

Yarri smiled a little and said, "We'll have help. My parents told me where to go to get it."

We slept on light, fluffy blankets that she'd carried with her. Like the tent, they were large when unfolded, but compressed into an impossibly tiny space. I did not dream, and when I woke in darkness, I could not begin to remember where I was, or how I had come to be there. It took far too long for my head to clear, but the tea helped. Yarri gave Dan and me several cups of it.

I hated the taste, but after the first half-cup, I could feel the energy running through my blood, and my heart began to feel like it beat with the sharpness and speed of horses' hooves on a hard road.

Quicker than I would have thought possible, we were ready. We packed everything tightly away. With the load split between three of us, food, shelter, and spare clothing weighed almost nothing. Dan and I slipped the kit-bags

Yarri had brought for us over our shoulders, and we were ready to go.

We walked through the forest at a quick pace, Yarri leading. For a while we said nothing, any of us, but we caught the rhythm of our pace and the silence became dull. So I asked, "Why did you have us wear the clothes we did? Why the gesture with my hair? Why did Kai-Lord Letrin respond so strangely to the two of us?"

Yarri said nothing for so long I thought she must have either not heard me, or else must have wanted to keep what she knew secret. But just as I was getting ready to ask her again, she said, "He had a wife once. Human, like you."

We worked our way along a log over a stream, and for a little while none of us said anything. Then, when we were over the slippery, mossy surface and safe on the other side, Yarri picked up the thread of the conversation. "His wife, whose name was Oesari, was a wonderful woman, beautiful and compassionate, and she cared for our people and her own with equal intensity. She gave Letrin hope for the future, and made him believe that our combined peoples could make our world better, that each nightling and each human had individual worth, that life was not for the entertainment of the powerful at the expense of the weak."

Oesari sounded a lot like my mother, I thought.

Yarri said, "The kai-lord loved her, and she loved him, and the two of them had a young son in whom all of Arrienda rejoiced. His name was Oerin.

"But your people live short lives, and suffer much for them. She became sick at last, and he could see the marks of age appearing on her face. So he made for the two of them a spell; it would bind both of them eternally to youth, so that they might love forever. So that she might live forever with him. And he would have been a better man had she joined him."

Yarri's voice grew soft. "She did not think immortality in the flesh would make her a better woman, however, and she was horrified when she discovered the price of the spell that he had created for them. The price was the life of their son, Oerin — the child both of them loved madly. The kai-lord could give his love immortality, but only at the price of their son. He told her they could have another — they could have a dozen, or a hundred, if they lived forever. But she wanted no part of this. She told him she would rather die.

"So he worked his magic on her anyway. And when she woke, strong and healthy and young again, and when she knew that she would never feel sickness again, or suffer the pains of age, she died in his arms of a broken heart."

"Though she was immortal?" I asked.

"It's said that immortals can die of a broken heart." Yarri said.

"Oh."

I thought that was a terrible story, and said so.

"And yet he loved her. He loved her, he loved their son, and since her death, he has been . . . hollow. Evil. He does things that hurt people, just because he can."

Dan said, "He was evil when he killed their son."

"Yes. I suppose he was. But until he had to make that choice, between the woman he loved and the son they both loved, he was kind. Good. The change in him was horrible."

"And let me guess . . ." I said. "The dress I wore belonged to Letrin's wife, the clothes Dan wore to his son."

"Yes."

"And she wore her hair long, in a single braid, and played with the tip of the braid when she became upset."

"Yes."

"So we might have been the ghosts of his past."

"You were scars, to wound him. To take some of the poison out of him." Yarri shrugged. "We decided if ever the opportunity presented itself that would allow us to use a human or two against him, we would do it. You're somewhat like the woman he loved when she was very young. I don't know that Dan bears any resemblance to his son. What we did might have helped. I think the clothing and the gestures may have saved your lives when he had the opportunity and the desire to kill you but stayed his hand."

"He murdered his son," Dan said, his voice even and thoughtful. "That seems a bad memory to be trying to call up when I was presented to him."

"He sacrificed his son to save someone he loved more than his own life."

I said, "Apparently not. Or he would have killed himself when she died."

"He truly did love her. He still does. Trying to make the two of you remind him of everything he had lost was a safe enough bet. Even all these years later, their ghosts follow him sometimes, and when they do, he weeps and locks himself away. Some say he keeps their ghosts in a box so that he can bear to move from day to day still breathing."

"And the box needs a ruby key to open it."

Yarri gave me an odd little smile. "That's the story."

"Has anyone seen the box?"

"No," Yarri said. "Not that I know of, in any case."

Dan said, "Has anyone seen the key?"

"My father said he thinks he caught a glimpse of it once, when he was tending to the kai-lord at bedtime."

"So the rebellion is basing its hopes on us retrieving a key that might exist to a box that might exist, and that will do . . . what?"

"No nightling knows this, but my father says he was told that one person does." She smiled, then. "And the kai-lord has set us to find *him*."

My heart sank. We were on a fool's mission, for a fool's prize, and the nightlings would die for nothing, and my mother would die for nothing, and . . .

"The kai-lord will never give the key to me, whether I bring him this child he demanded or not."

Yarri said, "Letrin gave you his word. He'll never go back on his word. He'll give you the key because he swore he would."

Dan and I looked at each other, and I shook my head. He shook his, too. "You want to use the ruby key to kill him."

"Is that a question?"

"Only partly. You do, don't you?"

"To destroy him. If what it does can destroy him without killing him, we will accept that."

"Then he's not going to give any of us the ruby key," I said. "Because he has no desire to die, or to be destroyed, and he's certainly not going to hand you the sword that will kill him. If it will. If it even exists."

"But he gave his word."

Dan, whose nose was in the law books every spare moment he had, said, "He gave his word because we are going out to obtain something that he wants — and cannot get for himself. But here is an example to prove he will not hold to his word. My father's best friend gave his word that he'd honor the deal he made with your people. In our whole lives, Genna and I had never known Uncle Banris to go back on a promise he made. Once — I think — he would have done anything for my father. And yet to live forever and become a king, he betrayed our father to his death. Now he intends to send everyone Papa ever loved into the Passing World with him. If he lives forever and becomes a king, what does he care that your people will no longer bargain with him? And what would he care that everyone in our village died to feed his ambition?"

"But that's *your caer*," Yarri said. "I'm talking about our kai-lord."

I looked at her, thinking that for all her cleverness,

she was far too willing to trust those who had not earned her trust.

I said, "Neither Uncle Banris nor your kai-lord wants to die. Ever. And whatever either one of them has to do to live forever, they will do. If that means killing children, even their own, they'll do it. If it means breaking their word, they'll do that, too."

"Then you think this mission he's sent you on is futile?"

"He may honor his word so far as saving my mother's life," I said. "Though perhaps not even that."

"But he won't give you the ruby key," Yarri said slowly.

I told her, "No."

"Then we might as well just travel someplace pleasant where we can hide for the rest of our lives. Because if you don't bring him Doyati, he'll send hunters after us soon enough." Yarri hung her head and balled her hands into fists.

Dan said, "We have to save our mother. We have to bring him this child he wants — this Doyati — but maybe we can figure out a way to use Doyati to force him to give us what he agreed to give us. The spell lifted, the ruby key in hand, and your people and my people freed. Perhaps if we're clever, we can also save the child."

We walked in silence for a long time. The forest was quiet, windless, and long-shadowed with moonlight. The sky above us, black littered with white stars, seemed cold and harsh. And the moon itself was an unblinking eye that watched us. When I looked up at it, I started feeling lightheaded again, as I had when Letrin grabbed me and stared into my eyes. I started seeing ribbons running over the face of the moon and feeling as if I were in many places at once.

So I looked away from the moon and focused on Yarri.

"We should figure out a way to save the child," I said. "Because if we bring him to Letrin to be sacrificed, how are we any different from the kai-lord, who sacrificed one person to save another?"

"Maybe the kai-lord doesn't want to kill the child," Dan said.

Yarri didn't hesitate. "He'll kill him."

Dan said, "Then my sister is right." He looked over at me and gave me a nod of approval. It was, I think, the first time he had ever said I was right about anything.

We reached a road, and then we started traveling faster. We had nothing to say, though. I could not stop thinking about the futility of what we did, nor could I take my mind from the tantalizing thought that we might find a way to win, even with everything stacked against us.

We could not meekly give ourselves and everything and everyone we loved over to death. We would not. If Kai-Lord Letrin cheated, then, honor be cursed, we would find a way to cheat. Or perhaps we could find a way to use his lies against him.

Suddenly, Yarri stopped, her hand raised, her body tensed. "Listen."

Dan and I stopped as well. I heard the wind in the trees brushing bare branches and whispering through new leaves. And then something else.

Faint, distant, but coming closer. A howling, almost as if from a pack of wolves. But . . . not. I heard something *wrong* in those long, quavering wails, something exaggerated, mystical, unearthly. Something that did not belong in forests or on roads where people walked.

Yarri grabbed both our arms. "We have to get off the road, but unless you do exactly as I say, even that won't help."

"What is it?" I asked.

"Death," Yarri muttered. "If it's what I think it is, fast, ugly death. Come on."

She bolted off the dirt road and beneath the trees, and Dan and I raced after her. She didn't go far into the woods, though — just deep enough that I lost sight of the road. "That gets us away from her view," Yarri said, opening her pouch and pawing through it. "Now to get us away from their noses."

The howling got a little louder and a lot more eerie.

She found what she was looking for, and with a soft cry of "Ha!" pulled it out. She said, "Stand downwind of me. Quickly."

I tested the breeze and did as she said, as did Dan. She had a bottle in her hands, and when she squeezed the little bulb attached to it, it misted us lightly. I smelled nothing. She sprayed each of us all over, quickly, and herself last, getting even the soles of our feet, then sprayed back just a ways along the track by which we'd entered the forest. Then she pulled a small knife from her kit and sliced two long strips from the bottom of her tunic. "We have to tie ourselves together," she said. "So none of us will run." So we did — Dan to her, and Yarri to me. "Crouch, keep close to the trunk of this tree, and don't move at all," she said. "They're blind, but they can find you by the faintest scent or sound."

"*What* are blind?" I whispered.

But she put a finger to her lips and crouched down; she closed her eyes tightly and pressed her forehead against the rough bark of the tree trunk. Dan took a place at her left, I at her right, and we did as she did.

For a moment or two, nothing changed but that the howling grew louder.

Then, a hard wind rattled the branches over our heads and tossed damp leaves up from the forest floor into the air, and slapped them against us. A cold fog rolled over us, wet as the fogs that plague the Highlands, but thicker, and laden with the sweet-rotten stench of spoiled meat.

The reek of death.

Such a smell terrifies. It knots the belly; it tenses the muscles; it sends a shudder through the brain. It screams, *Run! Or die!* I felt that urge. Everything in the forest felt it. The beasts that inhabited the ancient forest fled as if before a fire, and every bone and muscle in my body fought to bolt, to run, to flee mindlessly, to mark myself as prey. But to get away, away, away.

I took Yarri's, thin, fine-boned hand and held on to it for life and sanity. I prayed she was holding on to Dan on the other side.

Then the howling was right on top of us, and I wondered how I had ever mistaken the noise for wolves. Surely only from demons could such hideous sounds erupt.

The fog, lit by the moon, buried everything. I could not see the bark of the tree upon which my forehead rested.

The howling stopped, replaced by wet snuffling, and what sounded like hundreds of shuffling feet pushed past us on all sides — close enough that if any of us had reached out, I was sure we could have touched them. Or perhaps it was the fog that made them sound so close. I hoped it was that, and not the first thing, but I feared at any instant sharp teeth would sink into my neck and shake me the way a dog shakes a rabbit.

"You had their trail, you stupid beasts!" a woman's voice shrieked. "You've tracked them all the way from Hillrush — you will not lose them here. Two children did not suddenly sprout wings and fly away."

Two children. Two children from Hillrush? The monsters were hunting us.

I closed my eyes tightly and tried not to breathe at all.

The monsters were hunting us.

Before, they had been some new form of nature, terrifying but impersonal — I had feared them, but I had not thought they were searching for Dan and me. Now, though, the demon sounds and the snuffling and the death stench all became personal. The unseen woman and her monsters might go away, but if they did, that would be their mistake. They were tracking us, following us, and they would, I suspected, keep coming until they found us.

"Back," the woman shouted suddenly. "Go back. We'll find the spot where they left the road and you useless hounds lost their trail."

The beasts she commanded, sounding for the first time like nothing more than dogs, whined.

"Hunt," she said, and the howling began again, but this time moving away rather than toward us. Away was better. The stinking fog thinned and then sucked up after the huntress, all traces of it quickly vanishing.

We, however, did not move for a very long time.

Finally, Yarri pulled her hand from mine, and with the knife cut the cloth strips that had bound us together. "Oh, help," she whispered.

I stood up, stiff and cold clear through, both from the fog and from fear. I was still shaking. "What was that, Yarri?"

"The Blind Hunt," she said. "They hunt my kind for sport, and eat us when they catch us. The huntress hates nightlings. The Hunt wasn't just out for a run tonight, though. They were after you."

"I heard," I said.

Dan was on his feet and looking around. "Will they be back? Tonight?"

"Not tonight," Yarri said. "The huntress will think her hounds were drawn off their trail by something tasty, and she will run them back a long way searching for where the two of you doubled back on the trail she followed and went off in a different direction. That you walked so far in one direction before heading off in nearly the opposite direction has to have bothered her. She'll probably go all the way back to where you two and I met to see if that was where her hounds went wrong."

"We might have bought a day or two, then," Dan said.

Yarri shrugged. "There's no telling. She hates to hunt in the daylight though, and dawn is not far off. So we should be safe here for the day."

We helped her pitch her tent and made camp.

When we crawled inside, I looked at her, wondering how she had known what the hounds were. How she had been chosen as Dan's and my guide. "Why did you come for us in the forest last night?" I asked her.

"So that you could come to Arrienda," she said. "So that you could bargain with Letrin."

"No," I said. "That isn't what I meant. Why were *you* chosen? You're a child —"

"I explained about how the children of the slaves are ignored," she said, "although my time to remain unseen probably grows short. Before long, there will be those who will notice me in spite of my best efforts, and who will want to buy me as a housegirl." She shuddered. "But in any case, if you wondered why it was me instead of some other child of slaves — I volunteered. I knew your family, and I felt a . . . a sort of kinship with your parents, who were very kind to me. I hope that does not offend you."

"It makes me happy," I said.

Dan nodded agreement.

I settled onto the tent floor as she brought out the light she wore around her neck. "How did you know how to hide us from those . . . things? Beasts. Monsters."

She smiled slowly. "When you followed Yan through the gates of Arrienda and down to meet the kai-lord, did you see me?"

Dan and I both shook our heads.

"Yet I was at your side the whole time. When you bargained with Letrin, did you see me?"

"No," I said.

"Yet I was there. Slaves and the children of slaves are forbidden all magic. Yet slave parents pass down to children the quiet magics that have always belonged to all nightlings — how to hide in plain sight, how to move without sounds, how to trick hunters into going off on false trails, and a dozen other things. And because of need, I have been a good scholar learning these magics. That was not the first time I have crossed paths with the Blind Hunt."

I shivered. I could not imagine ever again being as close to them as we had been. I thought about them and found the memory of those creatures more terrifying even than they had been in the flesh, for I could imagine them ripping me apart. Yarri had faced them more than once and had escaped each time. I tried to imagine being that brave.

"We'll face worse than the Blind Hunt before we're done," Yarri said.

I did not want to consider that.

CHAPTER 5
THE AUDIOMAERIST

Dawn came, but the light outside did not make its way into the tent, which made sense. The nightlings created their tents to protect themselves when they traveled away from their cities or barrows.

Neither Dan nor I could sleep, and Yarri seemed to have endless energy. So we settled around her light-and-heat-ball campfire and her foldable pot, and we each pulled food from our kit-bags to contribute to the morning meal.

I did not want to think anymore about what was behind us, so I asked her, "Where are we going? How did you know where this person Kai-Lord Letrin wants would be? It seems to me if he wanted to set us a difficult task, he would not ask us to do something that any nightling from Arrienda already knows how to do."

"I don't know where Doyati might be found. No one has been able to find him for more than a hundred years."

And we had fourteen days? Suddenly, the task Letrin had set for us took on monstrous proportions.

"Then where are you leading us?"

"I have traveled before to speak with an audiomaerist known by my parents. Do you know what they do?"

Neither Dan nor I had ever heard of such creatures.

"Well," said Yarri, "audiomaerists have the ability to divine the locations of living things by listening to words and sounds spoken into the air, be they near or far, ancient or recent, or sometimes, I think, in the future. The audiomaerist we travel to will already know of whom we seek before we tell her, because you each have said his name several times. She'll focus on the resonances that attach themselves to this boy, and will track echoes of his name to his voice, and will track his voice through the air and across the ground to the boy himself. Then we will go get him."

I found this unlikely. "If he lives nearby, perhaps. But what happens when we discover that this boy lives on the other side of the world, across seas and over mountains, and we would need a year and a day, a ship and a caravan, and armies and swords just to reach him? You have to know that will be a possibility."

"Letrin had to ask something possible for us to accomplish," Yarri said. "Otherwise he could not have signed the contract." She frowned. "He may not want to pay you what he will owe you when you bring the boy to him. But he certainly wants us to find and bring him Doyati."

We ate. The food Yarri shared with us tasted much better than it looked. I've never been fond of dried food. It's most of what we eat in winter in the Highlands, and it all seems the same after a while — tough and stringy and dry. But the nightlings had discovered ways to make dried food tasty and fresh-seeming. Fruit, grains, and meats — we ate all of them, and when our stomachs were full, Yarri passed around some delicious sweet wine, and suddenly Dan and I were yawning and I couldn't keep my eyes open.

"You'll wake refreshed," she told us. "And you'll be ready for the hard travel and the probable dangers we will face tonight. This will be the last day we spend in friendly territory."

Which seemed a strange thing to tell someone on the verge of falling to sleep. Especially considering how friendly the *friendly* territory had been. Yet I slept.

* * *

I was falling.

I landed so lightly my feet barely brushed the ground. I was back in Hillrush, in front of Catri's house, but I knew the house was empty, just as I knew I was dreaming. I even had time to be surprised by that — knowing that I was in a dream — because I'd never realized that before.

I went inside through the kitchen door, into the middle of Catri's mother's kingdom, but Catri's mother was not cooking, even though it was past morning and she should have been working on the day's meals.

The house was quiet, and I had never heard quiet in Catri's house any more than I had heard it in my own.

Nothing in the house was different, but everything was wrong. I knew that wherever Catri and her family had gone, they wouldn't be coming back. I turned slowly, praying that I would see some sign of her, that I would be able to know she was safe.

Without warning, she appeared from the front room. She didn't see me. She walked right through me. But she was the ghost in her house, not me.

"Catri," I shouted after her, but she didn't hear me. I followed her, out the kitchen door and down the three steps, past the goats and the chicken coops, into a shadowed circle beneath the apple trees. She stood crying, silent, only a shadow herself. I reached out to touch her, to comfort her.

And I was falling again, wrapped in darkness.

I toppled into light, into a sunlit glade in the heart of a beautiful forest. All around me, great butterflies fluttered and deer romped and rabbits chased one another, full of spring madness. The air smelled of honeysuckle and apple blossoms. In the distance I heard water chuckling over a stream bed, and farther away, the comforting thunder of a waterfall.

And I saw my mother, and others who, back in the village, had been sick with the *saku*, but who had not yet wandered off or died. I hurried to Mama's side, reached out for her, and whispered, "Mama?" She did not hear me, but I could hear her.

"Where are my children?" she was asking everyone around her. "Where am I? Where is Jhon?"

But no one answered her. They, too, were wandering from person to person, asking where their loved ones were.

I tried to touch Mama to make her see me, to tell her I would take care of the younglings and to promise that I would find her, but my hand moved right through her and that broke whatever spell had brought me to her.

And I was falling again.

I dropped onto a hard, flat, bright plain. The sun beat down on me, the wind tore past me, and grains of sand like tiny razors scoured my skin. My father stood beside me, looking battered and nearly starved. Nor was he alone. Others in the village who had gone mad with the *saku* and wandered away to die were with him. I knew them, but again, I could not make them see me or hear me. I could not comfort them. I pressed my face against my father's tattered shirt, willing him to wrap his arms around me and tell me, "Genna-dilly, everything will be all right," as he had when I was little.

But when I opened my eyes, utter blackness enveloped me. Something watched me — I could feel it staring at the back of my neck. I turned but could see nothing. I listened but could hear no danger.

But then a voice I knew — a voice I had come to hate, said, "You're here? Here? On the roads? I'll find you, little Genna. I'll find you, and I'll find Danrith, and I'll kill you both."

The voice belonged to Banris.

I ran.

All around me lay darkness, and rough ground rose and

fell beneath my pounding feet. He pursued me, running hard after me, hungry for my life and soul.

"You belong here," he said. "You belong here, and you belong to me, along with all the rest. If I catch you, I will keep you. Or you will bring yourself back to me, and offer yourself into my hands. Either way, I'll have what I want."

I tried to wake up, for I knew I was sleeping. But I could not wake. The ground beneath my feet stayed uneven, and my footsteps over them had weight. I turned my ankle and the pain made me scream. I began to lose ground, and the pounding of footsteps behind me drew closer.

I fell, and the rock beneath my hand cut into me, and the pain should have woken me. But it did not. I screamed again, and scrambled to my feet, feeling my own warm blood on my palm, wishing I had one of Yarri's heatless lights. I put my palm to my lips as I ran and licked the dirt from my wound, and tasted my own blood.

I remember thinking in that instant, How very strange. I cannot remember having ever tasted something in a dream before.

And then a hard hand on my shoulder shook me, and a hand slapped my face — a stinging blow. I shrieked in terror, certain that Uncle Banris had me, and a second blow fell, and this time I woke up.

My head ached and spun, and my first impressions were confusing. Yarri's pale oval face staring down at me, wide-eyed, her features distorted by the shadows cast by her fireless nightling light. My brother, hovering behind her, rubbing the palm of one hand with the other hand. Voices that faded in and out of my ears — my mother, my father, people from my village, talking over and around and through one another. And Yarri, who kept saying, "Wake up, wake up!" And a sharp, awful pain in my right palm. I looked at it. Found a slash in my skin, a ragged cut filled with dirt and little granules of rock.

I could not understand what was happening to me. I looked at Dan and Yarri and muttered some inane thing about still being dreaming. But I already knew that I was awake. My stinging cheek and Dan's expression and the way he held the hand with which he'd slapped me — all of these told me that I no longer slept. And that something had happened that I could not explain.

Yarri studied my hand, and carefully pulled a piece of gravel from it. Then she took a little knife out of her kit-bag and worked two of the larger bits free. She cut a corner from her tabard, dropped all three bits of grime into it, and tied it closed with a bit of lacing that she sliced from her clothing.

"Why did you do that?" I asked her.

"Because the one we're going to see will want to have a look. Not everyone ends up with dream gravel embedded in their dream cuts, you know."

"Uncle Banris was chasing me," I said.

Yarri and Dan both stared at me.

"And Mama and Papa were in the dream. Both trapped, but in different places. And my best friend was a ghost in the kitchen of her house."

Dan said, "Catri?"

I nodded.

He stared down at his hands and his ears reddened. "I hope she's all right."

"Me, too." I would have teased him about the red ears, about his alarm at the mention of Catri's name, but I didn't have it in me right then. I'd been dreaming, but I had gravel in my hand, and a throbbing knee that, when I checked it, proved to be skinned and bleeding, too.

Yarri said, "I've heard about people who could travel into their dreams. Who could actually reach those places that the rest of us . . . well, only dream of. It's quite a useful talent, I've been told. Though I can't imagine why."

I was thinking.

"What if Mama and Papa really are trapped in the dream realm?"

"You know they aren't," Dan said. "Mama is home in bed. Papa is dead."

"We don't know he's dead," I said. Until I had seen him in my dream, I had been as certain as Dan was that Papa was dead, not lost. Suddenly, though, I found myself believing along with Mama that he might still live.

Dan said, "I *know* he's dead."

It was the way he always got. "Why do you say that?" I asked.

"Because I have his ghost," he said. "It is the ghost the caers of Hillrush have passed down since Hillrush has had caers. It is the ghost the kai-lord saw in me, and the ghost who gives me nightmares some nights. And that is why . . ." He closed his eyes tightly and swallowed hard, and I saw tears start down his cheeks. "And that is why I know Papa is dead. The ghost would not have come to me to be my advisor if he were still alive."

I rested a hand on Dan's arm. "I saw him in my dream. And Mama, and Catri. And I cut my hand and skinned my knee in the same dream. If that were real, it could all be real."

"Or they could all be dead now," Dan whispered.

"What if the part of them that really matters is trapped in the dream world, and the rest of them is where we can see it? Or could? And that is why Mama is sick. And why Papa wandered away."

"Then Papa would still have his ghost," Dan said with dreary finality.

That night we ran hard. The waning moon had moved not more than a finger's breadth through the sky before we came upon a tiny village nestled in the hills. We came over the crest of the hill and before us lay a handful of houses, lights shining golden through their oilskin windows.

We headed down the road. "The audiomaerist we've come to meet lives behind the main part of Peevish," Yarri said.

Dan and I looked at each other. "Peevish."

"There's a longer name, and it has something to do with someone's goats and the village washing, but the name's been shortened to Peevish over time. I don't know the longer name, though my parents said the old people here use it sometimes."

I thought sometime I'd like to find out how a village got its name from goats and laundry, but all I wanted to do right at that moment was find this wisewoman who could tell me how I'd cut my hand and skinned my knee in a dream, and what sort of dream I'd had in which such things could happen.

Yarri took us along a narrow path, and from the droppings, I could tell Peevish, like Hillrush, lived on its goats and sheep. She pointed between trees to a tiny cottage. It could only have had one room, and that room big enough for only one person with a few sparse belongings to live comfortably. "She only sees people one at a time," Yarri said. "So I'll tell her who you are, and then you'll have to each go in and speak with her separately."

"Perhaps she could come outside to meet with us," I said. I didn't like the idea of being alone with this audiomaerist with her unknown magic, but I liked less the idea of leaving Dan alone with her. I get annoyed with my brother, but ugly things can happen quickly — something I had learned the hard way. Splitting up seemed a bad idea to me.

"I do not think she'll agree to that," Yarri said. "She's . . . odd."

"Her oddness is not a point in favor of the three of us dividing up," I said. "If anything, it makes me think we should stick closer together."

We reached the little house. The tiny walled yard around it reeked of goat and chicken and dog, though I could not see or hear any sign of those. Yarri knocked on the door, and a woman older than the rocks on the road, by all appearances, opened it after a long moment. She peered up at the three of us with eyes that I would have thought near blindness — and then she did the strangest thing.

"By all the little gods, get in here, all of you. Think you this is a safe place for the three of you to be seen, or that you can walk so bold beneath the stars, carrying on you the onus that you do?" She shook her head and backed up, and we crowded into a tiny space thick with the stink of boiling herbs and overheated by a fire that burned far too hot and bright for cooking or heating.

The audiomaerist took a seat at a tiny round table. It had one chair opposite it. Beyond that, one plate and one cup sat on the mantelpiece, and a flat cot, the kind that hangs on the wall and unlatches to drop down at night, took up most of the far wall. On the sill of one of the three oilskin-covered windows, a gray-and-black-swirled tabby with a white face and belly and white toes on all four feet watched the three of us with an appearance of fascination that you don't usually see in cats. Unless, perhaps, you're a mouse.

The three of us crammed into a space that would have been uncomfortable for one. We all stood.

The old woman turned to Yarri. "You weren't supposed to come back here, but I can see why you brought them, but, still, they could be the death of me, as if you couldn't, and you know I don't need *him* stalking me." She said it all in one breath, as if she were afraid she would run out of air. In her hot, cluttered, crowded cottage that smelled overwhelmingly of goat and spoiling cheese, I could understand her fear.

"Show her the cut on your hand," Yarri told me instead of saying anything directly to the old woman.

I held out my hand.

"Here are the bits of gravel I dug out of it," Yarri said, and put her little handmade bag on the table.

The old woman ran one gnarled finger along the edges of my cut and hissed. She undid the little tie on the bag, and touched the grit, and suddenly she wrapped her arms around herself, closed her eyes, and began rocking back and forth, making keening noises. Dan and I both jumped, but Yarri held out her hands, a calming gesture. "Wait," she mouthed.

"You are watched and you are hunted, all three of you, by the roads and also through the nightworlds, including the world that hides the child you seek. Hunters are after you, powerful, deadly creatures who command Old Magic, and who are not bound by the waxing and waning of the moon.

"The one you seek hides from old and new evils. He has hidden for a long time, bearing many faces and many names, and your enemies have only the one name to follow. You seek a trickster, and perhaps you will find him, and perhaps he will find you. And if he finds you first, you may face danger from all sides. Those who hide often resent being found."

She opened her eyes, and stared at my brother and me and then at Yarri.

She pointed to Danrith. "You have two eyes to see the present, and two eyes to remember the past and know the future." She made a broad, sweeping gesture, certainly meant to be ominous or impressive, but in the cramped space, she managed to knock two jars of herbs from the shelves right beside her to the floor. We heard glass shatter, and then twin clouds of powder and dust billowed up from the floor.

The old woman began to sneeze.

An instant later, so did the rest of us.

The old woman began waving her arms, which only made things worse.

"Bother and pestilence!" she wheezed between sneezes.

My eyes burned and watered. I sneezed, I coughed, my nose ran, and I yearned to breathe in even the reeking air that surrounded her cottage. I reached for the door next to me and shoved it open. A breeze blew in, guttering the fire, sending the cloud of powdered herbs spiraling through the door, and cooling off the overheated room. Air I'd found stinking and awful not long before seemed as sweet to me as mountain air in a spring meadow. Well . . . almost as sweet.

But the old woman slammed the door shut, shrieking, "Are you mad? Have you . . . any idea what . . . (cough) . . . forces have been brought . . . to (cough) bear . . . in the search for you?"

"No," I said.

"Vast forces," she said.

"Could you . . ." I sneezed again. ". . . be more specific?"

She sighed, and blotted her running eyes and nose with a dirty sleeve. "No. I cannot tell the future. I can hear hunters talking, I can know that they pursue you, I can know they have Old Magic because they speak of it, but I cannot tell you who they are, because unlike you, they are careful never to speak their own names."

Yarri told her about our meeting with the Blind Hunt, and the old woman said, "That's one. But not all."

Dan said, "You started to tell me about the eyes in the present, and the past . . . ?"

The old woman leaned her chin on her hands and said, "I have no energy left with which to be poetic or mystical. Forgive me. Your ghost — the one who talks to you so often — has a role in your journey. If you listen to him, you'll find his advice good. It is advice only a warrior can give. If you allow him to control you, you will lose yourself. Be cautious."

She turned to Yarri. "You have magic you've hidden from your family and everyone else. It's useful, practical stuff, but the kai-lord would kill you for knowing it."

Yarri said, "He will already kill me for what I have done to get us here. Dead is dead."

"It is," the old woman said. "So use your magic. Heat, cold, the casting of shields, the spinning of light — your talents and the tools you have made will be the difference between life and death in what lies ahead. Keep everyone's trails confused and keep yourselves hidden, and you may live to see your family again."

"I will," Yarri whispered.

The old woman turned her gaze on me. "You must lead. Be the voice of reason, the hand of justice, the maker of plans. In the future, you will wear other faces and carry other burdens, but this time —"

I interrupted her. "I thought you said you couldn't see the future."

"Bah!" She waved my protest away as if it were a fly buzzing near her face. "Your future sees me. That's another problem entirely. You want to listen, or you want to argue?"

"I will listen," I said, trying to appear meek and apologetic.

She studied me with eyes gone shrewd, and after a moment burst out laughing. "You'll need to work on that," she said after she got her laughter under control. "Good fake sincerity could save your life one day."

I felt my face go red.

"Good. Better." She smiled. "You have a little gift, and a little curse, and they're both the same thing. The kai-lord marked you with the moonroads, and now" — her finger touched the cut on my hand — "the moonroads have marked themselves with you. You saw things there, and heard things, and you don't know whether to believe them or not."

I nodded. She had my complete attention.

"Your actions — your faith, your hope, your love, and above all else your persistence — can make them true or make them false. You can find what you saw. Or you can lose it all." She leaned forward, searching in my eyes for answers, and she frowned at what she saw. "You might not be the one, though, in which case you were doomed to fail before you started."

"The one what?" I asked her, but she shushed me.

And turned to her cat. "You'll go with them, of course. These three will be walking the moonroads, and we cannot think they'll find their way without your sort of help."

"I thought you'd want a favor," the cat said, and I shrieked, and Dan jumped, and Yarri stared with her mouth hanging open. "I might go with them, even if just for a while. They seem to be doing interesting things, and all you've been doing lately is making potions that stink."

"How did you make him talk?" Yarri asked our hostess.

The old woman looked disgusted. "I have done nothing with him but feed him at night and listen to his long-winded tales. If you value your sanity, don't let him tell you about the time he sailed the Warding Seas as a pirate's cat."

"I'll take them along the moonroads," the cat said. "But you're the one who must tell us which roads we'll need to follow."

"Dare I say the name of the one they seek?" she asked the cat.

"I can't hear the roads talking, old woman. You'd best tell me."

"In a moment, then. Better I tell you than them, better you hear it here than later. *He* can't see them here. Or me. I always feel better when he can't see *me*. Their hunters can't see here, either. I don't know what tricks they know, but I don't think I care to be spreading answers to questions they haven't thought to ask."

"I don't think they concern themselves with cats," I said, and the cat turned all his attention on me, and looked straight into my eyes, and from his mouth I heard the words, "Neither do I," while in my mind, just as clearly, his voice said, *And you, Dreamer of Moonroads . . . do you think I'm a cat? Here, kitty, kitty, have some nice fish?*

Then he added, for everyone, "But let us just be cautious, shall we?"

Of course he wasn't a cat. How could he be a cat? I'd had cats twining around my ankles all my life, tripping me after I'd milked the goats, begging favors, and none of them had ever spoken to me, either aloud or by dancing through my thoughts.

I found myself standing as if at the fork in a road, and one branch went to places I knew and could understand, and the other took me where I had never been, and where things were different and terrifying and wrong. Where the world that I knew fell away and strange bones poured out of the melting skin of the universe.

I wanted to run back home. I wanted never to have picked up those buckets or sneaked out the door with my brother. I wanted to have the old life and the safe road back; but my feet were already on the new road, and I knew in my gut that the only way off that road was to travel it to its end.

The old woman said, "You have quite the path ahead of you. And the cat can be a help to you, if you keep him in his place. But remember, you three — you're traveling with bad company. Ruinous company."

"I'm good company," the cat said, sounding to me a bit put out. "I caught all your mice for you, didn't I? I got you help when you fell ill. I listen to your endless complaining."

The old woman ignored the cat. She said to all of us, "I would tell you that everything will be well for you, but I cannot make promises. You have a hard road before you, though not the hardest, and if you have a fine prize within your reach, the abyss that lies before it will more than likely devour you before you win it. And more than you." She shrugged, a stiff, arthritic movement of her shoulders that made me feel for her just a little. I would have been much more sympathetic had she not just finished announcing the likelihood of my death and my brother's.

I knew we faced danger, but hearing it so coldly stated is another bitterer thing.

"You'll leave by the moonroad," she told us. "You'll not come back here again, no matter what happens. I'll neither see you nor help you — I have another path, not yet completed, and your presence will most likely destroy it."

And in my mind, the cat said, *And I ask myself again, what is she waiting for to complete this path about which she so often speaks? I think she's gone well past her grace period already. I would think her time for grand destinies lay in the past . . . not the future.*

I almost laughed, and only kept myself from it by biting the inside of my lip. I liked the cat. I felt I shouldn't, but I did.

Yarri said, "Our search, old mother. Our search. Where are we to go?"

"To the nightside of existence. The moonroads."

"Those are myths," Yarri said.

The cat laughed, and the old woman said, "The cut on her hand and the gravel you pulled out of it aren't myths. I can get you started in the right direction. Only she," and she pointed to me, "can call them and walk them and pull you onto them with her."

"I can, too," the cat said. Nobody paid attention to him.

"These roads. They're dreams, right?" I asked. "But dreams made real? I found my mother and my father and my best friend inside of my dreams, and then Uncle Banris chased me, and I hurt my hand. But they're really just dreams."

"No," the old woman said. "You think that because you dreamed your way onto them the first time. Had the reckless nightling spun her shield that day before sleeping, the moonroads would never have lured you onto them. It will be harder for you now, because they have bitten pieces of you, and you have taken away pieces of them." She sighed. "They are not dreams, and nothing like dreams, and if you let yourself think of them in that manner, you'll not survive. They are real. The moonroads run through the shadows and layers of this world, but this world turned sideways, bent in the middle, twisted by an old, foul magic. They should not exist. They drag life from this world into its echoes, and pour poison into all that they touch. But no one has found a way to end them, and they'll be where they are long after you and I are dust."

"They have their uses," said the cat.

"As do nightshade and darkbell, cat," the old woman snapped, "but the uses are ugly ones." She turned to me. "Stay off the moonroads as long as you can, walk them as little as you can, and flee them forever as soon as you can. They'll claim a bit of you each time you walk them, and keep the bits and dig into your soul with them. It would be best for you if you had never stepped foot on them at all — but that can't be helped now, can it?"

And to the cat, she said, "Letrin lied when he said they had two weeks. He made his bargain on the morning after Offering Night, so that was the full moon right there. They've spent two nights running here."

The cat hissed. "And roadclose comes at the beginning of the waning crescent. Which means they have only five days to find the person they seek and get back to the sunworld."

The old woman nodded and turned to me. "Remember that. If you have not found your quarry by the fifth night, and, what's more, found a way to escape the moonroads before dawn, you will be trapped and you will have missed Letrin's deadline, and he will own you all." She pursed her lips, and her face became even more wrinkled, something I would not have imagined possible.

Yarri sucked air through her teeth, hissing, and the cat turned his attention on her. "That's my line, nightling."

To all of us, the old woman said, "You'll need the road named Coldfall. That will be your first road and perhaps your last, for beyond Coldfall the echoes will not speak to me. Nor can I find the one you hope to capture, you understand. He has hidden himself so well, and for so long, that my magic could no more pin him down and shake him loose from his hiding place than I could unspin the spool of life itself. His name echoes in thousands of places, from countless tongues. Nevertheless, his own voice lingers on the Coldfall Road, and if you follow it, perhaps you will find him, or perhaps he will find you."

She looked at the cat. "You know Coldfall?"

He sighed. "The worst of bad roads. Inhabited by all manner of lowlifes, and dangerous to traverse at the best of times. And with hunters coming for us, this will not be the best of times."

Then the cat stretched languorously and yawned, curling pink tongue to roof of mouth in apparent contempt of the terrifying future he had just finished painting for us. "And now, old mother," and he glanced at Yarri as he said at last, “before you send us off to nasty places, why don’t you tell me the name of this poor soul I’m helping these urchins hunt down to feed to everyone’s enemy.”

The old woman sighed. She dropped her voice to a whisper, and all around me I felt magic curl tight enough to stop the air from moving. And she said, “Doyati.”

The cat went rigid and his back arched and all his fur stood on end so that he looked twice his size.

“You know Doyati?” the old woman asked, voice still soft.

“Far better than I’d like,” the cat said. “Far, far better.”

Chapter 6

. . . And the Cat

"You've already crossed the moonroads," the cat said to me. He rode on my shoulders. "If you have not walked them in the flesh, you've walked them in spirit, and they have marked you. So for you, finding a road isn't going to be that hard. As the old woman said, you've got the roads into your blood now, and your blood is on them. The moonroads and the nightworlds will call to you — they're nasty that way. When you sleep they will try to drag you in soul-first, and when you're awake, from time to time you'll see some corner of a moonroad try to slide itself beneath your feet, so that you'll step onto it all unwary."

I shivered. "I don't like the sound of that."

"You shouldn't," the cat told me. "The moonroads want to be walked, but those who can find them are not usually the sort of folk a gentle young girl like you would want anything to do with. The moonroads feed off their passengers, and at the same time feed them. None walk them and remain unchanged. Although," he said, and dug his claws into my shoulder, making me wince, "I do know a few tricks for taking the worst of their bite out of them."

The four of us were hiking away from the old woman's tiny cottage and her goat-stinking, dog-stinking yard, and I was beginning to catch promises of scents other than cooked fish and onions and wood-fire smoke and animal dung.

Behind me, I could hear Dan telling Yarri about figuring guilt and innocence in a trial by use of two drops of daylight taandu essence mixed with verbena and one drop of the suspect's blood. He'd been at me for hours with that business only days before, so excited was he to have learned something so complex and full of spell-work and questioning techniques and the reading of results.

I pitied Yarri. But better her than me.

I returned my attention to the cat.

"So really," the cat was saying, "the problem is not so much finding a moonroad as it is staying off one when you don't want to find it. During the moony half of the month, anyway."

"How did I get to the ones in my sleep the first time?" I asked. "And why were my parents there, and my best friend?"

"Well, I'd guess the charming fellow who wants you to hunt down his oldest enemy for him is probably the one who made sure you would find the roads that would let you do it. Letrin is a fiend, but good enough at magic for any ten monsters like him — he could have opened your eyes and your mind to the roads with a single touch, were he so inclined." The cat leaned forward a bit and turned to look into my eyes, and said, "Did he touch you?"

I thought about it, then nodded. "More than once."

The cat gave a little purr and settled onto my shoulder again, and started kneading my neck with his paws.

"Watch the claws," I told him.

"Sorry," he said. But he sounded not the least bit sorry.

"So the roads will find me, just like Doyati will perhaps find me," I said, annoyed. "So I might as well go home and all my answers will come to me and my problems will solve themselves."

The cat laughed, a happy laugh that didn't seem to me the sort of sound a real cat would make even if it could talk. This laugh didn't have much dignity in it. "You're actually funny," the cat said. "Imagine that." He flowed from my shoulder to the ground, boneless as poured milk, and turned thrice in a circle, his ears and tail up, his whiskers all spread out. "That which comes unsought is most often unwelcome.

And when you find Doyati, you're going to want a few things in hand to deal with him — and later, with Letrin."

"And Uncle Banris?" I asked.

The cat laughed again. "Certainly Uncle Banris, if you're going to live long enough for *him* to be a problem."

"You're such a comfort. Thank you," I said, not meaning it at all. "If Doyati is Letrin's enemy, why isn't Doyati going to be my friend?" I asked.

"Because," the cat said, "you're bringing Letrin and his worst weapons right at someone who has spent a great deal of time and effort avoiding that very confrontation — and you hope to give Doyati to Letrin as a gift to save yourselves."

"Oh."

"So shut your mouth and open your eyes and look at what I'm doing," he said, and I did as I was told.

Without warning, I found myself very close to the ground, looking out at my boot-shod feet some distance from me, the socks I'd knit myself poking over the tops; a skirt of homespun that went down to the socks, with deep pockets in the front; and Mama's beautiful deep-green hand-knit sweater, made from wool she'd sheared, washed, carded, spun, and dyed. It was my best sweater, full of little magics. And warm, too. I looked like every sturdy farm girl who came to market in Hillrush on market day. Dark hair braided back, hazel eyes, freckles. Nothing special. Except I'd never been able to see all of myself at once before, or any of myself so clearly. I'd never realized how much I looked like my brother. Or Papa. I looked down and discovered I had cat paws, and noticed the whiskers sprouting from my face.

Don't get excited, the cat whispered inside my mind. *You aren't a cat. I'm just letting you look through my eyes for a moment, because it will save you time and me explanations.*

Through his eyes, I saw something flash — a tiny spark low to the ground, like the flicker of a firefly, only quicker and brighter and more orange.

There, he said. *That's what you're after. That little flash. Not necessarily orange, though. You'll see different roads as different colors. But when you see the spark, step toward it, and it will come to you.*

I thought of how I might someday need to find the road in twilight by a riverbank, with the fireflies lighting up the air around me like fallen stars, and the cat's voice in my head said, *Don't borrow troubles you don't have. Worry about the things that really are problems.*

As quickly as I'd been looking through his eyes, I found myself once again looking through my own. The sudden shift made me dizzy, and I swayed and almost fell down.

Yarri and Dan both reached for me, and Dan, looking scared, said, "Are you unwell?"

"I'm . . . fine," I said.

The cat snorted. "Happens to everyone who goes looking for moonroads for the first time. She'll be well enough."

I nodded.

"Why are they called moonroads?" Dan asked.

"Because you can only move onto them or off them when the moon shines, of course. Dark of the moon, skies covered by clouds, or times when the moon is not in the sky, you'll have to stay where you are, wherever that might be."

I thought of Uncle Banris reaching for me on the moonroad, and Dan and Yarri dragging me back to my own world. I thought of Mama and maybe Papa trapped on the moonroads, their bodies left behind to wander or die.

And then the cat told me, "Neither Dan nor Yarri can find the moonroads or see them or call them, which means that for them to travel by moonroad, they're going to have to rely on you and me. We can cast for roads at the same time — that is, call them to us — but you must never step onto a moonroad that you've found if I have already moved onto one that *I've* found. We would end up in completely different nightworlds, and we might not find each other until we come back here. And in the meantime, such terrible things could happen to one or the other of us that we would never be able to return."

I looked at him, unable to believe what I was hearing. "You and I could start here, and each find an . . . opening . . . and they might go to two different places?"

"Not might. Would."

I shivered.

"And each time we go through, we'll end up someplace different?"

"Mostly. You get to know the terrain after a while. You get the flavor of the different roads, and you'll learn from that where you are and what might be close, but — the roads aren't like roads here. They move around on their own."

"Then how will we make any progress?"

"We'll walk," the cat said, "and as long as we keep moving, progress will eventually come to us. What remains to be seen is if it will kill us or save us when it reaches us."

A firefly shimmer, cool green, tempting, flickered at the corner of my left eye, and suddenly I felt the rich weight of yearning tighten my belly. I turned toward it, smelling air after lightning, tasting cool rain on my tongue, hearing bells so faint I could have believed they might exist nowhere but in my own imagination, except that I had never imagined music so captivating or so alien. I walked toward the place where I had seen the shimmer, and the cat said, "Not that way. That's *a* road. It isn't *the* road. They can all connect with one another sometimes, and if you work at it hard enough, you can usually find your way from one to the other . . . but they'll fight you to keep you where you don't want to be."

More lights gathered around the first bright sparkle, and the temptation to go to them grew. So I forced myself to back away from the road, blinking my eyes to make them water, so that I didn't see the little sparks.

That was when Dan said, "Do you hear the howling?"

I did. I'd been hearing it for a while, faintly, a pack of demon hounds belling after some prey, but I was busy, and I'd ignored it.

The cat was circling in front of us, eyes half closed, tail straight up in the air and crooked at the tip, whiskers straight out and trembling.

Yarri said, "I hear them, too."

We all grew very quiet, listening. It was — it could only be — the Blind Hunt, and I could tell from their excitement that they had the scent of something they wanted urgently, and they had that scent strongly. We were what they wanted. They began to draw nearer, and a shiver ran down my spine.

"Cat," I said.

"It's them," Dan told me. "Hurry."

"*Cat!*" I said again, and when the accursed cat still ignored me, circling and circling instead in his search for the right road, I grabbed him by the scruff of the neck and half lifted him off the ground. Tendrils of fog began to curl around my feet.

He hissed, but I said, "Do you hear the hounds?"

He listened for only an instant, and his ears went flat back on his head. "Do you still see the road you found?" he asked. I felt his small body go rigid in my hand.

"Yes," I told him.

"Then hold hands with your brother and the nightling, and step into the lights. Where we end up cannot be *that* much worse than what we leave behind."

The green shimmers and flickers, the smell of sweet, storm-washed air, the beckoning pull of the road, and the real warmth of my brother's hand in my right and Yarri's small, cool grip on my left — that is what I remember of that first voluntary step onto that first moonroad. That and the fear in my belly, as the baying of hounds drew nearer.

I took a step toward . . . into . . . *onto* light that gathered into a shimmering tunnel but did not grow brighter. The pale firefly flickers wrapped around us. I hadn't the feeling of being on a road so much as I had of falling down a hole — the same falling, in truth, I had felt in that moonroad dream. I clung to Dan and Yarri, and they clung to me, and we swept forward or downward or upward, weightless, seeming to fall and fly and race forward all at the same time.

I think I might have screamed, but I could not hear myself. I could not hear anything but the bells all around me, ringing with no tune, but all in harmony. I opened my mouth and tasted rain again. If it had not been for the fact that I could feel nothing under my feet, I would have never wanted to leave that road, it was so wonderful, so magical.

And then Yarri, Dan, and I pitched forward into darkness and landed on hard ground. I fell flat on my face, dragging both of them with me.

"Ow!" Dan said.

"Get off me, you oaf!" the cat snarled.

I did feel something small and heavy and warm and soft beneath me. I pushed myself to a sitting position and muttered, "I'm sorry, cat."

My eyes began to adjust. I could see Dan's shape to my right, sitting up, rubbing a knee. And Yarri to my left, pulling something out of her kit-bag, then whispering and waving her hands in graceful circles and spirals.

"What are you doing?" I whispered.

"What the old woman told me to do. I'm shielding," she whispered back.

"Good."

"The only good I've seen." The cat got up into my face, his front feet on my chest, his hind feet on my lap, and said, "You're an idiot." He jumped off my lap and walked in a little circle, shaking each paw, stretching carefully, and finally he sat down and began licking himself, angrily, with his back to me.

"I'm *sorry*, cat," I said again. "I couldn't see you on the road, and with the bells and the rain and the falling —"

He kept his back to me but turned his head all the way around to stare at me. "With the *what*?"

"The bells ringing. And the rain in the air . . . though it wasn't wet, actually. And all the tiny green lights spinning around us while we were falling through them."

He still stared at me, saying nothing.

"On the moonroad," I added, attempting to be helpful.

"Sounds like the wizard's tent at a Harvest Faire," he said, sounding grumpy. "Everyone experiences the moonroads somewhat differently, and every moonroad is a little different. No one I have ever known got lights and music and smells and tastes all in one road. On that road, I got nothing but a faint whiff of storm coming." He returned to licking himself. "You're a freak," he added, in between licks.

I wasn't very sorry anymore that I'd fallen on top of him. My brother and I exchanged looks. "Cat," I said, "we have the huntress after us. Should we not start running? Somewhere? Or at least be doing something?"

"I *am* doing something."

"Something *useful*," Yarri said.

"You think they'll come racing down the moonroad after you, just like that?" The sarcasm in the cat's voice was sharp enough to slice third-day bread.

"They won't?"

The cat sighed heavily and stood up and glared up at me. Cats don't have a great range of facial expressions, but what they lack in the ability to smile or frown, they make up for with body language, and the ability to express condescension in a multitude of degrees. He said, "Where are we?"

"I don't know," I told him.

"You took us on a road that went who knows where," the cat said, "with no idea how you called the road, and no idea why it chose to answer, and you leapt onto it thinking,

I would guess, of nothing but those who pursue us — or, perhaps, of lights and rain and bells rattling in your head. So which sign do you suppose you left them that they could find and call this road you charged onto all willy-nilly?"

"It wasn't waiting for them?"

He scoffed. Cats should not scoff. It made me want to smack his furry round head.

"No," he said. "The road wasn't waiting for them. Moonroads don't wait for anyone. You leap when you find them, or you're left behind. If we stayed here and none of the creatures watching us right now were Letrin's spies — or in the pay of your uncle —"

"He's not really our uncle, you know," Dan interrupted.

The cat ignored him. "— we could hide here forever, and they would not find us unless they tripped over us."

I'd been feeling almost good, if annoyed by the cat's insufferably smug behavior, until he mentioned creatures watching us.

"What creatures?" Yarri and Dan asked at the same time. I turned all around, looking to see what was watching us.

There was a twilight feel to the place where we were, even though we'd landed beneath a stand of enormous trees that added shadows and layers to the darkness. Their branches spread wide and low to the ground; they had grown together and intertwined over ages, until they almost could have been one tree. Lights danced among their upper branches, blue and gold and green and pink and lavender.

Beyond the trees that sheltered us, I could make out a meadow. It looked lovely, and smelled of night-blooming flowers. And those same lights bobbed and floated and chased across the waving grasses.

Somewhere nearby, I heard water hurrying over rocks and between boulders.

"I don't see anything watching us," I said.

"That's because you're an idiot," the cat said.

Dan came to my defense. "She's not an idiot."

"You know even less than she does. And the nightling is as much a vacuum as you are."

Dan's voice rose. "If you're going to insult us, you can just . . ." And then he caught himself. And stopped.

I'd been thinking the same thing, but there was no good end to that sentence. The cat could . . . what? Leave us? We didn't know Doyati, or how to find Doyati. We didn't know the roads, or which ones could take us someplace useful, or which ones would lead us into a nightmare. I had no idea how to call a road to me. The one I'd found simply came, and here we were. I had no idea how to deal with a huntress who ran blind hounds.

I had almost nothing useful to offer to our little group. A farm girl's magic, no wisdom, no guile, no power. I had a few recipes and spells for healing and curing that my mother taught me. I had the moonroads . . . or they had me. I had the old woman's statement that I was in charge, though Yarri was older, and Dan had law training and Papa's advisor ghost, and the cat knew more about everything than I did. My sole claim to having any part of this was that I had made a bargain with a monster because I had no other choice. On my own, I had no way to keep that bargain. And neither had Dan.

"If he wants to call us idiots, we're going to have to let him," I told Dan. "We can't save Mama or the younglings or our friends, or the village if we don't have him." I turned to the cat. "Does that satisfy you?"

He just looked at me. I couldn't read his face. I couldn't read his body. He was just a cat at that moment, and I might as well have been talking to the tree beside me.

He stood there, staring up at me for the longest time. And then he sighed, and this time it wasn't an irritated sigh. "Come along," he said. "We have to find out where we are. I'd ask the trees, but they don't often talk to anyone but one another. And the maddards have never said a sensible thing to anyone."

We all rose. I looked at the trees. "They can talk?"

"They can. They usually don't. They might give us away to the kai-lord, of course, or your uncle, so let's not be too hasty to start any conversations."

"And . . . maddards? What are they?"

He raised a paw and waved it toward the meadow, and then toward the top of the tree. "The little blobs of light. The maddards are inside them. They're usually harmless, though they'll come float over anyone trying to hide, just to see what's going on. They're curious, and fear attracts them."

"So . . . everything is watching us." I shivered, suddenly chilled.

"More than you can imagine, or that I care to mention," the cat said. Inside my head, his voice added, *And most of what watches us I don't wish to speak of in front of your brother or the nightling. You I trust to be calm and sensible. The other two are holding together so far, but I suspect they could be rash. Or flighty. We don't need to be dealing with a panic right now.*

So the watching, talking trees and the watching blobs of light were not bad enough. Worse things spied on us, too. It figured. We'd landed in such a pretty place, but I supposed I couldn't count on it to be kind.

We started walking, the cat in front and the rest of us following. Since he didn't know where we were, I couldn't guess how the cat decided where we needed to be. But since I knew even less than he, I didn't complain. I simply reminded myself that for a little while, at least, no huntress pursued us, so no matter how bad things got, they were not as bad as they could have been.

I hoped.

CHAPTER 7
MOONROADING

For a long time, it was hills and meadows and more hills for us, with a cloud of maddards gathering above us and trailing along behind, so that we must have looked like the faire coming to town to all those who watched our progress. The sky never got brighter. It never got darker. The air smelled sweet and stayed comfortably right on the edge of cool. I grew thirsty, though, and tired, and Dan began to stumble as we walked. The cat, not in a talkative mood, told us to shush if we began to complain.

Yarri trudged, head down, as silent as the cat. When I asked her in a whisper what was wrong, she only said she didn't belong in the place where we were, and we needed to get out of it as quickly as we could.

The cat, I remembered, had said something to that

nature. That the moonworld would set hooks in us and keep us if it could. That it would change us.

The cat suddenly stopped, and his back arched, and his fur puffed out in all directions. He started to growl, low in his throat, and his ears went back, and he began to advance on something that he saw or smelled or sensed, but that I didn't. He began spitting.

"I wish I had Papa's sword," Dan whispered.

"Can you see what he sees?" I asked.

"No. But it must be something."

It turned out to be an abandoned camp, but one not long abandoned. We found the firepit with the fire out, but hot coals still beneath a small pot of stew that cooked over it. The stew was hot. Not bubbling, but if someone tossed a bit of wood on the fire, it would have been in no time. We found three small, abandoned tents. Inside them, gear the campers had carried.

"If they ran from us," I told the cat, "it doesn't seem they would be dangerous to us."

"They were bolkins," the cat said, as if he expected me to know what bolkins were, "and they didn't run from us." He turned to look at me. "Right. Bolkins. A pack of bolkins might run us down and catch the three of you if they were hungry enough. And throw you in their stew. They're mean little monsters, with long claws and fast legs and sharp teeth. They do trade sometimes, and if you catch them when they're well fed and happy, they aren't so bad. They're not the best trading partners, though, since they're hungry about half the time, and as likely to eat the prospective trader as bring out their beads and baskets. But they don't scare easily. And, greedy as they are, they usually hold their ground against threats."

"And something scared them off."

"Right. You understand the problem, then."

"They ran from something horrible. Do you know what?"

"Yes," the cat said and didn't say anything else. He was walking in small, tight circles, and he seemed agitated. "It's late," he began to mutter. "Late, late, late."

Yarri and Dan moved closer to me. "What's he doing?" Yarri whispered.

"I'm not sure. But I think we're in big trouble."

Both Dan and Yarri stared at me as if I'd lost my mind, and Yarri said, "Do you think so? Really?"

Well, yes, it had been a stupid thing to say. We had been in big trouble for quite a while, hadn't we?

"Road," the cat said. "The road Darkriver. We can take it out to a place I know and hole up for the day. Come on."

I saw, then, what he had caught. A little swirl of yellow-gold light, the sound of a waterfall. I moved toward it, and the cat said, "Their hands, idiot. Take their hands. They can't see what you see."

I almost couldn't make myself stop for them. The road smelled of bread cooking, and I felt Yarri and Dan grab hold of my hands as I held myself in place just long enough to be sure they had me. The light raced at me, and around me, and I stepped willingly, eagerly, into it. And into weightlessness, and the glorious thundering of the water crashing all around me, and bread baking so near I could almost taste it, and the yellow-gold of a field of dandelions. Beautiful, beautiful, beautiful.

This time, when we fell onto the ground, the cat kept himself out from underfoot.

We were back in our own world, and the moon was on the western horizon, setting, and behind us, the sky pinkened with dawn, and to our left waited the dark mouth of a cave. I looked at the cave and didn't like it.

"Barely made it," the cat said. "The soul-drinker would have finished off the bolkins and come back to make a snack of us, and everything would have been lost."

I paused a moment on the name *soul-drinker.* And shivered. "Do I want to know what a soul-drinker does?"

"Do you need to ask?"

I considered that briefly. "No." And added, "But why did we only almost make it out?"

The cat jumped from the ground to my shoulder and leaned into my face. "I knew where I needed to go, and what road I needed to call to take us there without, ah, detours. But where I needed to go was here — and *here* the sun was almost rising. The moon was almost setting. Once the moon has set, there can be no more moonroads until it rises again."

I thought about this for a moment. "I thought the moon and sun circled the world like dogs circling a bone. And that the world was a ball, too, so that each was always rising somewhere."

"That's close enough to the truth to be useful," the cat said. "At least you don't think the world is flat. The moon *is* always somewhere. But it isn't always rising right here. And I know of a nice, safe hideout inside that cave where you are going to eat, and sleep, and where Yarri can hide from the sun. And as I was trying to get us out, the moon was setting *here*."

"Then we could have found a road somewhere else."

"Yes. But not one where I know an excellent hideout." He leapt to the ground in that boneless arc that cats make look so simple, and said, *Take the others into the cave. You'll find the place where you're supposed to be. Stop there, stay there, eat, and sleep. Don't go exploring, out here or* especially *in there. I need to hunt my own dinner, but I'll be here for you before the moonroads are back.*

He trotted away from us and from the cave without another word.

"He *left* us?" Dan said.

Yarri stared after him. "Should we go after him?"

"No. He said we need to get inside and out of sight," I said.

"But he *left* us?" My brother found that hard to accept.

In truth, so did I. It wasn't as if we were familiar with the area, or if he had left us in a nice little cottage with windows and doors that could be barred. We were standing outside, in a clearing in front of a cliff, and were supposed to find our way through a cave to somewhere that we'd recognize when we saw it.

The look of the cave mouth gave me no comfort. A narrow vertical cleft jagged upward through sandstone to about the height of a man, with the base wide enough for us, but the top of the opening nothing but a crack that ran upward as far as I could see. Inside was darkness, and nothing but darkness, and it was all I could do to crouch and move inside.

Dan and Yarri squeezed in after me. We could see nothing.

"Do you suppose there are bats in here?" I asked. I'm terrified of bats.

"Bats," Yarri said, "and lizards, blind snakes, various toads and frogs, worms, all sorts of insects. Maybe rats. Fish, but again, probably blind ones. And cliffs and ledges and dead ends and drop-offs. Probably some larger predator who has found this a convenient den —"

"Yarri," I said. "Still your tongue, please. And turn on your light."

Yarri didn't say or do anything for a moment. Then she said, "Oh! You didn't want to know what was in the cave, did you?"

"I wanted you to say, 'No, Genna. I'm sure nothing is in here but us.'"

She tapped the little light she wore on a chain around her neck once we got to the first sharp turn, and we and the inside of the cave were illuminated in cool, blue-white light. We couldn't see far. The low, narrow passageway turned sharply to the right just ahead of us.

"I don't see any bat guano," Yarri said after a moment. "So there probably aren't any bats."

I didn't believe her. In my mind, they were all just waiting around the next corner. And I did see spiderwebs, so my skin started crawling anyway. Outside, I don't mind spiders much. But in low places, where I'm sure they'll drop into my hair and I won't know, just the thought of them makes me want to shiver. Or scream.

"Genna, you have to go," Dan said. "We can't spend the night here."

We could. We wouldn't be comfortable. But we could.

Still, I had to believe the cat had brought us to this place for a reason, and I had to trust that it was a good one. So I started forward. I could hear Dan and Yarri shuffling forward, and I could hear Yarri whispering to Dan.

But worse than that, I could hear whispers from ahead of us. I reached behind me to wave them to silence, and hit my brother in the head.

"OW!" he yelped. Ahead of me, a thousand voices shouted, "OW!"

I tried to turn and discovered I could not — the passage was too narrow. "If anything in there didn't know we were coming, it knows now," I whispered. My angry whisper scuttled forward to add its rustling-paper sounds to the diminishing chorus of shouts. It also skittered back to my brother and Yarri, and they fell silent.

Around the corner, I was pitched back into darkness again.

"I need Yarri's light," I told Dan, keeping my voice a low murmur.

"I need, I need, I need, I need . . ." said the cave.

After a moment, light came around the corner. I could see my brother's arm holding the chain. I grabbed it and put it around my neck. The next part of the passage jagged sharply left and moved upward.

I thought upward was good. It probably meant I wouldn't land in a lake. I'd heard of such lakes from the men in our village who had explored the caves in the hills around us. Of how one man might be leading others and have the ground drop away abruptly so that he tumbled forward. Landed in a cave lake. Was battered by the fall and drowned.

I did not want to die in the darkness.

Partway up the rising passage, I had to get on hands and knees and crawl. I already had a skinned knee, and the sandstone was coarse. It hurt.

But I thought I could see a door at the top of the passage. Well, just the bottom corner of it, actually, because the ceiling was so low, but that corner looked to me like a real, actual, oak-and-brass door built into the rock. I felt a sudden surge of relief, and crawled faster, hearing the soft shuffling as Dan and Yarri sped up behind me.

I found myself envying Yarri's breeches. Her knees wouldn't hurt at the end of this passage. My skinned knee was already bleeding, and the other knee was getting scraped. And my gravel-skinned palms hurt, too.

At the top of the passage, space had been carved out to permit one person to stand. I reached the landing and looked around. A corridor went on into darkness, straight and level and carved square, receding into the darkness as far as I could see — admittedly not far, because Yarri's little light cast a small circle. But I saw no doors set into the smooth rock except for the one I stood in front of, and the cat said I would know where I was supposed to go when I got there.

The door seemed an obvious sign to me, so I opened it and dangled Yarri's light into it.

Dan, behind me, said, "What's in there?"

"You wouldn't believe me if I told you," I said.

He stood up and moved past me, and Yarri reached the top of the climb.

"I don't believe it," she said.

I didn't, either. Before us lay a room that would have been good enough for Letrin's palace in Arrienda.

Tapestries in the boldest and most amazing colors hung before us on the walls, depicting men hunting stags and women dancing in circles with crowns on their heads. And men sailing in great ships that made me think of hawks and eagles with their wings spread. And women reading books and painting pictures and writing on huge sheets of paper or perhaps sheepskin.

Their clothing was gorgeous, but nothing like the clothes we wore. Or, for that matter, the clothes the Arriendans wore.

The walls around us were of carved sandstone, and pillars of marble held up the corners of arches. The huge room had an enormous bed in one corner, covered with clean quilted velvet covers and piled with pillows. In the room's center sat a massive wooden banquet table and forty chairs. Forty. I counted.

A hearth big enough for roasting an ox took up much of the far wall. No fire burned in it, but I could see the makings were already set, and plenty of firewood stood to one side. If we had flints or sulfur quicklights, we could have a lovely fire to take the chill off the air in the room. And perhaps cook something from the collection of the wonderful things I saw in the open stone pantries on the right wall — fresh apples, dried pears and dried cherries, potatoes and beets and other root vegetables, jerky and smoked fish and smoked venison and rashers of bacon, and so much more. My mouth watered at the sight.

Dan had begun working his way around the room, starting at the food wall. "Here's a little wheel to twist," he said, and an instant later, "Genna, it has water in it. Good, sweet water. And when you twist the wheel, it stops and starts."

And a moment later, "A little room with a privy! But —" Echoing noises. "Oh," he said, sounding elated, "when you press a handle, water washes the inside of the privy. You should see this!"

I hadn't moved. I was taking it all in.

Yarri had gone in the other direction. "The wardrobe holds a man's clothes," she said. "I've never seen anything like them before. They're cut in such wide lines. Perhaps he's very fat."

I turned and barred the door behind us. It had the sort of sturdy triple barring — brackets and oak bars at top, middle, and bottom — that suggested the owner feared intrusion. If he feared, knowing what he'd had to do to get into this place, then I feared, too. I guessed that perhaps monsters lived deeper in the cave.

I didn't want to find out I was right.

"Genna?" Dan's voice sounded far away. And tight with nervousness. Or fear. "You need to come see this."

I turned, and Yarri stopped digging through the owner's wardrobe and commenting about his odd taste in clothing. I couldn't see Dan. Apparently, neither could she, for she said, "Dan? Where are you?"

"In here." The voice was muffled, but I thought I had the direction and headed toward it. It seemed to be coming from behind the tapestry in which a single man, in clothing like that which Yarri had pulled from the wardrobes, held both hands in the air, one pointing and the other held palm up. In the palm-up hand, a ball of light that didn't actually rest on his hand sent scatters of little bubbles of light in a spiral around him.

From the pointing finger, lightning blasted into a tower, shattering it.

The man had black hair and green eyes, and his teeth were bared, and his expression was both furious and triumphant.

Dan's head poked out from behind the tapestry. "Are you coming?"

Yarri and I both ran.

We slid behind the tapestry; there was little room, and I felt smothered. We scooted sideways along the stone wall. And then, in the middle of the tapestry, suddenly we had room. An inset had been carved into the stone, and in the inset, there was a door.

And on the door, there was a lock.

The cat had said, *Don't go exploring.*

When I'd seen the long passage outside this extravagant room, I'd thought he meant we should not go exploring down the dark passages of the cave, and he need not even have mentioned that. I would never have gone voluntarily any deeper into *that.* The thought of bats, spiders, bears . . . bats, sinkholes . . . bats . . . No. No exploring in caves.

Looking at the door before me, though, I realized that he'd been warning us off the secrets the room held. *Eat, sleep,* he'd said.

But the door was plain. Sturdy. Locked.

Something interesting had to be on the other side.

"I don't think we should break the lock," Dan said in a voice that made me certain that he thought we should do exactly that.

I knew we shouldn't. Of course I knew.

"We can't break the lock, Dan," I said. "We don't know

who this place belongs to, but destroying his property would be wrong."

Beside me, Yarri said, "We need not break it, if you really want to see what's inside. Such padlocks are simple to open." She turned to me, eyes shining in the dark. "If you *wish*."

The cat had said, *Don't go exploring.*

But the cat had left us to find our way to safety, while he had gone to chase down mice.

I looked at Yarri, filled with curiosity. I wanted to know what sort of secrets the cat wanted to keep from us. "Are we shielded?"

"Always," she said.

"No word of this to the cat," I said. "Open it."

She rested her hand on the lock, and for a moment I heard metal clicking and clattering softly. Then the lock opened, the handle turned — though with difficulty, as if it had not been used in a very long time — and the door creaked inward.

Darkness inside.

"Let me have my light back," Yarri said.

I took the chain from around my neck and handed it to her. "Pity you didn't bring one of those for each of us," I said.

"I can make them. I didn't think about it, but I'll make you and Dan one later."

With her chain once more around her neck, she tapped the light, and it came to life.

My heart nearly failed me. A man as tall as a giant pine stood before us, his back turned to us. He wore only a loincloth, and had his arms outstretched, raised as the man in the tapestry had held his arms. One hand pointing, one hand held palm up with fingers spread wide.

I started to back out, but Dan was staring intently at him, and something in his expression made me stop.

Dan fished into his pockets, pulled out something small — I think it was a pebble, but knowing Dan, it might have been anything — and threw it hard at the middle of the man's muscled back.

The sound was loud. Pebble on stone, pebble bouncing off a dozen other things none of us could see, pebble clattering at last to stone floor.

The giant did not move.

"Statue," Dan whispered.

"Statue," I agreed. My heart was jigging like a troupe of spring dancers, but I could see that the gigantic man was made of stone.

I'd seen statues before — little ones. The statue of Spirit in the meeting hall. And the stags that guarded the gates of Arrienda. I'd never seen anything like this.

Yarri's hand slipped into mine, and I saw Dan's slip into hers, and without any of us saying anything about it, we all inched forward.

Yarri's light revealed the place one small circle at a time. We could only guess at the ceiling, so far above us it was. And there were hints of balconies lower, but what might be on them we could not guess.

We could not estimate the size of the room, either, for our light did not reach from one end of it to the other.

"We have to remember where the door is," I said.

"It's open," Dan reminded me.

"But if there are other open doors, how are we to know that one is ours?"

"By the tapestry?" Dan suggested.

"Leave something in it," I said, "to make certain it does not close by accident. One of our kit-bags."

Dan looked at me. "Who is to go and do that?"

"You."

He swallowed, let go of Yarri's hand, and whispered, "Don't go anywhere without me." He raced off, long legs pumping, and disappeared into the darkness. We stood utterly still, Yarri and I, feeling smaller than we had when he was with us. I had not realized until he was gone what a comfort he'd been to have around.

Moments later, I heard his footsteps again, and then he skidded into view, hair askew and eyes a little wild. "Kit-bag is propped against the door," he said. He took Yarri's hand firmly.

I pretended not to notice that he was scared. He returned the favor.

We walked deeper into the room and found tables with books chained to them, and with instruments on them that looked both fascinating and dangerous. We found shelves stacked full of glass jars and vials and tubes, some empty and in racks, waiting, and some full of things that did not bear close inspection. Inside their murky depths swam shapes and forms suggestive of monsters, the demons of old tales, and the stuff of nightmares.

"What *is* this place?" Yarri asked.

Neither Dan nor I answered. We didn't know.

I stopped our little party at a line of bookshelves where stacks of books, bound not in leather but in silk-covered boards with titles embroidered on the spines, rose from the floor to far overhead. A ladder on wheels hooked to a bar that ran the length of the shelves. I thought the design clever, and said so.

"It's a great lot of books," Yarri said doubtfully. "Why are there so many, do you suppose?"

I didn't know. I'd thought Papa had a great lot of books, having a shelf of them downstairs and another upstairs, but these books could have filled our house from floor to ceiling, room by room, until not the space to wiggle a thumb would have remained anywhere, and there would have been more books left over. Enough to fill our village, perhaps.

Yarri and Dan were both leaning forward, looking at titles.

Uncertain that I should be so bold, I lifted one of the books from the shelf and blew dust from the spine.

Haggareth Tobar, the spine said. I could read the letters, but the words made no sense to me. Yarri was even more bewildered. "This is all scribbling," she said. "What do these sticks and circles mean?"

Dan said, "The ghost knows them." He pointed to the book I held. "The ghost said that one is *Treatise on Airspinning*."

"And now," I said, "I know no more than I did. What is airspinning?"

Dan said, "He says airspinning is a form of sun magic, and that we are clearly in a sun wizard's workshop. He suggests we get out as quickly as we can, because he does not think we'll like what happens if we're here when the sun wizard comes home."

The three of us looked at one another.

I put the book back on the shelf as quickly as I could. But I was not quick enough. No more had the book slipped back into its place on its shelf than light shimmered above us. We jumped, I shrieked, and we all turned.

The giant stone man no longer stood in a loincloth but was dressed in grand robes like those in the tapestry of him. In his outstretched hand, light shimmered in an enormous, spinning, shimmering ball, and little bubbles of light burst from its surface and rippled over the whole of the room, so that we seemed to be underwater, with the sun high above us. The ceiling, painted with stars, glittered. The balconies, each holding shelves of books and tools, beckoned.

Diagrams of terrifying things covered the bare places on the stone walls — skinned men with their muscles and bones labeled, plants and animals and the parts of them scattered and drawn large, with writing and arrows pointing to each piece, bewildering machines and arcane tools and words,

words, words, naming things, pointing to things, describing things. And not a one that I could read.

We stared back at the stone man, at his pointing finger. No lightning came from it.

Yet.

We fled back the way we'd come, all of us hanging on to one another for life itself, with our feet flying and our hearts in our throats, and we said not another word until the door was shut behind us, and locked by Yarri, and we were out from under the tapestry and shaking in a corner on the far side of the room.

"Dinner?" I asked, first of the three to break the silence.

"Privy," Dan said and bolted off, to return a moment later with the gurgling of water louder than a roar in our terrified ears.

"Camp meal," Yarri said when each of us had made our own quick, desperate visit to the privy and regathered at the wall beside the door that would take us out of the cave. "We should start no fire, take nothing from the shelves, and maybe sleep on the floor."

"Definitely the floor," Dan said.

So in a rich hall provided with every fine food, with a soft bed, with every luxury, we three ate as if we were camping out. We slept with the bedrolls shoved together and the three of us within touching distance of one another. We jumped at every faint noise — and there were noises that echoed from behind not just the wizard tapestry but from behind all the tapestries, that made us huddle closer and shut our eyes tight against the demons we had awakened.

The cat was standing on my chest, staring at my face, breathing on me. His breath reeked of fish.

You listen less well than goats in the barnyard, he said. *We'll not mention your transgressions out loud, but it is purest luck that you did not stir the stone wizard to blast you into cinders.*

I observed the cat through slitted eyelids, then closed them completely and rolled to one side, trying to knock him to the floor as I did.

How did you get in? I asked him. *We barred the door.*

I'm a cat. Small. Agile. I fit through little passageways, down chimneys, things of that sort. Why didn't you listen to me?

I had no good answer to that. So I didn't offer one.

You woke the wards, he told me. *If they quiet again in a hundred years, it will be a miracle. No telling what sort of trouble that will stir up.*

I still said nothing.

I should leave you here, he said.

I sat up. I felt I hadn't been asleep at all. I ached, and my eyelids felt like lead. But the vile cat was right. *I'm sorry,* I thought. *I should have told them we were not going in.*

He studied me, tail lashing, ears halfway back. *Just figured that out, did you?*

I won't do it again.

Not if you value your life. Or anyone else's.

The cat was in a snit. I supposed he had every reason to be. So I did my best to be meek and agreeable.

"What do we do today?" I asked.

"We go to find Doyati, of course."

"On Coldfall Road."

"Eventually. I have no wish to call Coldfall first. I know what I intend, so the blind hounds will be able to follow me. I thought to let you choose our road again, and then, when we landed wherever you might take us, to call Coldfall from there."

"Why didn't we do that yesterday?"

"We would have, had I been able to get Coldfall to come," the cat said. "I was calling it the whole time we were walking, but you took us someplace I had never been, far from anyplace familiar. I was lucky to get the road that brought us here, and you saw how long that took."

Danrith handed me one of the kit-bags he'd packed. "Yours," he said.

"Then how do you know the same thing won't happen today?"

Cats can look exasperated. I know this because when the cat looked at me, I would have melted had he been given the power to melt me. "I don't know," he said in scathing tones. "That's my big plan. Hope this time you don't drag us halfway past nowhere, hope I can find Coldfall, hope the huntress and her dogs don't track us down, hope Doyati is home when we get where we're going. It isn't much of a plan, but it's all I have. If you can suggest better, I'm all ears."

Into the long and awkward silence that followed the cat's outburst, Yarri finally said, "I'd say you were mostly tail."

Dan laughed. I smiled in spite of myself. And the cat's stiff, bristling posture relaxed, and he sighed. "Well," he said, "we have a long way to go, and moonrise is almost here. And we'll have less time today, because the moon will be setting after dawn — it's hard to call a road once the sun has risen."

We ate jerky and dried pears, chasing it with cold water drawn from the little covered well that babbled in the corner.

When we finished, and squeezed ourselves and our bags out into the twilight, the cat hurried us toward a tiny clearing. "Find something," he said to me. "Quick as you can. The hounds have had all day to cast about for our scent. They could appear at any time."

The moonroads want to find me, I thought. They want to have me walk on them. They're calling to me. I tried to relax my mind. I tried to catch little flickers of light. Fireflies. Look for fireflies.

But it wasn't fireflies I saw. It was, instead, a glowing snake of pale pink light that slithered toward me along the ground. I'm terrified of snakes, but this one I wanted to touch. I could feel it pulling at me, promising me . . . something. Something wonderful. I started to step toward it, and the cat said, "Take your brother and the nightling."

They had been right beside me. I'd forgotten them again. At that moment, that fact didn't bother me at all, though I knew it should have.

I took their hands and stepped again, and the moonroad slid under and around me, and its vague promises curled through me, and I thought if I could never leave it, I would be forever happy. It made me warm. It filled me with bubbling laughter. It sang songs I thought I almost knew, and would certainly like to learn, if only I could catch hold of them. I floated in it like a swimmer in a warm and comforting lake.

And then the moonroad dumped me onto the ground, flat on my back, from high enough that it knocked the wind out of me and left me lying, stunned, staring up at a twilight sky that lacked stars or moon. Just streaky, red-bellied clouds. Wind screamed around us, hot and dry, and the ground beneath us growled and lurched.

"Oh, you're joking," the cat groaned and said, "on your feet, all of you. Quick, hold hands, before we all die."

He circled in a crouch, as if he were hunting, with his ears flat against his skull, and his mouth half open. His tail lashed. But it didn't take him long. "Here," he said. "Hurry. Get them on the road."

The shaking beneath our feet grew worse. With Dan's and Yarri's hands in mine, I ran for the little shimmers of light the cat had called, and we were falling again. This time there were no songs, no promises, nothing to offer comfort. This time there was only a pale gray light and silence and the falling. I tried to talk but again could not hear my own voice.

We stepped into the midst of leaning, crowding, dun-brown buildings, into a narrow side alley that twisted so that we could only see a few steps before us and behind us.

The cat said, "Why there? Why did you take us there? Had we tarried another moment, the living ground would have devoured us. The only worse place you could have landed us would have been the one where the huntress and her hounds were waiting."

"I'm sorry. I thought of how the roads wanted me to walk on them, and I —"

At a distance, we heard men singing, their voices strong and fierce. And we heard the tramp of many feet in unison and the rattle of armor.

The men were not singing in a language I knew, but Danrith's eyes rolled back in his head, and he began singing with them.

"Gah harri, harri gae!
Gah jurri, nang bae!
Tonga gae, tromga jie!
Mosga!
Hosga!
Kie!"

I punched his arm. "Dan! Danrith! Snap out of it!"

The whites of his eyes rolled back where they belonged, and he looked at me sidelong and said:

"Right foot, foot down!
Left foot, hit the ground!
Spear down, turn blade!
Thrust!
Twist!
Pull!

"Soldiers, Genna. Ghost soldiers. They're coming for us."

The cat looked at me, I looked at Dan and Yarri, and Dan, Yarri, and I held hands.

"First one to find anything," the cat said.

I started looking. I suspect it was fortunate for us the cat found a road first. We stepped onto it, as the sounds of marching and singing grew louder.

CHAPTER 8
DOYATI'S WORTH

We landed in a chilly, rough wasteland. The ground was rocky and flat, the stunted, leafless brush rattled as the steady wind, stinking of sulfur and ash, blew through it.

I landed on my feet this time. That was something. But Yarri shrieked, and I turned to see that she was holding her right ankle.

I hurried over to her. "Let me see."

She was reluctant to move her hands.

"Let me *see*," I told her again. "My mother has been training me as the apprentice yihanni since I turned eight. I'm good at bones and tendons by now."

Yarri removed her hands, and I pushed the leg of her breeches upward and her thick socks down. Her leg was as big around as the thinnest part of my wrist . . . and I have bony wrists. But her ankle — oh! — that already had fist-thick swelling all the way around it. I made her wiggle her foot, and she could, so the bones were unlikely to be badly broken. That was good. But the swelling was darkening quickly, which suggested she was bleeding hard inside.

I took a deep breath and fought to calm myself. I'd practiced on livestock, but only with Mama watching me because, after all, our animals provide us with much of our food and our clothing and raw materials for tools and other things, and children cannot be allowed to ruin them.

I closed my eyes and swallowed my fear, and kneeling on the rocky, hard ground, I let my fingers read her hurts. I let them feel patterns in heat and cold, firm and infirm. My fingertips read prickles of pain, and I pulled those away, a little at a time, much more slowly and clumsily than Mama would have managed.

You could hurry, the cat said in my head.

Maybe you could. I can't, I said right back. My fingers kept pulling at prickles inside her ankle, drawing them out. Had I been more experienced, I could have done the work with my eyes open, but I completely lose touch with what my fingers are feeling if I look at what they are doing. Mama said that would change with experience. I hoped she was right, because I felt helpless not being able to see anything that was going on around me.

At last my fingers could find no more pain or wrongness. I dared open my eyes.

Her ankle was of normal size again, though it bore a nasty bruise — something I hadn't yet learned to fix.

"How does it feel?"

She hugged me tightly and grinned. "You were very good. Thank you."

I hugged her back, and the cat said, "Really? Must we? Or could we perhaps get started before all sorts of uglies show up to eat us?"

Yarri stood and carefully put weight on her foot. "It's still sore, but I'll be able to walk."

The cat looked at us, picked a direction that seemed random to me, and started walking. We followed.

"I think I understand where you're going wrong when you call the moonroads," he told me. "The roads that want you are not the roads you want. The roads most desperate to have you walk them are hungry. They're filled with the endless starvation of the soul-drinkers, or earth that has wakened to self-knowing and that desires the blood and bones of other living things to feed it memories and secrets. Or pack-hunters like weyrdwolves or canniboars who talk to the roads, even if they cannot walk them."

I said, "You might have told me that sooner."

"I might have," the cat said, "had it occurred to me that you would seek roads that wanted you to walk them rather than places you needed to reach. Next time you call a road, think of one that goes someplace safe. Pleasant. Useful, even."

The cat, finished chastising me, fell silent, and Dan leaned over and whispered to me, "I felt that one."

I looked at him. "What do you mean, you felt it?"

"Until now, you took my hand and we went someplace else."

"No falling, no colors, no music?"

He gave me a look that was almost as exasperated as the cat's had been earlier. "Right. That's why I'm telling you I felt something this time. It was different. Like a . . . like a rope tied to the inside of my belly, pulling me forward. And it felt like it took longer. It wasn't just here, there. It was here, and then the pulling, and darkness, and there. Or there and then here. You know what I mean."

"I do." I looked to the cat. He had stopped walking and was sitting on the ground, head cocked, eyeing the three of us. "How about you, nightling?" he asked. "You starting to feel things when you go over the moonroads?"

Yarri shook her head.

He turned to stare at my brother, while to me he said,

"You're contagious, Gennadara. To humans, anyway. Something about you is passing on your awareness of moonroads to your brother. If it continues, he'll soon be able to see them. And once he can see them, he can walk them. Interesting."

We all agreed it was interesting, but we were all still shaken by having come so close to being caught by the ghost warriors, so that seemed far more important to us.

I asked Dan, "Who are the ghost soldiers? How did you know they had come for us?"

Dan said, "I didn't. My . . . my ghost said he knew them. That they were from his time and had been mercenaries. Allies. But something happened to them, and they were all killed and their spirits captured."

"I know what happened to them," the cat said. He trotted a few steps ahead of us. "During the Long War, when nightlings fought humans for dominance of all the lands, the sun wizards sometimes . . . ah . . . harvested the spirits of recently fallen enemies and bound them to objects that could be used to summon the spirits at need. Horns, drums, swords — that sort of thing. While many questioned the morality of such magic, none questioned its efficiency. The nightlings are particularly vulnerable to ghost warriors, and for a time it seemed that the sun wizards would win the battle over the nightlings' far larger forces by the creation of such weapons."

The cat's whiskers twitched, and his ears swiveled forward. He stopped, crouched, his tail started to twitch, and his hindquarters wriggled. We all froze and dropped into the grass. Previous things that had caught the cat's attention had been deadly, and we wondered what new horror we faced.

However, he pounced, and an enormous bird shot into the air with wings thundering, squawking. It dragged the cat partway into the sky behind it, until some of its tail feathers came loose and cat and feathers fell back to earth. The cat, twisting wildly, missed his landing and fell gracelessly into the grass. He stood, turned to face us, and through a mouth full of tail feathers said, "I meant to do that."

Then he stalked ahead of us again, all injured dignity and silence, while Yarri and Dan and I burst out laughing.

Here, kitty, kitty, have a nice birdie, I thought at him, and he huffed out the feathers stuck to his mouth in response.

Sometimes he was much more than a cat. Sometimes, though, he wasn't. That heartened me somewhat. I don't know why.

Yarri said, "So what happened with the ghost warriors?"

The cat glared at all of us, then growled. "The nightlings found ways to break most of the weapons that bound the warriors' spirits, and since the nightlings vastly outnumbered the humans, they won the war. And hunted down the rest of the weapons and destroyed them."

"The Long War ended in a draw," I said.

"You're an idiot," the cat answered.

Dan asked, "Then how are there still ghost warriors?"

"A few weapons survived, hidden away by humans who did not want to find themselves at the mercy of the nightlings. The one I know of is a war harp currently owned by a bard who is himself a warrior of sorts. He's been a thorn in the side of the kai-lords, for sure, though he lives mostly on the moonroads and in the nightworlds. Letrin would gladly kill him if he saw profit in it."

"Why is this bard after us?"

The cat said, "I don't know any more than I know why you have the huntress and her hounds after you. My guess is, you've made enemies with this quest of yours. Perhaps Doyati knows you seek him and wants you dead."

Yarri eventually asked, "Will the huntress or the bard be able to track us here?"

"Perhaps. But the fact that they tracked us to Barranak is more worrisome."

"The village we were just in?"

"City. You only saw the Beggars' Quarter. Barranak is vast and in places glorious to behold. It's ancient. And complex. And dangerous, even if you don't have the Blind Hunt or ghost warriors after you."

"Barranak is where Doyati is?" I asked.

The cat said, "It would be the best place to look for him."

I felt my stomach tighten, the way it did before I threw up. That was the wrong answer.

We had been trusting the cat to get us to Doyati. He'd said he knew him very well, and the cat had seemed to be certain about where he was taking us. My world, Dan's world, Yarri's world — all of these depended on us finding Doyati. If we failed, our worlds would die. And we had only four days left before the moonroads would close. I said, "You don't know where Doyati is?" My voice sounded tight and shrill.

"I didn't say that," the cat told me. "I just said that Barranak would be the best place to *look* for him. We can *find* him in any of several places, but if we find him in Barranak and things don't go well, he will still be able to hide there again."

Dan said, "You mean if things don't go well with us. If he won't come with us and Kai-Lord Letrin kills us."

"Well . . . yes. That's what I mean," the cat said. "The nightlings will still have another chance someday of beating Letrin, so long as Doyati lives."

I almost grabbed the cat by the scruff of the neck and shook him, but I held my temper. "How could you find him in more than one place? How could he be in different places at the same time? That makes no sense."

The cat stared at me through slitted eyes. "He's walked the moonroads for a long time, little girl. The roads changed him. He can do things no one can imagine."

"Like be in many places at once?" I glared at the cat.

"Like be in many places at once," the cat said.

My brother beat me to the next question. "Why does the kai-lord want him so badly?"

"We've been at this a while, and the road I want isn't coming to me," the cat said instead of answering. "Why don't we sit, eat something, and walk again when we're rested."

I could not see where we'd made any progress at all. The place had no landmarks, nothing that we could point to and say, "We're closer to this," or "We're farther from that." So I was grateful when we found rocks to sit on, and Yarri set up her heat-ball cook-fire and set the folding pot on its little frame. Each of us poured some of the water from our canteens into the stew pot, and then added dried vegetables, dried meat, and dried herbs. The heat-ball brought the water to a quick boil, and before long, our food began to smell delicious. All we had to do was wait.

That was when the cat said, "*Now* I will tell you about Doyati. He's the son of Letrin's older brother, Marquin — the rightful heir — who would have been kai-lord had Letrin not killed him at the same time he killed his and Marquin's parents, the kai-lord and kai-lady."

Yarri gasped.

"You didn't know of that?" the cat said. "You believed the tales Letrin has spread about how good and kind he was before he killed his son to save his wife's life?"

Yarri nodded.

"All lies. Letrin always desired power. His brother, Marquin, was, if not a kind and gentle man, at least honest and fair. He would have almost certainly been a good replacement for his father when the old man finally died. Marquin married a human woman, and she was wonderful. Kind, funny, caring, and lovely. She was like a rainbow in Arrienda. Everything about her brought joy to those who knew her. Nightlings and humans both loved her."

The cat sighed. "Letrin envied his brother. Marquin had the loyalty and trust of his people, the faith of his father, the love of his wife. And he had a son. A baby boy named Doyati, who would secure the line of succession after Marquin, so that Letrin would never become kai-lord."

"So Letrin killed them all?"

"Not right away. Ten years before he killed anyone, he married a human woman named Oesari, who was, in her own right, very sweet. A good woman." The cat curled his paws under his body and sat staring off at nothing, as cats are wont to do. "Two years after that, by human reckoning, he and his wife had their only child, a son they named Oerin. And then, six years after that, Letrin murdered his parents and his brother, though of course he didn't do it with his own hands. He hired brigands and secretly breached the magical wards and great walls of the palace for them so that they could gain entry — *then* he happened to be traveling with his wife and child when the murders took place.

"Doyati's mother, however, escaped with the baby during the massacre. Letrin hired hunters to find her and the baby and kill them both.

"Publicly, Letrin mourned, he wept, and everyone sympathized with him and tried to comfort him. He clung to his distraught human wife and made everyone believe she was his strength and the reason he was able to hang on. He gained everyone's sympathy. Arrienda supported him. The nightlings believed him, because he had been very careful to set up his alibi. The killers were captured and publicly executed, the bodies were burned, and Arrienda's people believed justice had been done."

I said, "If he was away when everyone was killed, and the brigands who killed everyone were captured, then how do you know justice wasn't done?"

"I'm getting to that." The cat's ears flattened, and he narrowed his eyes at me. "Letrin was made kai-lord in his father's place amid great acclaim, and for two years peoples of the other nightling realms looked to him and his wife and their son as examples of enlightened rule. When Oesari, his wife, grew gravely ill and he sacrificed their eight-year-old son to save her, the nightlings forgave the atrocity because of the depth and the sincerity of his love for her. And when the woman he claimed he had made immortal died of a broken heart in his arms — not so immortal after all — all of Arrienda mourned, and many of the Highborn offered him their daughters to wed."

"But if no one saw, how would you know what Letrin said was not true?" Yarri protested.

"Because a few saw after all."

"You?" I asked.

"No. I'm not that old. But Doyati's mother saw the first

massacre. And some of her loyal retainers, with whom she had managed to maintain contact, saw the second."

"She had spies?"

"She had *friends*," the cat said. "Yarri's parents are among them. Though Doyati's mother has long been dead, she has friends still. Her friends, well placed, saw Letrin kill his wife and son at the same time and use their bodies and souls to make himself immortal."

Yarri's hands clenched into fists, and she turned away. "You're lying, cat. My parents would have told me this."

The cat laughed. "You think so? You've been a messenger for the conspirators against Letrin since you were half your age. Your parents dared not let you know anything, lest you were stopped and questioned."

I sat back, considering Letrin. "Then the kai-lord wants to make sure Doyati cannot return as the rightful heir and overthrow him."

"Precisely."

That made sense to me. It felt true, no matter how much it upset Yarri. But the more I thought about it, the more I felt certain our cause was doomed. Doyati, safe in hiding, would not care to come face the wrath of the Kai-Lord Letrin. He would not choose to let himself be sacrificed to save a little human village at the corner of Aeiring, a minor trading partner with the glorious city-state of Arrienda.

We meant nothing to Doyati.

Meal finished, we packed up our camp and began walking again, following the cat.

I trudged forward, my heart heavier with every step. The kai-lord wouldn't accept *me* as a sacrifice, and that made everything we did pointless from the very beginning.

"He won't come with us," I said.

"You might be right," the cat said. "But you might be wrong."

"You think Doyati will willingly die on Letrin's word so Letrin will spare us if he does? I wouldn't, even if I believed Letrin. And I don't. The kai-lord has no intention of letting us go."

The cat jumped up onto my shoulder and this time didn't dig his claws into me. *So then.* He spoke into my mind, to me alone. *You face a dilemma. You can continue on what you now understand is a fool's mission, with nothing but betrayal at the end.*

Or you can quit, which is both sensible and understandable, and you can hide from Letrin, who may someday stop searching for you. You, after all, are nowhere near as important as Doyati, and he has been hiding from Letrin for over a hundred years. If you started running now, you'd have a fairly good chance of escaping him.

I considered that. I might live, and Dan might live.

I would even help you, the cat added. *If you wanted.*

The cat made a certain sort of sense. And he would be an enormous help if we decided to flee. I didn't know that I trusted him completely, but he had kept us from death more than once. If we ran, we might hope to live.

However, if we ran, my brothers and sisters would surely die. And my mother. Everyone in my village would be sacrificed to Letrin's evil. My friends, their parents. Cousins, uncles, and aunts. I might live, Danrith might live, but everything we had to live for would be lost.

If we kept going, on the other hand, we could pretend we thought we might win, only to lose anyway at the end.

If we could catch Doyati and give him a sleeping draught (which we did not have) and drag him back to Letrin against his will (but the cat said he was more fearsome than soul-drinkers), we would watch as Letrin took his prize and then betrayed us anyway.

I was the one the cat was asking. The oldest child. The firstborn. All duty and all blame fell on me; the old woman had said I would be the one who bore the duty of choice, but being firstborn had given me that duty anyway. What I decided, we would do. If I chose wrongly, the fault would be mine alone.

Three children. A cat. And a prince who had been in hiding since he was a baby, more than a hundred years ago, if I understood the story. I thought a little longer, but I knew what my answer would be. I'd known it all along.

We keep going, I told the cat. *We find Doyati, whatever it takes.*

Any chance for Mama and the younglings, however poor, was better than no chance at all. And we would have no chance at all if we quit.

I could have sworn I saw that cat smile. "Well, good for you," he said aloud.

We had not been hiking long when the cat suddenly said, "Here it is!" and Yarri and Dan and I joined hands and all stepped onto the road he'd found. Cool and meadowy and full of the sound of the whispering of tender leaves in springtime, the moonroad spun us around and down and even deeper down, until we fell gently to our feet. We had barely caught our breaths when the cat said, "And now Coldfall," and something in my heart contracted at the sight of the red sparks he drew to himself, brightening and tightening until they coalesced into a terrifying spiral.

"I don't want to," Yarri whispered. Dan clutched my hand, and I grabbed Yarri's arm, and I dragged the three of us forward and into that spiral before the road could slide away from us. And before I lost my courage.

Coldfall was not like any other road, or perhaps it was the first road I'd learned to see more clearly. Things moved around us as we fell. Creatures, shadows, glowing eyes that stared at us in bodiless pairs. Broken people, twisted animals. Monsters. They slid past us or dropped behind us as we raced by, and some of them opened mouths and screamed without sound, and others reached out to try to grab us, though their hands slid through us as if either they or we were made of nothing but smoke.

And some saw us and laughed, and even though I could no more hear the laughter than the screams, it was somehow worse. It was as if they knew — absolutely knew — what was about to happen to us.

I yearned for wings or a way off the road. I wished Dan still had Papa's sword.

I tried to breathe, but my terror clogged my throat. Hands grasping and eyes staring and shadows wrapping themselves around the three of us and trying to slip inside, as if they wanted to wear our bodies like coats.

We crashed onto the road, all three of us feeling filthy and ill-used, and the cat landed in a heap on us, hissing and spitting and with his claws out.

"Up, quickly," he said. "The old woman said this was the way, though I didn't want to believe her. This way, though, nothing good lies between here and what we seek." He got to his feet, and stared over my shoulder, and puffed himself to twice his size.

"Run," he whispered.

We did not look behind us. I could feel the weight of something back there. Something big. Wet-mouthed. Hungry. Beneath my feet, the ground shook. I could hear the moist noises of its movement. I could feel it staring at me. I got to my feet and bolted after the cat that streaked away from us, and Dan followed me, and I hoped that Yarri followed him, and that her ankle would hold. I could not hear her when she ran, so I did not know, and I feared that if I looked behind to check on her, I'd see the horror making those wet, crunching, smacking sounds . . . and then Dan passed me and Yarri shot past Dan and *I* was the one at the back and falling behind.

The uneven ground caught at me, and thorns snagged my clothing and my legs. I pumped my arms and legs and felt my lungs burn. Yarri flew over the ground, her feet barely touching it. She caught up with the cat, and then paced him. Dan held a middle distance behind the two of them.

I lost ground as mud sucked at the soles of my boots and my braid and my skirt and my sweater caught in briars. The squelching noises, and the fog of dark red hunger radiating from the monster, and the grinding of huge teeth, and the rush of air pressed forward by enormous bulk, grew louder and stronger behind me. I felt a drip of moisture on the back of my neck. Smelled wet, death-stinking heat — like the thing's breath — wrap around me. A shadow darkened the ground in front of me, and I wanted to pretend that a cloud had run over the moon.

But the brush just behind me crackled and crunched.

Whatever it was, it grabbed at me. I squeezed my eyes tight — I was so frightened, I couldn't open them again. So I couldn't see the arm come down behind me, but I could feel the movement of the air around it and smell a new stink, nearly upon me. And then my feet were moving but there was no ground under them anymore, and I was looking for a moonroad, any moonroad, something that I could slip away on, but there was nothing, and the ground was getting farther away, and the sound of smacking and

slurping grew closer.

The straps on my kit-bag broke. I fell.

Behind and above me, I heard a little crunching and a sigh, and I hit the ground so hard I couldn't breathe or move. The darkness and the weight moved over me, and I felt for a moment like I was lying in a storm of sticky rain. And while I waited for it to crush the life out of me, it moved on, going after Dan, Yarri, and the cat.

It was the most hideous monstrosity I had ever seen, worse by a hundred times than any nightmare I'd had or ghoul I'd imagined hovering over my bed as I cowered under the covers in the dark. It stood taller than our three-story house, and it looked as if it were made up of all the bits and pieces of all the creatures it had ever eaten, all sliding around beneath a layer of clear, sticky, slimy skin. It had two arms, but they were of different sizes, lumpy, misshapen — they seemed unfinished. It had two legs, but those, like its arms, had bits and pieces of things that were not rightful parts of the monster pushing right up to the surface and sometimes clear through it. I swear I saw a wing that looked like a bat's poking out of the back of the monster's left heel, but that wing and one like it would have been big enough to make a horse fly. I shivered briefly at the idea of a bat that big —

bats! — but the monster made bats seem like kittens by comparison.

Over its enormous, lumpy shoulders, I could see the top half of what had to be its head, but that was covered in moss, or grass. Or weeds.

It dripped slime as it thudded forward, and it went down a wide path between mounds, bent over to pick up something that screamed, but didn't bring anything to its mouth — not that I could see anyway. Instead, it swung its huge, shaggy head in all directions, and only for an instant I saw that it had no eyes — only sockets where they should have been. It sniffed loudly, and then thumped off in a new direction.

It hadn't stepped right on me. That felt like a miracle. It hadn't realized my kit-bag was not me, and that, too, was terribly lucky. I should have been dead, but I was still breathing, and if every bone in my body ached, I was grateful to be alive to feel the pain.

I waited until I couldn't see the monster or hear the noises it made. Then I sat up carefully. I hurt everywhere, but I couldn't find any broken bones. When I stood, my back and shoulders throbbed so much I wanted to lie back down again. But I couldn't. Not with such a horror wandering around looking for something to eat. I hoped

that the cat hadn't given me up for dead and told the other two to grab on to his tail so that he could lead them somewhere else. I hoped. I had to find them before the monster did.

I started moving forward, only to realize I had no idea which way forward was. I'd been following running people and a cat, and I hadn't had time before that to get a good look at the world around me. I didn't know which way I'd fallen, or whether the slimy monster had spun me around. I only knew that nothing looked familiar.

The ground was an endless series of tall, uneven, grass-covered mounds. Muddy paths wove through them, all of them covered by tracks, and by the same sort of monster slime that covered me. The occasional scrawny tree topped one mound or another, and some of the mounds sat within circles of tall, narrow standing stones. I held very still for a moment, watching enormous, vaguely manlike creatures with slowly flapping wings — bat wings — flying some distance from where I stood. They were hunting. One would drop to the ground and lift again an instant later with its squealing, kicking prey clasped to its chest. Then another would plummet, and another. The faint, sharp sounds of squealing and screaming reached me, and I tried to block them from my ears. The flying hunters congregated at the tops of the standing stones to eat what they'd caught, and they cackled and chuckled among themselves. They had to have been twice as tall as my father or the other men in our village, with wings that would have spanned the narrowest part of the village.

I'd be a snack for any one of them if they saw me.

I shivered with an awful thought. Had they caught Dan? Or Yarri? I doubted they would bother with anything as small as the cat. I wondered how long it would take one of them to spot me.

Not long, you idiot. You'll be wanting to get inside.

The cat! I couldn't see him, but I could hear him.

I can't find you, I thought.

I'm coming to get you. Lie down on the ground. Try to look dead. They don't eat dead things. And keep talking to me. I'll find you.

Is Dan safe? I asked him.

And Yarri. And me. Thanks for asking. He sounded insulted.

I ignored him, the way I ignored the barn cats that sunned atop our water barrel and who always looked at me like I'd thrown them out of their own home when I moved them to get water to cook our supper. *What was the mon-*

ster that nearly ate me? I asked.

The gurleeg. A type of taandu monster. Be glad he didn't catch you.

He did catch me. He was getting ready to drop me into his maw when the straps of my kit-bag broke. I fell, and he ate the kit-bag instead of me, then walked away. I hurt, I added.

I didn't hear anything from the cat for a while.

Cat?

Nothing.

Cat?

Still nothing. I almost screamed out loud.

But then the cat showed up, right in front of me, and whispered, "I'm sorry. I was getting the other two into shelter. I didn't know."

Chapter 9
The Bard and the Harp

Still startled by the cat's sudden change in attitude, I followed him down a tunnel and into the tiny room that lay inside one of the earth mounds. Yarri sat with her back to me, scratching symbols into the dirt floor. Dan's eyes were red and I could see tear streaks on his face. The instant he saw me, he smiled — and then he glared at me and looked away.

A central fire cooked a pot of boiling roots and greens and vegetables. It smelled bitter, but I was hungry. "You see . . . she wasn't dead," the cat said.

Yarri turned around, and I saw she'd been crying. "I thought the cat was lying to us," she told me. "I thought you were dead and he was going to leave us here and run away."

The cat yawned, licked a paw with an air of complete focus, and when he was done, said, "I'll consider that an option the next time I have to risk my own skin to save your lives."

"You should have kept up with us," Dan told me. "If you die, how are we going to help Mama? I can't see the roads yet! The kai-lord made his agreement with you. If you died, we would be left with nothing."

"I ran as quickly as I could."

Yarri said, "You can't fall behind and not call for help. You have to let us know you're in trouble. You could have died. We might never have known what happened to you."

"We could have lost everything," Dan said. I heard both fear and anger in his voice. "Not just you. That would have been bad enough —" His voice broke. He cleared his throat and turned around to look at me. "If you die, everyone in our village dies. Yours is the signature on the contract. Not mine. Not Yarri's. Where contracts are concerned, only those who have a signature on the paper have a voice in the agreement. If you die, Kai-Lord Letrin can use all the punitive measures written in, because dead is the same as defaulted."

Yarri was nodding. "You have to be *careful.* Fast. Responsible. We have to be able to count on you."

It was all true. I'd wanted sympathy for being almost eaten by the taandu monster — the gurleeg — but instead they were reminding me that my life wasn't *my* life anymore — that as long as other people would die if I became careless, my life belonged to all of them equally.

They were right.

I was being childish, feeling the way I was. But I still wanted just one of them to say, "Oh, poor Genna, almost eaten by that horrible monster."

Just one of them.

Instead, the cat glared at all of us and said, "All of you — enough. Eat. Rest. Though this is one of the places where Doyati goes to ground in times of need, I cannot sense Doyati in this place, not with you squabbling like old hens in a cage. I need to listen, and you need to be quiet. Quiet words, quiet thoughts."

"Who made the stew?" I asked.

Yarri said, "The food was here when the cat led us in, already waiting." She closed her eyes for a moment, waved a hand over it, and the food glowed bright green for a moment. "It's safe. No poison." And then she studied me, her fine, downy eyebrows knitting together in puzzlement. "You lost your kit-bag."

"The gurleeg," I told her. "When he picked me up, he caught the kit-bag rather than me. The straps broke as he was going to eat me, and I fell to the ground, and he ate the kit-bag instead."

Dan stared at me, shock on his face, then turned on the cat with a fury I'd only seen in him once before, when he stood between Banris and Mama, threatening Uncle Banris when he began shouting at her. "You said she just fell behind!" he shouted at the cat. "You said she was fine. You said she just tripped, and the monster went right by her."

"I need quiet," the cat said. "This isn't quiet."

"You lied to us!" my brother yelled, while Yarri scooted across the room and pressed her head against mine and whispered, "Oh, poor Genna. Almost eaten! We didn't know."

Dan roared, "You lied, cat! Lied! If I had Papa's sword, you'd have no tail."

The cat stalked toward the tunnel. "If I can't find quiet here, I'll leave and let the three of you fend for yourselves."

I said, "Dan. I'm fine. Let it go."

Dan turned to me, and I saw tears on his cheeks again. "I thought you were just being stupid," he told me. "Slow and girlish. Like the girls in the village get when they want us to watch them. I didn't know you'd almost . . . died."

I hugged him, and then hugged Yarri, and they cried, and then I cried. I'm ashamed to say it was all very satisfying. Like imagining going to your own funeral and seeing everyone sobbing and tearing at their hair, realizing at last that you were the most wonderful person they had ever known. Only for real, and without having to die — which, having almost died, I have to say was a great improvement.

When we'd cried ourselves dry and I'd had my fill of all that wonderful pity, we ladled portions of the stew into gourd halves that sat on a narrow shelf at the back of the little dwelling. And we ate, though the food managed to be bitter without being in the least flavorful. I thought longingly of salt, almost as costly in Hillrush as daylight taandu essence, and of how even a pinch of it would have made the meal palatable. I'm sure the stew was good for us, though. Those foods that taste terrible usually are.

Afterward, we studied what remained of our belongings. I still had my home clothes because I'd been wearing them. Everything else, though — my bedroll, my supply of food, the beautiful dress and the delicate shoes I had worn when I faced the kai-lord, as well as the handful of useful tools the kit-bag had contained — were all gone.

"No sense dividing the rest of the food between the three of us," I said. "I haven't a kit-bag anymore to carry my share in. I could carry your kit-bag," I told Yarri.

She shook her head. "Mine has the tent. You haven't been lucky, and we don't want to lose the tent."

I hadn't been lucky. So I didn't press my case.

As best we could, the three of us readied ourselves for sleep. The mound-house had no running water, no little privy, no outhouse. What it had was a hole dug at the end of a dead-end tunnel, a wooden hatch, and atop the hatch, a small chamber pot. Halfway down the tunnel, a hole in the tunnel ceiling let the smells out. A small barrel under the hole caught rainwater, which I guessed would be used for cooking, drinking, and, I hoped, washing.

We each made our trips down the tunnel, poured half a dipper over our hands when we had finished, and hoped for the best.

Yarri and Dan then spread out their nightling bedrolls. Those looked clean and soft and inviting. My bed would be the pile of straw bagged in a rough homespun sack that lay in one corner, well away from the central fire and its occasional sparks. I wished that my own bedroll was not at that moment in the belly of the gurleeg. My berth would certainly be full of fleas and bedbugs and no telling what other vermin, and the straw would poke and itch. But I didn't doubt it would be better than sleeping on the ground, which was going to be all the bed I had when we next slept outdoors.

So I said my thanks to Spirit for straw in a bag, and remembered to be grateful instead of complaining, and we noticed that the cat had gone up the tunnel, so we talked.

Well, mostly Yarri talked, and Dan and I listened. "I was so afraid I'd lost another friend," she said.

Almost in unison, Dan and I asked, "What friend did you lose?"

And I added, "What happened?"

She rolled over to face us, her eyes luminous in the dim firelight. "Her name was Nali, and she was, like me, a daughter of slaves. We were the same age, and so on our first year, our fifth year, and our ninth year, we were presented together with all the other same-age slave children to the nightling Highborn."

"Presented?" I asked.

"Slave parents have no rights to keep and raise their own children. When the babies are first born, again when we are mostly trained, and again when we are ready to begin light work, we are gathered up and presented at the annual Child Day. Those Highborn who want children pick through all the slave babies and children presented, and select the prettiest or the cleverest or the most docile. And they take them. Sometimes they choose to raise the children as their own. Sometimes they simply want a companion and life servant for a child they already have. And sometimes they want someone they can frighten and hurt. What they want us for doesn't matter to anyone. They're Highborn. Their word is law."

Dan sat up, furious. "That's ridiculous. Common Law states that all people are born free, live free, and die free, and that none may own another, or deprive another of life or family, lest he be served justice."

Yarri said, "Nightlings have no Common Law. And slaves are not people. We're possessions, with which our owners may do as they choose. Some parents of children taken away during Child Days thought as you think, and tried to get their children back. The Highborn now frequently order the entire birth family killed to prevent this from happening."

I tried to make that idea fit in my mind, but it wouldn't. There was no place for something so evil, so cruel, so unjust.

Yarri sighed. "But anyway, Nali and I were together for all three Child Days. I'm plain, my skin is ordinary yellow, my hair is wild and flyaway. I'm no one special, and each time the Highborn looked right past me. Nali, though, was beautiful, with skin as blue as a twilight sky and hair of blue-black, long and wavy and thick, and eyes the color of good topazes. Her family and my family were friends, her brothers and sisters played with mine, and she and I were always together.

"Our third Child Day, everyone was afraid for Nali, so her mother shaved her head and her father powdered her skin to make it an ordinary pale blue, and she stood with her shoulders slumped and stared at nothing, and picked her nose, too."

I sat up and wrapped my arms around myself and shivered. Mama's sweater could not warm away the chill inside of me.

Yarri said, "It didn't matter. She was so beautiful nothing could hide her, and a huge Highborn — one of the taandu monsters — claimed her and dragged her away. I never saw her again. Nor her parents, her brothers or sisters, her aunts or uncles, or her grandparents. I was not allowed to speak her name again, for fear that our family would be linked with hers and would suffer the same fate as her family. My father thought his position as the kai-lord's clothing master would be sufficient to save us all, but my mother thought not."

I shivered. "You don't know where she is? Where any of them are?"

"That's what slavery is," Yarri said. "People you love vanishing, and everyone around you pretending they don't notice, so they won't vanish, too."

I did not know how she could bear such a hard life, and I did not understand why she had to.

We talked a little longer, but I could not shake the horror of her story. Eventually, our conversation faltered and sputtered to silence, and we tried to sleep.

My mind was full of Doyati and blind hounds and warrior bards with ghost armies to command and great squelching gurleegs and giant bat-winged men. And taandu monsters. I wished I had asked what taandu monsters were, and at the same time, was grateful that I had not.

I would have thought that the worry and terror of the day would have kept me from sleeping. But it didn't.

And more is the pity for that.

I noticed the scents in the dream before anything else. That should have been a warning. The air was sweet with honeysuckle and night jasmine. Dark. Unutterably dark. Somewhere ahead of me, I heard singing.

The voices were strong and deep, the song they sang simply enchanting. I found myself moving toward the music, my feet starting to dance on their own. A little light — a pretty fire in the middle of a forest — guided me forward. Over the fire, meat roasted on a spit, and a hand somewhere beyond the light kept it turning. The juices sizzled as they hit the flames, and the smell made me so hungry — especially after my dinner of roots and greens — that I could hear the growling of my stomach over the end of the men's song.

Before the echoes of the first song died away, one of the men started a song about home long lost and long forgotten and about yearning to be with the loved ones he had left behind. I thought of my village and my family and friends, and the tears began pouring down my cheeks.

It's hard, isn't it, to be so alone, so far from home and loved ones, not knowing if you'll ever see them again, a man whispered inside my thoughts. *You're a brave girl, a warrior in your own way, but wouldn't it be better to have someone bigger than you to help you? A man who could fight for you? Who could chase away the monsters that pursued you? Wouldn't it be wonderful to have a hero who could win the battle you face for you and your friends?*

It would be good. I wished I had my father with me. Papa would have known what to do if a monster chased him. Papa would have been able to deal with the kai-lord and keep the hunters off our trail.

You're tired. You're hungry. Come sit with us. Eat and sing, the man said.

Dreams that include eating and singing are good dreams indeed. I found myself sitting on a log, close to the fire, and unseen hands passed me a bone with some of the cooked meat on it. The wonderful flavor of roast wild boar filled my mouth, and juice dripped down my chin, and for a little while I ate and listened while one man, alone, sang a ballad of the woman he had loved and lost. Two others then sang a funny song about a trickster who stole away a magic staff from a sleeping wizard and found that he wasn't nearly as clever as he'd believed. By the time the singers got to the verse where the thief, with donkey ears and raven's beak and lobster-claw hands, was begging the wizard to take back the staff, I was laughing so hard I could barely breathe.

And then it was my turn to sing.

And the man who sat beside me in the great darkness said, *You should sing about your adventure. About you and your companions, about the dangers you have already faced, and those you seek. It would make a grand song.*

It might have, had I been able to sing somewhat better than a flock of crows. Had I known anything about tune-smithing, or about setting words in a bardlike fashion. But though I love to sing, I sing as crows sing, and friends and family alike cover their ears with their hands or flee to other rooms, laughing. So I only sing when I am alone.

But the men began humming. Melody blended with harmony, and in a fashion I could not explain, I felt the words of a song falling into place in my head.

The kai-lord brought us,
The Kai-Lord Letrin
To feast at his table
To sit in his hall
My brother and I
We only drank water
We ate bitter greens
And we waited his call.

A nightling, she helped us
She told us the secrets
That Letrin was hiding
Behind his kind eyes.
We dressed in fair clothes
And I played with my braid
And I asked for a key
And I beat all his lies.

We fled from his anger,
And Yarri, she hid us,
And wrapped us in magic,
To meet an old hag,
To find a cold road,
And —

Sharp pain seared into my arm, and something hot and stinking of fish shattered the smells of flowers and roasting meat. Faint light replaced darkness.

The cat stood on me, his claws dug into my shoulder while he breathed into my face and growled at me.

"You idiot," he said.

I looked up at him. "What is the matter with you, cat?"

"What were you doing?"

"Dreaming."

"Really? Lick your lips. Smell your fingers."

I licked, and discovered bits of meat juices around my mouth. And my fingers were greasy. And my stomach was full. Happily full.

"The roads," I whispered.

"You're a menace," the cat said. "I come over here to find a warm, soft place to sleep, and you've left your body here and taken your mind wandering. And when I finally track you down, you're sitting with the warrior bard and his ghost harp, telling the bard and his ghosts names and secrets, betraying the people with you. Did you mention me in your song?"

I sat up. "No." And I thought about that song, about how it had just come pouring out of me. "I was telling the story, and I hadn't yet gotten to the old woman. Or you."

"But you told them Yarri's name, didn't you? And that she helped you."

I shuddered. Yarri had not let me know her name until we were away from Arrienda, because she said Letrin would learn of it and kill everyone she knew if he discovered she was a traitor. "I told them," I whispered. I had given those who hunted us Yarri's name. I did not know what they would do with it, but I knew what they could do. I sat up and covered my face with my hands. "I didn't mean to," I told the cat.

"I'm sure that will be a comfort to Yarri."

I bit my lip to keep from crying. "She'll be safe with us. We'll keep her safe."

"Perhaps you will. Tell me this, though — how will you keep her family safe?" the cat asked.

I had failed in my duty to the people who counted on me. Now everything Yarri cherished was in danger. Because of me.

"How do I take it back?" I asked the cat. "How do I fix it? There must be some way that I can fix it."

The cat stared at me, offering me no words of comfort or of reassurance. His tail twitched, and his ears, half back, let me see his anger.

A bit of tasty food, music, some songs, and I forgot my danger, forgot my friends, and said something unforgivable.

"But," I told the cat, "you said the ghost warriors fought against the nightlings in the Long War. Surely they would not be working for the kai-lord now."

The cat sat blinking at me, inscrutable. After a moment, he said, "You shouldn't think. You'll get yourself in trouble. You would have been safer telling everything you know about Yarri to the huntress. *She* would rather die a thousand times over than ally herself with Letrin. Or any of the nightlings. The warrior bard, though? Tofsin is more a mercenary than any of the ghost warriors trapped in that harp of his ever were. He would loan out his soul for enough gold — probably already has. Letrin has enough gold to make Tofsin's greedy heart sing, and all the reason in the world to pay someone to find out who told you to ask for the ruby key."

"Oh, Spirit forgive me," I whispered. "I don't know why I talked to him. Well, sang. I can't even sing."

"It was an enchantment," the cat said. "There are ways to beat it. A child like you wouldn't know them, of course."

"Then why are you angry at me?" I protested. "How can you blame me?"

And then I heard what I was saying, and I stopped. Of course he was going to blame me. And when, in a few moments, I woke Yarri and told her what I had done, she would blame me. And finally, when her entire family went before Letrin to be executed, they would blame me. I was the one in charge. People were going to die because I'd failed to keep a secret with which I'd been entrusted.

It wasn't fair, because I had not received the magic or the training or whatever it was that would have let me defeat the warrior bard and keep my secret safe. But it was life. As my mother said when one of my sibs or I started to complain about fairness, "You're alive, aren't you? That's all the fairness you get."

I could not escape from my mistake.

"I have to wake Yarri," I said. "I have to tell her what I've done."

I cried first. Then I woke her. And told her. And in telling her, cried again.

Her response, though, was not what I'd expected. I'd thought she would be furious with me. Or cold. That she would hate me. Maybe that she would try to hurt me. I had been ready for any of that.

I wasn't prepared for her to roll into a ball and start screaming, "I forgot! I forgot! I'm sorry! Sorry! Take it back!"

She wasn't talking to me. She wasn't talking to the cat, or Dan, who was somehow managing to sleep through all the noise. The cat stopped glaring at me and padded over to her.

"What did you do?"

Her voice was muffled because she was still rolled into a ball. "We . . . I . . . after we were all so upset last night . . ."

"I was here," the cat said. "I remember the hysteria."

"I always shield all of us," Yarri said. "I keep us shielded, day and night, except when you're looking for moonroads. The audiomaerist warned me that I must."

The cat waited. I waited. Dan slept.

"I had shields around everyone while we ate," Yarri said. "But they must be renewed frequently because so many things are constantly checking them. They wear thin. And we talked last night, and I was so tired — and I forgot."

"So," the cat said, "you have as much responsibility for what happened as Genna, who ended up bespelled because of what you did."

Yarri rolled into an even tighter ball and began to sob. "I'm so sorry. I was so stupid." She lifted her head and stared at me, her huge eyes dazed and glassy from tears. "My family. They kept hidden in plain sight for time out of mind, but with a moment's thoughtlessness, I have betrayed them. I have killed them." She shook her head and collapsed back onto her bedroll, her arms wrapped around her head.

I went to her bedside and sat next to her.

"I'm sorry," I told her. "I didn't mean to tell the ghost warriors or the bard about you. There was music. Food. Singing. Magic for certain." I patted her shoulder. "I thought I was dreaming. I didn't know it was real."

One hand lifted and weakly waved off my apology. "*My* fault," she said. "What *I* did, I did from carelessness."

The cat said, "Crying won't fix things."

Yarri sat up slowly and pulled a silk handkerchief from one pocket of her tabard. She wiped her eyes and blew her nose, and the handkerchief glowed a little, just for an instant. It looked clean again. She put it away, and took a deep breath, and straightened her shoulders.

"I have to go back," she said.

"You can't go back," I told her. "The kai-lord will kill you."

"He may well be gathering up my family now," Yarri said. Her lower lip trembled as she said it, but she took another deep breath to get herself under control and kept going. "My parents, my aunts and uncles, my grandparents, my brothers and sisters. He will have the guards take them to the deep places in Arrienda, away from all light and fresh air." She turned to face me. "The guards will begin to torture everyone, as the kai-lord commands, and some may live, but surely some will die. My friends, too, will be captured, along with their families. Those people I spoke to often. Everyone I have touched, I have betrayed by my moment of stupid carelessness."

I reached out and held her hand. "I'm sorry I distracted you," I told her. "I never imagined what cost our talking when we were tired might have."

She leaned over and hugged me. "Nor I. But what remains is . . . duty."

The cat said, "Yarri, I think you should stay here, where you'll be safe."

Yarri pulled away from me to look at him with disdain.

"I'm sure you would hide. I'll go be with my family, though. If I can make some sort of deal with the kai-lord, maybe only I will be punished. If I can't, at least maybe I can be with them until the end."

The cat sat watching Yarri, but I was watching the cat. He seemed . . . pleased. Perhaps a bit amused. Cats are hard to understand at the best of times — one minute sweet as you rub their tummies but the very next instant attacking your fingers as if they were mice. *This* cat — he was impossible.

Though he could talk to us, as normal cats could not, I never once felt that he was telling us even part of what was going on. He knew more than we did, and he wasn't sharing.

"Well," he said after a moment, "if you truly want to go back, we have time to catch a road to Arrienda and still allow me to get back here. If you hurry, of course."

Yarri swallowed hard.

"I still think you should hide here," the cat said when she didn't stand immediately. "You're only a child. No one will blame you for being afraid."

I said, "Quiet, cat."

He glanced in my direction. I could not read his face or body language. I had no idea what he might have been thinking.

Yarri started to pack her bedroll, but the cat said, "You won't need anything where you're going. But Genna will need everything in there."

"Oh." Yarri's pale face turned ash gray, but she stood. "You're right, of course." Her hands shook, and she looked to me as if she might throw up at any moment. I had no idea whether nightlings ever threw up, though — they seemed too elegant to ever do anything so human.

I stood with her, leaned over, and whispered in her ear, "I think you're brave. I hope I would have the courage to go be with my family, too."

"You think I'm right?"

"Yes. We'll miss you so much. But I'm doing everything I can to save my family. You have to do everything you can to save yours."

"Give Danrith a hug for me, will you?" she whispered.

"I will, I promise."

"You can still do this," she told me. "As long as you and Dan and the cat keep going, you can beat Letrin. I believe in you. And you'll be fine without me. I wish I could keep a shield over you as you go, but it would break every time you walked a moonroad."

"We'll be all right." I hugged her again, feeling my throat go tight as tears welled in my eyes. "Be safe. Be lucky." On impulse, I pulled off the sweater my mother had made for me and gave it to her. "Wear it until we meet again. Dan and I won't be long, and in the meantime, it has its own magic. It will watch over you."

She shrugged into the sweater, which was huge on her, and took off the little necklace with the light crystal she wore. "When you want light, you'll have it. When you need darkness, you'll have that, too. Just tap the crystal and think what you need."

The cat growled. "The night is still young, but we must get outside quickly," he told her. "You'll let me stand on your shoulder, and I'll take you by moonroads as close as I dare to Arrienda. You'll have to travel on your own from the place where I leave you, though."

He turned his attention to me. "You and your brother will wait for me here. Don't go outside, don't go to sleep, and keep your voices down, for there are creatures who hunt below the ground as well as those who hunt above it, and without me to listen for them, you won't know if they're coming. If Letrin doesn't get me, I'll be back. If I'm not back when the food runs out, flee and save yourselves. You won't find Doyati without my help."

I hugged Yarri once more, and said, "Good luck, and be strong. We'll come for you, and we'll bring Doyati."

Then they were gone, hurrying out of the tunnel, up to the surface where gurleegs and giant bat-men and no doubt other horrors awaited them.

CHAPTER 10
DANRITH OF HIGH HOUSE

When the cat and Yarri were gone, I shook my brother. "Wake up," I whispered. "I mustn't go to sleep, and I need you to help me stay awake."

He murmured something in his sleep that sounded like, "Save the women and children."

I shook him again, harder, and said, "We *are* the women and children, you idiot. What remains of them, anyway. Wake up!"

"Circle the men . . . pikes to the fore . . . wizards to me . . ." he mumbled, and I thumped the top of his head with the flat of my hand.

"Wake up!"

His eyes opened and he looked at me with complete confusion. "Varlet! Knave! Dost thou disturb a man in battle for our very lives?"

Clearly, the ghost looked out at me, something that made my skin crawl and made me want to go hide in the tunnel. But I needed my brother back. And quietly. The cat's admonishment about things that hunted beneath the ground as well as above it had not passed from my memory.

"Your battle is long over, warrior, and you are long dead. Go away," I said. My voice squeaked at the end, and I barely got the words out.

Danrith's expression changed, though. The ghost disappeared, and Danrith whined, "I was *sleeping*, Genna. Why did you *wake* me?"

"Hush. Keep your voice down or we may be eaten."

The spoiled, sleepy child went away, too, as he took in where we were.

"Where are Yarri and the cat?" he murmured. He rubbed his eyes and frowned.

His frown got deeper by the time I finished telling him.

"You let her go?" He stood, twelve on the outside, but older for what we had been through. "She won't win a deal from the kai-lord! She's the child of slaves. She has nothing to bargain with."

I pulled him back to his bedroll. "*Quiet,*" I said, as firmly as I could while being quiet myself. "If I told you that you could spend your last days with Mama and our sibs or you could hide, but no matter what you did you would not save them, what would you do?"

"I'd be with them," he said without hesitation. He bit his lip and his cheeks and ears turned red. "But that's different." The flush of his cheeks darkened. "I'm not a helpless little girl."

He and Yarri had talked together often as we traveled, usually when I was paying attention to the cat. I'd thought nothing of it . . . but seeing the way he blushed when speaking about Yarri, I thought again.

"I promised her we would come for her," I told him, trying to offer him some comfort. "I promised her we would bring Doyati."

But Danrith was not comforted. "Doyati is only part of the answer." He sat on the floor and started going through his kit-bag, pulling out food items, tools, and other things that Yarri had packed in them, and spreading them out on the bedroll. "I dreamed about this," he said, "though I didn't know it was about this at the time. I was dreaming about the nightling kai-lords and the human kings —"

"There were never human kings," I said. "Only maraeshes who rebelled against the nightlings."

"There *were* human kings," he said, and his eyes burned with an intensity that frightened me. "And human cities as great as the city of Arrienda and as powerful. Humans were once the ruling race, and nightlings served them as humans now serve nightlings."

He seemed so sure. But even if it had been true once, it was no longer true, and it had nothing to do with Yarri or Dan or me, or with our bargain with the kai-lord.

So I asked him, "Why does this matter now?"

He took the kit-bag Yarri had left for me, and started adding the food and tools he'd pulled out of his own bag to it.

"I saw the last fortress fall," he told me. "And all in it die at the hands of nightlings. Long ago. What I saw — it wasn't like the stories of how we came to have Offering Night. The men fought so hard, Genna. They threw themselves at the nightlings with weapons we don't even have anymore. Our people had real wizards, and the wizards were warriors, too. They weren't entertainers at faires or makers of trinkets. They were heroes. But there weren't enough of them, and the archers and the swordsmen weren't enough. The nightlings had tricked them."

"So the humans in your dream, they lost a battle."

He shook his head. "They lost the *last* battle, Genna. The humans lost the whole war."

He was trying to tell me something that he thought was obvious, but I didn't understand.

I said, "The maraesh and all the caers said we made our peace with the nightlings as equals. That we and they realized our war was destroying all of us, so we negotiated a way to live with each other without killing each other. That we gave each other Offering Night, and rule, covenant, and law."

"Right. That's what everyone says. But it wasn't that way. The nightlings took us all. They claimed all surviving humans as their property, and set people to work in farms and villages, no matter what they might have done before. They put rule and covenant over us as burdens, and lied about promise. They killed all the wizards. All the warriors. All the record-keepers and the kings and the scribes. They destroyed all the human cities and schools of magic and law and history. Only those people who did not understand the power humans wielded before were allowed to live. And of those people, they taught a few and set those over the rest. Nightling masters gave human captives a false history. They lied, Genna. And as humans settled into the nightlings' lie, they forgot what they had been, and believed they were what the nightlings told them they were. Unprotesting, they bore the nightlings' burdens, and did for them in daylight what the nightlings could not do for themselves."

"So humans were nightlings' slaves?"

"More like farm animals. They still are, I think. *We* still are. Not the slaves of all nightlings, though. Most of the nightlings aren't much better off than we are. The kai-lords own them, too."

"But what you're saying — what the ghost tells you — it isn't true. Yarri and her people might be slaves, but humans are free now. We buy and sell property, make contracts, marry whom we will."

Danrith shook his head. "The ghost says before we do any of those things, we go to the human, trained by nightlings, who gives us permission or denies us. The caer. The priest. The yihanni, or the yervi."

"Even if you're right," I said, throwing my hands wide, "and I cannot believe you are, what are we supposed to do about this? Go marching across the moonroads — you, me, and the cat — and declare war on the kai-lords and their vast armies one by one, and beat them into submission with our socks and kit-bags?"

"No." He wasn't looking at me anymore. "Right now, I have to go save Yarri."

"We have three days left," I told him. "Three days to find Doyati, convince him to go with us to Arrienda, and then get off the moonroads. We don't have time to go to

Arrienda, then come back. I do not know if we have time even to find Doyati before our days run out."

"I didn't say *we*," Dan said softly. "I said *I*. I have to go save Yarri."

"You can't save her. You're twelve."

Danrith sat across from me, as strange to me in that moment as if we had only just met. He was thinking, a frown tight across his brow, with his fists clenched and his knees pulled up to his chest.

"You aim to save everyone in the village, and you're only fourteen," he said. "Yarri has nothing to bargain with before the kai-lord," he added, and I knew he was right. I'd known it before she left. "She's his slave. He owns her. But he doesn't own me. Not by contract anyway. If he bargained with you, he might bargain with me. I haven't made a deal with him, and I know what he wants."

"*We* made a deal with him. I spoke for both of us. And he wants Doyati."

"He also wants human slaves. I can give him what he wants, and I don't have to worry that the deal won't work."

I stared at him. "You can't."

He looked at that moment so much like Papa, back when Papa was still well. He looked stubborn and certain.

And strong. "The oldest child has duties. But the oldest male child has duties, too, and while your duty is to our family and to our village, my duty as caer-in-training is first to our people."

He sounded like Papa, too, but I still wanted to hit him. "What are you talking about, you lunatic? What we're doing *is* for our people!"

"This is bigger than our village, I think. Since not long after the Long War, our people and their people have been forbidden to meet each other. We thought they were all monsters. They thought we were, too — most of them. If we, who represent humans, abandon Yarri, who represents nightlings who help us, then we show we have no honor. We'll prove we're exactly the monsters they thought we were."

"We're children."

"The ghost says not. He says if we do not stand by our friends, all nightlings who might see us will say that we abandoned their kind when danger came. And before we have a chance to matter, that chance will be dead."

"If we bring Doyati, we help the nightlings."

He shook his head. "In my dream — in the dream the ghost gave me — I saw something, Genna. I saw our people as they were before rule, covenant, and promise. And I saw what the kai-lord of Arrienda and the other kai-lords have done to us since." He looked over at me, and his face was young, but his eyes were suddenly old. "Yarri is fighting him. Doyati, if you can win him to this cause, will fight him. Other nightlings are fighting him. If we join them, if we add our strength to theirs and stand with them, we can throw down our owners and become free again. But as long as we fight apart, not trusting one another, we are helpless."

I sat back, searching desperately for an argument. I could not, for the longest time, think of a single thing to say to him that didn't start with *Are you mad? Have you lost your mind?* He intended to sell himself to Kai-Lord Letrin to win Yarri's freedom, or perhaps simply her life, and do it to win battles we were not even fighting and almost certainly would not survive to fight, while neglecting the one we were — the one, I might add, that was almost sure to kill us all.

And yet, I could not say he was wrong. I wanted to. Oh, how I wanted to.

But while I was working to save our lives right away, he and his warrior ghost were looking at how we might keep such horrors from ever happening again. Both were important.

He meant to leave me alone to do something I had to do, and I did not know if the thing could be done alone.

I said as much.

He said, "When we found Doyati, were we going to hit him over the head so we could drag him to Letrin against his will?"

Even though I was afraid, even though I was worried, I still laughed out loud. "Of course not. I mean, I thought of it, but that was just in passing."

"How were we going to get him to Letrin, then?" he asked.

"I was going to talk to him. Try to convince him to help us."

"No tying him up and carrying him? No dragging him by his hair?"

I giggled and shook my head.

Dan said gently, "Then you don't need me. You're ten times the talker I'll ever be. People like you, they trust you, and they see something in you that makes them want to help you. You're kind, mostly. When we're not fighting anyway." He grinned at me. "I've seen you smile at people, or just stop to help them if you notice they need it, and forever after, they like you. If there's any way to get Doyati to help us, you'll find it."

"You think so?"

He nodded vigorously. "Mama's life is depending on you. And Catri's, and everyone else's. If I didn't think you could do this alone, I wouldn't be able to leave. But, Genna, we owe Yarri. Without her, we would have wandered in the Nightling Forest forever. We would never have found the audiomaerist, never have met the cat, never have learned how to travel the moonroads —"

"You can find moonroads now, too?" I dared to hope.

"Not yet. But I can see them once you or the cat finds them."

"That's good. That's . . ." Normal conversation faltered, as the weight of what I was agreeing to hit me. I was agreeing to be alone. I wanted him to stay with me because I was afraid to be alone. I was afraid to fail alone. If he were with me, if I could not convince Doyati, perhaps he would think of a way. Without him, I carried the entire weight of getting the child to Arrienda.

But Dan was right. One of us had to go help Yarri, and if this came down to which of the two of us was likely to convince Doyati to help, then the person to solve that problem would be me. Dan's quick temper and tendency to bluntness would be more likely to turn Doyati away than win him over.

"If Doyati were stubborn, *you* might hit him," I said at last.

He smiled. "I'm still your brother," he told me.

I bit my lip. "You are. You always will be. Do what you must do. I'll find a way to do what I must do. If the little gods approve, perhaps we'll meet again." I hugged him.

"It's done," a nearby voice said, and Dan and I jumped and clung to each other. And the cat strolled out of the tunnel. "We got there, though morning caught me on the way back. I barely made it."

I was starting to get teary-eyed, and even though Dan sounded right in what he said to me, I hoped the cat might say he was wrong. So I said, "Danrith wants to make his own deal with Kai-Lord Letrin, to sell himself into slavery for Yarri's freedom."

The cat sat on the floor, his head swiveling from one of us to the other, his unblinking gaze making me more nervous and anxious than I had been before. "Letrin will use every tool he has to extract the names of his enemies from Yarri. He has unthinkable power. You can only imagine part of how he will use it. I've seen much that you cannot imagine, and even I cannot guess everything."

"I'm right to go then?" Dan asked.

"Not entirely. You would do much to lend credibility to your cause if you did this thing, but only if Genna succeeds. If she fails to bring Doyati to Arrienda, you will be Letrin's slave for far longer than a human lives, for he will use all his power to keep you alive — to make sure you last a very long time — and he will make sure that every moment you live you will wish you were dead. You will have sold yourself for nothing."

"Then he shouldn't go?" I asked.

The cat sighed. "You two have become something more than the children of a caer and a yihanni. Much rests on your shoulders that you cannot understand."

I nodded, doubtful. I was still trying to find my way through our obligation to people we didn't know to the part where my brother had to become the slave of a monster. "Isn't there someone else who can bargain for Yarri?"

"No," the cat said. "You cannot, because you must continue on your way, so that you can find Doyati and win him to your cause. You will have to convince him that now is the time when he must come out of hiding and risk his life on the merits of your bargain with Letrin. You must somehow convince him that your bargain for the ruby key will meet with success."

"It won't. We'll have to find something else we can do."

The cat walked over to me and rubbed the top of his head on my arm. "If Yarri is not kept safe from Letrin, at least long enough for you to bring in Doyati, the battle is already lost. Even now, Letrin is with her, pushing her for what she knows. She has little brothers and sisters, too. A mother and a father. Nieces and nephews. Every moment you hesitate is a moment that Letrin's gaze might fall upon another of them."

"I have to go," Dan said.

"You did the right thing," the cat told me. "Give your brother the freedom to do the same."

I stood. My head almost touched the domed ceiling, brushing the scaffolding of beams and arches that kept it in place. Dan stood. He had to crouch.

"We are the two people left who can still do things, Genna. If we were pieces on a game board, we'd be the only two who could still move. We have to move in different directions, and we have to be quick."

I hugged him, and he hugged me back. "Stay safe," I told him, knowing he could not be safe, that he went toward his own destruction.

"You, too," he told me.

I then said something I'd never said to any of my brothers or sisters, even though it was true — most of the time. "I love you."

And he told me, "I love you, too."

"I'll take him," the cat added. "And come back for you."

I could only nod. I was fighting back tears, choking on them, watching the brother who had pestered me nearly mindless while I was trying to read or knit or milk the cow walking off to bargain his own life away to save the lives of strangers. Well, Yarri and strangers.

He was only one more member of my family, but he was the last one I could talk to. I wasn't ready for him to leave me. I didn't want to be alone.

Like Yarri, he and the cat disappeared up the tunnel and were gone.

It didn't occur to me until a dim, muddy daylight shone down the mouth of the tunnel, just a bit later while I was waiting for the cat to return, that when the cat came back from taking Yarri away, he said he'd barely made it back before the moonroad had closed. That daylight had come to Arrienda.

So he couldn't have taken Dan there.

But he'd taken him someplace.

That was when I panicked.

CHAPTER 11
ALONE

First, I ran up the tunnel and peered out, quickly, in every direction, hoping that the cat might still be searching for a road, and that I might scream to my brother to run away — that the cat was a liar. A traitor.

Neither of them was anywhere I could see from the tunnel mouth, and when I ran to the top of the mount to get a better look, three of those bat-winged horrors peeled out of the lazy circle in which they'd been soaring, riding the air, and tucked their wings to their sides, and plummeted toward me so that I ended up jumping off the mound and falling into the tunnel and rolling down it, landing like a tossed bag of apples at the bottom. The flying creatures peering down at me from outside were too tall and too wide to get in.

I shivered, though, and crawled away from where they could see me, and cowered in the chamber-pot tunnel until they were gone.

Then, I am ashamed to say, I flung myself facedown on Dan's bedroll and kicked and screamed and cried to put a three-year-old to shame.

It was not the smartest thing I've ever done.

I heard a grinding noise and felt rumbling in the ground beneath me. That shook me out of my self-pity. I rolled away, and an instant later, an enormous maw with circles of teeth set in rows swallowed the whole of the bedroll on which I'd just been lying and stretched a wormlike body out of the tunnel it had just dug, and after almost no pause, came straight at me. I crouched, then jumped for the long-handled cast-iron skillet on the shelf near me, grabbed it, and as that maw came at me, started swinging the skillet with everything I had. I connected, and teeth and bits of worm flew everywhere. The worm tried to back down its hole, but I kept moving toward it, cutting off its escape. Smashing it was the antidote to my rage and fear and despair about my brother and Yarri, and my dread at what the cat had done with them, and I kept advancing, kept swinging. With every solid strike, with every chunk of worm that flew across the room and splatted into a wall or a shelf or a beam or a bit of tunnel, I felt stronger. Braver. More ready for whatever I had to do to find Doyati and then get my family back.

Too soon, I had nothing left to smash. Pieces of the worm's tooth-lined gullet festooned nearly every surface of the tiny hovel; his slimy body plugged the tunnel he'd made. The room was going to start stinking before too long, I imagined, but still fresh, the dead worm didn't smell like much at all.

Always be grateful for small mercies, because sometimes those are the only sort you get.

I put down the skillet. Suddenly, I was more tired than I had ever been in my life. I went to the rainwater barrel and dipped out enough water to wash my face and arms. I got one of the little earthenware pots, too, and filled it with water, and pulled off my broadcloth shirt and homespun skirt, and did the best I could to get the worm gore off them. I didn't dip anything into the barrel, of course. Fouling someone else's drinking water would have been unspeakable.

When my things and I were as clean as I could manage, I wrung them out and put them on wet. I carefully shook off the last surviving bedroll — the worm mess didn't even stick to the nightling fabric. It slid right off without leaving even a stain behind.

And then I sat. I didn't have any tears left, and I couldn't find my anger, and I had misplaced my fear.

I sat in the mound-house because I did not know what else to do. Had the cat betrayed us all? We were scattered, Yarri and Dan and I, and the cat had been the creature who had done that separating. He had led us from the old woman, who seemed not to know anything about him but that he talked and that he knew how to walk the moonroads. He had told me that he was not really a cat. He had gotten us out of dangers that I'd gotten us into.

But when he chose the moonroads for us, we ended up in places as deadly as those I'd found, and we had only his word that the Kai-Lord Letrin knew Yarri's name, or that taking her back and putting her into his hands was really the best method of dealing with the situation.

He'd claimed to be taking Danrith to Letrin, too, and in a fit of what — looking back on it — had to be me losing my mind, I'd let him lead my little brother away.

Never mind this was what Dan thought he was supposed to do. Dan was still a child.

And I was gullible and stupid and foolish.

We were not heroes. Dan and I were children, and witless ones. The cat was working for the kai-lord, and he'd split us up so that there was no way we could hope to accomplish Letrin's impossible mission. When it was too late to do anything but scream, he would send Letrin's hunters after me to gather me up, and probably Doyati as well, and Letrin would have everything, and we would have nothing.

I sat with my arms wrapped around myself, gently rocking back and forth, thinking about what I might do that could save the situation. How I might find a moonroad that would take me back to Arrienda, how I might breach the magical stone door and find my way, through the endless layered maze that was the city to my little brother, how I might rescue him. How I might yet hope to save Mama, and the younglings, and how I might yet bring justice to the false caer Banris, whose fault this whole mess was.

The cat didn't come back.

Well, I knew he wasn't going to, didn't I?

The thing we had needed to do more than anything was stay together, Yarri and Danrith and I.

And by the cat's suggestion, we were as far away from one another as worlds and time could take us.

* * *

But I could call moonroads, though I had never managed to call a moonroad I wanted. And I had three days. Perhaps, if I went aboveground, I could call a moonroad to me that would take me to Doyati. I didn't know him or what he looked like or what sort of creature he was. But the old woman had pointed us to the road that would lead us to him by listening for his name.

Doyati, I thought, getting up at last and going to the earthenware pots and plates on the shelves. This hovel, the cat said, belonged to Doyati. Or at least he used the place sometimes. So the pots would belong to him as well, and touching them, maybe I could connect to him.

Doyati.

Doyati!

I decided that the cat would not win. Letrin would not win. I would wait at the tunnel mouth until the moon rose, and I would call a road to take me to Doyati. If the first road failed me, I would call another, and then another. I would not stop until I had found my way to the boy who could save all of us. I *would* find Doyati, no matter what it took. I refused to believe things could end any other way.

I started up the tunnel, and nearly knocked down the oldest man I had ever seen, who was hobbling down it. He was hunched so far over he had to lift his head just to look forward. He leaned on a walking stick with well-worn hand grips. I could barely see his eyes for the wrinkles on his face, and when he smiled at me, three yellow, worn teeth flashed briefly.

"Grandfather," I told the old man, "you've come down the wrong path. Let me help you find your way to your own home."

He cackled until he began to wheeze. And he told me, "This *is* my home, child. My name is Doyati."

I stared at him. In my mind, in my worst moments, Doyati had been as tall as a house or the statue Dan and Yarri and I had found in that cave. He'd been young, and I'd seen him with sharply pointed teeth, glowing red eyes, claws like a bear's, and a voice like a thunderstorm. In my best moments, he had looked a lot like Letrin, only younger.

I said, "You don't look like Doyati."

He smiled, showing gaping gums, and said, "And how would you, young invader of my house, know what I look like? We've never met."

"The cat talked about you."

His beady eyes disappeared completely into the wrinkles of his face, and his lips pursed. "I would think you mad," he told me. "But . . . describe the cat."

"Black and gray and brown. Stripy, with the swirly sort of stripes. White face and belly and white feet."

"Ah. Him."

So the cat had told the truth when he said he knew Doyati. If this was Doyati, anyway. I found that hard to believe. This old man hadn't been young since the Nightling Forest was grass and seed.

"That cat's a terrible liar," the old man told me. "But most cats are, don't you think?"

Clearly, the old man was more than a little crazy. "I don't know any other talking cats," I told him, before I realized that I knew one, and therefore was hardly standing on firm ground for questioning the sanity of someone who might know two or three.

The old man said, "*Cats!* You know ordinary cats, don't you? The one who walks along the stall wall, and knocks the curry brush on your head. You look up at the cat, and the cat looks down at you, and in his eyes, you see . . . what? Guilt? No! You see, 'Did not do it. Ask the dog.'"

I laughed. This was true of every cat in our barn.

"That cat steals fish from the table, and when you catch

him with it in his mouth, he stares you down. 'The dog stole it,' his eyes say. 'I was just holding it for him.'"

I nodded.

"Right. Cats lie. They steal. They sneak. The talking cat just lies better."

"He took my brother away on the moonroads," I said.

The old man brushed past me and went down the tunnel into his home. Three steps behind him, I was positioned perfectly to hear the thin wail when he saw the awful mess I'd left in his house.

"Spirit and little gods preserve us!" he shrieked. "What massacre was this?" He turned to me. "Did *you* do this?"

I hung my head. I knew I should have cleaned the rest of the worm remains before I left, but I'd been in such a hurry. "Yes, grandfather. I'm sorry. The worm came up out of the floor —" I didn't even get a chance to finish.

"*Sorry?* Never be sorry for killing a dire-worm." He rested his arm on my shoulder and pushed his face close to mine, and he blinked at me. "Why in the name of all that is good would you be sorry? Child, those things are a menace. You should gather up the teeth, drill holes in them, and wear them on a chain around your neck. The list of people I know who have killed a dire-worm I could write on my hand. The list of people who have been killed by dire-worms . . . that would take a scroll that would stretch from here to near eternity."

I looked at the mess. It was dreadful, but he didn't seem to be bothered by it. Instead, he seemed excited.

"How did you do it?" he wanted to know. "Enchanted arrows? Spell of exploding flesh? Rain of fire? No, not that. The worm would be cooked and we could eat it. Wand of destruction? Oh, a wand of destruction would be a fine, fine thing." He turned to me. "Speak up, girl."

"I hit him with your skillet. A lot."

He rocked back on his heels, and his eyebrows slid up his forehead like ragged caterpillars. "You're an interesting girl. Interesting." He pursed his thin lips and his mouth nearly disappeared into wrinkles. "So you had to get close to him to kill him."

"Well, he got close to me," I said, not wanting to make myself sound like a hero. I had, after all, squashed a worm. It had been big, it had been scary, but it was only a worm. "If he hadn't been chasing me, I wouldn't have hit him."

"It will do," the old man said. And then, "Do you have any food? I don't remember when I last ate."

I'd wanted to talk to him about my brother, to find out where he thought the lying cat might have taken him. But the old man was my elder, and I would not be able to call a moonroad until sunset, or moonrise. I kept my patience and remembered my manners. If he were hungry, my needs and my story would wait.

"I could make stew," I told him doubtfully.

"The fra-hawks are hunting overhead," the old man said. "The sun is up. The moon is down. You can go nowhere until all these things have changed. Make stew."

So I cooked while he dozed on the straw-bag bed, and cleaned the worm mess, and saved the teeth — for after all, they were impressive, and I thought Danrith would be awed and envious that I had won them in a fight. If we lived to see each other again.

If this old man were Doyati, and if I could win him over, I could, perhaps, save our plan.

Perhaps.

Probably not.

When the stew was ready, I woke him, and filled a half-gourd bowl for him, and brought him water in another half-gourd. And then I took food for myself, and spread out my bedroll at his feet so I would have a place to sit and eat.

"The cat left you, did he?" the old man asked.

"Yes. He took my brother, but not where he said he was going to take him."

The ancient man who claimed to be Doyati ladled stew into his mouth and chewed it for a very long time. I kept my patience; elders have earned their respect.

At last he swallowed, and took a sip of water. "Good stew," he told me. "It has been a long time since I've had anything with meat in it. A very long time." He coughed, and took another sip of water, and when I was about to burst waiting for him to say something helpful, he finally spoke.

"The cat took your brother elsewhere. An audiomaerist could tell you where, I suppose. But you don't have time to chase after your brother, do you? You were to bring me to Letrin, and you have to get me there before the moon in its quarter becomes too weak to get you off the moonroads."

"How did you know that?"

Doyati laughed softly. "Letrin sends hunters after me from time to time. They rarely find me — those the cat leads to me he thinks are harmless, though, and they usually are." He gave me a long, thoughtful look, then turned to study his skillet. "Usually. But Letrin has wanted nothing else for me but my death since I was born, so if you came knowing my name, and knowing the cat, you are here to try to take me back to Arrienda. To Letrin. And to my death."

And there he had me. He knew everything he needed to know about me, while I realized I knew nothing about him.

"Why does Letrin think you're a boy?"

"Because I could have been. *Should* have been. We both have nightling fathers and human mothers. Letrin inherited the long life of the nightlings from his father, and he assumed that I did, as well. I, alas, inherited my life span from my human mother. I have lived over a hundred years, and now I am near death."

"Then it won't matter if you come with me," I blurted, and as the words came out of my mouth, I wished I could unsay them. "I didn't mean that as it sounded, honored grandfather. I know life is precious, but . . . surely he will see that you are no threat to him as you are. And even if he . . . if he . . ."

Well. How does a girl ask a stranger to come be killed as a favor to her?

I didn't know, and I certainly couldn't think of the words.

Doyati read my meaning well enough in my silence, though. He smiled a little.

"You look at me, and I am near death. So you think even if Letrin would not have pity on me — and he would not, for there is no pity in the kai-lord — he could kill me without me being much the worse off than I already am. And you would be able to keep your end of the bargain, thus saving your family and your friends and your village. Am I right?"

I nodded.

"To you, it looks simple enough. But it is not simple."

I waited.

"The nightlings have built their hopes around me. They believe that I — their rightful kai-lord — will come save them. That I will free them from Letrin and set their world right. They believe in me, and because they have their belief, they have hope."

I looked at that old, bent-over, helpless little man, and I said, "You can't save them, can you?"

He hung his head, and I could see liver spots on his scalp through the few remaining tufts of snowy-white hair.

"I can't save them," he admitted. "I can't do anything for them at all. Had I been braver when I was a young man, I might have at least tried. But I waited too long, because I was afraid. Now, I can do nothing. I'm no match for Letrin. I never was. All I can do is hide and give the nightlings hope."

This made no sense to me. "They hope for you to rescue

them — but you're never going to rescue them, so they're hoping for something that will never happen."

"I know."

"Then you're hurting them," I told him. "If they weren't waiting for you to come along and save them, perhaps they would do something to save themselves."

He smiled a little at that. "Where would they even start?" He shook his head. "No, child, they will never act on their own. Letrin has them terrified of their own shadows, and with reason. When he finds those who rebel, he destroys them and everyone they care about. He rules by fear, and he has a great talent and long practice in that art."

"Letrin is only one man, and if your people rose against him, he could never win. They're already taking action on their own. Starting to save themselves. Yarri risked her own life to help me reach you. I've made a bargain for the ruby key. Things are happening."

"Here you make two errors. You first error is to think numbers could overwhelm the kai-lord, but you forget Letrin has friends and allies. You miscount the numbers. The kai-lord of Arrienda holds treaties with the masters of Rasannai, Belinkann, Fairanarri, Metanai, and the list goes on. A successful overthrow of a hereditary kai-lord could lead to unrest in the other great kaidoms, so at the first sign of true rebellion, Letrin's allies would offer forces to crush any rebels."

He fell silent. This time I did not wait for him to shake himself back to attention.

"What is my second error, then?"

"You think the ruby key has value to someone other than me. That some other hero could step in and use the key, and in doing so, conquer Letrin."

"There must be someone," I said.

"If life were a better, happier thing, there would be someone," Doyati told me. "But life is not, and there is no one else." He sighed and put his bowl in his lap, while his head sagged closer to the floor. He propped up his head with twisted, gnarled hands . . . and the effort made his arms shake.

I feared he would not survive the effort of simply talking to me. I wondered if I might somehow take him to Letrin after he died, but the thought made my skin crawl.

Doyati said, "If I were what Letrin thought I was — nightling-favored, full of magic, and still young — I could use the ruby key to break him. But I'm not. And I can't. I have nothing more special about me than you have about you. And while I feel sad for you and your people, you're a tiny number, growing smaller all the time. Once there were millions upon millions of humans, but your numbers now lessen every year. Your villages shrink and disappear. In two, perhaps three, generations, you humans will be no more, and the whole of the world will belong to the nightlings."

I did not believe what he told me about humans. I did, however, try to use it. "If we are to be lost, then why wouldn't you save us? You're human by half. So we're your people as much as the nightlings."

He said, "No. My people are all of Arrienda, and they deserve to have some hope in their lives, even if it is false hope."

My stew grew cold in my bowl. Doyati told me what I did not want to hear. He was saying, in his old, cautious, gentle way, that he was going to send me back to Letrin alone, and that he was going to consign me and everyone I loved to death.

Not because by doing so he could save the Arriendans, which at least I might have understood, since it would have been simply a bigger version of what I asked of him. No. He balked because he wanted them to keep hoping for something that would never happen, and while they hoped and waited, he would leave them slaves to Kai-Lord Letrin.

I wanted to scream at him. I wanted to hit him or throw

my stew at him or shake him until he came around to my way of thinking. At that moment, I understood Danrith and his temper. But I ate my stew, and I watched him eat his, and I tried to think of words that would win him, that would move him, that would make him love my mother as much as I loved her. And my father. And my friends. That would make him understand that my people mattered, too, and that they deserved a chance to live.

He'd had a human mother. She had come from one of the villages, or perhaps from the big city. But she'd been human. He and I had something in common, then, if only he would remember it. I could *make* him remember it.

I thought hard, and for a few moments I was quiet.

Then I realized I knew something that he would almost certainly have known, too, and little gods have mercy on me that it was a song. "When I was small," I told him, "my mama used to sing to me."

And I sang, trying with all my heart and soul to sound like my mother, who had a lovely voice, when I sang it.

"Hey nara, nara long,
This my little baby's song
Dream of home and distant lands
Safe within your mama's hands."

He had stopped eating. He was watching me, and I saw him suck in his bottom lip.

"Dream of hills and vales and farms
Cradled in your mama's arms
Dream of eagles high above
While held near by mama's love."

He was swallowing hard, blinking fast. He looked away from me, staring down at his feet.

"When you are young I'll hold you close
You're the one that I love most.
When you are grown and I'm long gone
This your little baby's song.

Hey, nara, nara long,
This my little baby's song."

My voice broke as I sang the last lines, thinking that I might never see my own mother again.

Then I heard a whimper in the back of his throat, and looked up to see tears dropping to the floor. "My mama sang that song," he whispered.

I'd hoped she had. It was an old, old song.

"I always thought I'd have children of my own to sing that song to. Someday. I thought."

I told him, "My mama sang me that song as well. And now she's dying, and you can save her, if you'll just come with me. You can save a great many people, a lot of mothers like your mama. You can do something good."

He shook his head, while tears ran down the creases in his face and wet the dirt floor.

I told him, "You could still be a hero, Doyati. You are old, but you are not dead. Only the dead cannot act, my papa always said. If you save us . . ." My hands clenched into fists, crimping the fabric of my skirt as I fought to keep my voice steady. "If you save us, and I live through this, perhaps I will have a son someday. If I do, I shall name him Doyati, to remember you and how you saved me and my mama and my people. This I promise you. I shall tell him about you, and he and all who know him will remember you with gratitude."

I tried not to think about Yarri and her people, who would not be saved. For whom all hope was gone because this dying old man was not the Doyati she and the nightlings had believed in and risked everything to reach.

I forced myself to think instead of my mama, my sibs,

Catri, Danrith, the baker and the miller, the priest, the many yerva who came each week to take lessons from my mother. People I had known all my life. People who would disappear as if they had never existed if I failed.

I tried to look calm, and I tried to sound calm, but my body was knotted tight — with fear that I had said something to break the little spell of that old song. With fear that he would again tell me, "No."

But he buried his face in his hands, and his bony shoulders shook. He sobbed until he was gasping. Then the sobs died away, and slowly he regained control of himself, and slowly he caught his breath. At last he raised his head and looked into my eyes. "I'll come with you," he said. "I'll walk the moonroads with you, and we'll go see Letrin together. I'll stop hiding. I'll do something good at least once before I die."

I stood and hugged him and kissed his wrinkled cheeks. "Thank you," I said. "It isn't enough to say thank you. But, thank you. What could I ever do for you?"

"Have a boy. Name him Doyati," the old man said, and looked up at me with eyes strangely bright. "That will be enough."

CHAPTER 12
WALKING WITH DOYATI

Doyati woke me up by poking me with his walking stick.

I hadn't even realized I'd fallen asleep.

"Pack your kit-bag," he said. "The moon will be rising soon, and we should be on our way."

Packing took me only an instant. The bedroll folded into a square not much larger than an apple and dropped neatly into my bag.

"You missed two dire-worm teeth," he said, and handed two especially large ones to me. "They can be useful. Hold on to them."

I thanked him and took the teeth and dropped them into the pocket in the kit-bag where I had placed the rest.

We walked up the tunnel together in near silence. He wheezed a bit, and grunted once when his foot came down wrong. When we got outside, the sky was surprisingly clear.

The moon, low and small on the horizon, looked pale and watery, as if I saw only its reflection in a wind-ruffled lake.

"You seem a nice girl," he told me. "How did you come to be hunting down an old man to send him to his death?"

So I told him of my father and mother, of Banris and his bargain with Letrin, of the nightlings' and Yarri's demand that I ask for the ruby key — and of my adventures since, with Yarri and Dan and the cat, as well as with the huntress and her hounds, the warrior bard and his ghost-haunted harp, the audiomaerist, the moonroads, the gurleeg, and the dire-worm.

"You think the cat betrayed you to Letrin?" he asked when at last I finished. We had by that time wandered through a maze of mounds, ducking into tunnels to avoid the bat-winged creatures he called fra-hawks, and we seemed to be nowhere closer to someplace important than we had been when we started.

"I'm almost sure of it. The sun had risen and the moon had set in Arrienda when he returned from taking Yarri. Yet he took Dan *someplace*."

The old man nodded. "Yet, what better place would there be to deliver him than to Letrin . . . if he were betraying you to Letrin? That he would take the boy elsewhere — especially when the two of you were already planning on delivering yourselves into Letrin's hands within the next three days, saving the cat the trouble — makes no sense. He's far too lazy to put himself out that way without need," Doyati added.

"Then you don't think the cat betrayed us?"

"Didn't say that at all," the old man said. "You yourself told me you have more than one creature in this world who wants you dead."

I considered that for a moment. The second possibility hit me with full force. "You think the cat took Dan to Banris?"

I imagined Banris talking to the cat, offering him a deal if he delivered us to him instead of Letrin. It made a kind of horrible sense, if I pretended I didn't know Banris.

"I don't think that's it," I told Doyati. "First, Banris hates cats, and cats as a tribe return the sentiment. Second, he doesn't listen to anyone unless that someone has money and power. Third, he would never, ever talk to a cat, thinking such a creature too far below him. He barely talks to farmers."

Doyati laughed. "Well, he fancies himself a displaced prince." In that moment, while he was laughing and his eyes were bright, he seemed to me a different person. Younger. Stronger. When the laughter stopped, though, the cloak of age slipped back over him and destroyed that little illusion.

He said, "You may have a point about Banris. Perhaps the cat serves Letrin after all. He was right about the huntress never willingly serving the kai-lord. . . ."

Doyati paused and frowned. "I cannot imagine why she would seek you out, but since she has, perhaps she made some deal with the cat for delivery of your brother. Yarri as well, for that matter. You have no reason to assume the cat took *her* where she intended."

That thought had not even occurred to me.

"What about the bard?"

Doyati said, "He's just the sort to be Letrin's man, if there's gold in it." He studied a mound that looked to me just like every other mound we had passed and said, "Ah. This way, then."

And I said, "Why? Why are we wandering? The moon is up. I should be calling roads to us. I should be finding a way to Arrienda, because we have so little time and I have such little knowledge of the roads."

"That's why," Doyati said. "I may not have magic, but I have had a hundred years to get the roads in my blood, and my blood on the roads. I know them, and they know me. I will get us both to Arrienda, one way or another."

I did not want to ask him the question that came next to my mind, because I feared the answer. "What happens when we get to Arrienda? What happens to me, and what happens to you?"

He glanced sidelong at me. "You killed a dire-worm today and were ready to march out of that mud-mound and search the roads until you found me. You talked me into joining you, though my role is to be the sacrificed calf in a doomed feast." Doyati smiled faintly. "Genna my dear, you have accomplished what others have been trying to do for the last hundred years. You've gotten Letrin what he wanted. I would suggest perhaps you are less helpless than you think, and further, that however this ends, I would not be the man to bet against you."

I didn't agree with him. But I didn't argue with him, either. Arguing with one's elders is never appropriate.

Doyati said there was a place where we could find a road that would take us to another road that would take us very close to Arrienda, and that *these* moonroads were lightly traveled and mostly safe.

We came to a circle of flattened land around which a low stone wall had been built. The stones in the wall were black and glossy, sharp-edged, and, I realized when Doyati hoisted himself over the wall and I could see his skinny legs through them, transparent.

Mounds butted close to the wall on all sides.

"This is sacred space," he told me. "It is a place of sacrifice and magic, and gurleegs and fra-hawks alike respect it. Those who stand on this ground must hold magic, or when they stand on it, they will die. Neither fra-hawks nor gurleegs have any magic. They've learned, and passed on to their young the dangers of this place."

I was halfway over the wall, my foot about to touch that sacred ground, and I barely stopped myself.

He looked at me. "What are you waiting for?"

I stared at him as if he were a madman. "You said you had no magic."

"I don't," he told me. "But I *hold* magic. I can walk the moonroads. Get in here before a fra-hawk picks you off the wall and eats you."

I moved quickly then.

He said, "You might as well sit. The hour is not favorable for finding the road I want, yet it is the road we must take. So get comfortable and I shall begin to call it."

I had Yarri's kit-bag on my back, and made a pillow of that, deciding to rest while I had the chance. No telling if I might end up fleeing some monster Doyati had forgotten to mention when we landed in the place he'd chosen. I stretched out on the short-cropped grass, closed my eyes . . . and then found myself watching him through slits. He yawned, he stretched, he managed to pull himself a little straighter. He looked up at the sky and around as if checking for danger. Or observers. And then he began to spin little bubbles of light off his fingertips. Blue and gold and green and pink and yellow and white, one after the other after the next, and each he sent into a moonroad that came when he called it.

He'd said he had no more magic than I had — but I did not know how to do what he was doing. He said he *held* magic, as if that were different than *having* magic. I did not understand. Was holding magic some trick for the magicless? Or had he been lying to me when he claimed to have no magic? Lying to me seemed a popular thing lately.

I held my breath and did not move. I dared not disturb him with questions, and I did not wish to let him know that I was watching him, in case what he was doing was supposed to have been secret from me.

At last, he sagged forward again, and one final moonroad came to him. He poked me with his walking stick. "Up, girl. The road has come at last, and we must hurry."

I stood, slung my kit-bag over my shoulders, and when he reached for me, I took his hand.

We slipped into the scent of winter, with snow on the way. I felt coldness, hard wind. And the weight of emptiness, the feel of isolation, pulled on me.

We fell. I could not feel his hand in mine. It had been dry, papery, the bones birdlike, the skin cool when I took it.

But I felt nothing of it. I could not feel him with me. He seemed to have ceased to exist.

And then we pitched forward into sleeting rain, bitter coldness, the sting of falling ice crystals against my skin, and the old man yelled, "The tent. Quickly. Or we'll freeze to death."

I could barely see. The air around us was white. Doyati clung to my sleeve, and I did not question him. Had he taken a step away from me, he would have been lost in the storm, and we would not have found each other again save by the greatest of luck. The wind screamed in my ears, and the cold stabbed through me like knives cutting away flesh and muscle and bone. I longed for my mother's knit sweater and the warmth she had spun into it for me. I hoped it was serving Yarri well.

With fingers that almost wouldn't move, I dragged Yarri's tent from the kit-bag and snapped it as she had done. It unfolded into the graceful, fully formed structure we'd used. I could barely hang on to it in the wind, but managed to drag it to the ground. I couldn't remember how she'd fixed it in place, but I discovered I didn't need to. As the tent's corners touched ice, each dug into the surface like the roots of trees digging into soft earth. We walked around the tent, found the tent flap, and dragged ourselves inside.

I could not say the little shelter was warm inside, but the wind didn't touch us, and the sleeting rain stayed outdoors where it belonged.

"That's a nightling kit-bag you're carrying," Doyati said.

I nodded.

"Let me see it."

Warily, I handed it to him.

He rummaged through it. "Your nightling packed heavy. Good."

He brought out the heat-ball Yarri had used to cook our meals. Doyati began rolling it between his palms, then sighed and handed it to me. "I'm old and dried up. I haven't the energy to make it work well. Roll it in your hands as quickly as you can."

I followed his instructions, and after just a moment, its pale yellow became the soft amber red of a small fire and, a moment later, pure white light too hot for me to hold.

Doyati laughed. "You've enough energy for both of us. That will warm the tent until we're ready to leave, I wager." And he smiled at me.

Our wet clothes began to dry. He dug through Yarri's kit-bag again and brought out food items and cups.

"Reach out into the cold and scoop snow from the ground," he told me. "We'll gather enough water to make a good strong soup to warm us from the inside. And then we'll wait until the moon is at its peak near Arrienda. We'll not sleep here, but we might as well rest while we can. We will be lucky to live through the final leg of the journey — let us go to Letrin with full stomachs and all the strength and courage we can muster." He chuckled, which startled me. If I'd been certain I was facing my death, I would not have managed such a cheerful attitude.

Maybe it was simply because he was so old. Maybe knowing that he'd be done soon, and that he would no longer have to struggle to move from place to place, or to chew food, or to wrap his poor, twisted hand around a stick just to drag himself to a standing position gave him some comfort.

I didn't say anything. Rather, I gathered the water, and thought about Yarri and about my brother and about the people from my village who might still survive. I had hope. Like the nightlings in Arrienda, I had hope, and my hope was built around Doyati. Unlike their hope, mine had some substance behind it.

We ate, and he asked me about my brothers and sisters, about my mother and father, about the life I had in the village. He had a hundred questions, but all of them were small and personal. He asked them eagerly, and took in my answers hungrily.

Finally, he did not have another question for me, so I asked one of him. "Who are the people who have mattered most to you?"

The joy he'd seemed to take from my stories of my parents and my sibs and my life in our humble village faded from his face. "I had my mother when I was young. I had her for . . . a while. Years, but I don't know how many. She grew old, and died, and then I was alone." He shook his head. "I was in hiding, with my cousin determined to have my life, and in those days anyone might have been an enemy. Anyone might have been waiting for me to let down my guard in order to kill me and take my head to Letrin for the bounty. So I did not let myself know anyone." He shrugged. "The cat came to visit me sometimes. He's not much company, and he goes more than he stays."

I tried to imagine that. No friends, no family, no one with whom he could sit at mealtime and talk as we were talking. Not just for a day, or a month, or a year. For a hundred years, or as much of that as had passed since his mother died, with only the occasional visit of that know-everything cat.

As I thought of it, the empty coldness of the storm-ridden place in which we hid began to fill me. He must have felt like that inside. Abandoned.

"I'm so sorry," I whispered. "There's a city filled with people who wanted to love you, and you never got to be with them. That's . . . cruel."

"I was afraid for a long time," he told me. "Perhaps, had I not let fear be my guide, I could have had a better life." He shrugged. "I'm not alone now. It's already a better life."

I turned away. I was taking him to his death; I was hardly the person who was making his life better.

I could feel him watching me. "Well. Stomachs full, bodies warm. All we now need to accomplish is rest," he said. "But not much."

"We still have time," I said. "For what remains of these two full nights, and two more, the moonroads will still be open."

He stared at me as if I were foolish. "You've lost time traveling through the nightworlds," he said. "The moon will rise in its third quarter tomorrow, and for all save the most skilled, the moonroads will close until the next half moon."

I was out of time? I was certain I would not be able to rest. I had too many worries about my family, about my friends, about what I faced when I met again with Letrin.

"How?" I asked him. "How could I have lost two days?"

"The nightworlds do not all spin in unison," Doyati said. "Some turn faster, some slower, and some move not at all. Along your way, you've had to wait, or to walk a long distance searching for a road, and one or another moonrise here has passed you by."

Panic rose in me, but I pushed it back. We still had this moonrise, and Doyati knew the way to Arrienda. Time pressed us, but with the moon not yet risen, we had nothing to do but wait. I said, "I've had rest, but you have not. Why don't you wrap yourself in my bedroll while I stand watch."

He said, "Because I'm the one who knows what I'm watching for."

"Then," I said, thinking of all the time he had spent alone, "perhaps we can simply talk."

"Very well." He leaned against my pack. "That sounds a pleasant enough way to spend a few hours."

Something the cat had mentioned came to my mind, and I said, "I have a question. The cat said that the gurleeg was a taandu monster. And that there were other taandu monsters. But we were not in a place to talk about such things at the time. Do you know what he meant? What a taandu monster is?"

Doyati nodded slowly. "As a human, one of the dayfolk, you know about daylight taandu essence, don't you? How it works, what it does?"

This I knew well in theory, for Mama had been teaching me theory for years. I hadn't much in the way of practical knowledge, but that would certainly come. "Taandu trees distill the essence and power of the sun into their sap during daylight, and in the spring, when the sap rises, we can tap the trees and give ourselves their power. We can use thought and will to turn the energy into potions that heal, that fertilize, that strengthen, and that inspire."

"And that drive the unwilling mad with love," Doyati said, "or crush their wills, or whatever the skilled yihanni might wish. My mother was a yihanni, too," he added. "I know these things. Daylight essence, like the sun itself, is direct, straightforward, powerful, and honest. What you put into it is what you get out, whether for good or ill. No surprises. Correct?"

"Yes."

"Night taandu sap takes on the essence of the moonlight that powers it — or the moondark. It is indirect, changeable, unpredictable, surprising, and dangerous. A talented yihanni could turn it toward healing, but the one who drank the potion would affect the results far more than the elixir's maker. The drinker could decide that to be truly healed, he would have to be able to grow wings and fly — and night taandu essence would grant him what he willed. But there's more to it even than that. Moondark essence, made from the sap drawn on the night of the new moon, will grant the drinker his most deeply held desires. Not the desires he claims to want. The desires his inner self yearns for. Moondark essence will turn him into the living embodiment of the state of his soul."

I thought of the gurleeg, of the horror that it had been, and I said, "The gurleeg was once a nightling? One of those pretty, colorful, delicate creatures with great wide eyes?"

Doyati said, "A gurleeg was once a nightling of greedy and predatory nature, who desired power over others, and who sought to bring them pain and fear. Sadly, gurleegs are a common result among those who drink from the darkest draughts of taandu essence."

"Why, then, would anyone *ever* drink such a potion?"

"When you were in Arrienda, did you see the Flowers?"

"Growing along the corridors. Yes. They were magnificent, and the gardener who planted and tended —"

"Not the plants," Doyati cut me off. "The most exotic and breathtaking of the nightlings, those whose outward forms are an incredibly beautiful reflections of their inner selves."

"The ones with the butterfly wings, and the faces like little gods? I could barely take my eyes off them."

Doyati yawned and closed his eyes for a moment, then rubbed them open again. "Perhaps I should sit up. Sleep desires to claim me by stealth." He sat up straight. "Yes, those are the Flowers. They are, above all others in nightling society, cherished and adored. And the same moondark essence that makes a gurleeg makes a Flower. No yihanni can control what lies written within the heart, so no yihanni can make a safe night taandu essence."

"Then why isn't it given only to good people? Or why don't bad people avoid it?"

Doyati said, "Could you look into the heart of a man and see the good or the evil that resides within? As wise as he was, did your father recognize the depth of treachery in Banris? Did you suspect the double-dealing of the cat?"

"No."

"Then do not ask others to perform miracles you can't," he said. "Monsters always hide among us. Sometimes they hide even from themselves, convincing themselves that they are good and deserving, or at least better and more deserving than others. Taandu monsters are perhaps the least dangerous monsters around us, for we can see them for what they are."

He yawned again, and his eyes closed.

I'll give him a few minutes, I thought. He's old, and he has been worked hard. And the moon has not yet risen. . . .

". . . Tonga gae, tromga jie!
Mosga!
Hosga!
Kie!"

The singing of the ghost warriors woke me. I did not know how I had fallen asleep, or how we could have been surrounded by them if I had not. But surrounded we were.

I grabbed the old man's arm and shook him. "Grandfather! Wake!"

He snored gently.

He had no weapons on him, nor had I on me. Well, he had his walking staff, but that wasn't nearly as useful as a skillet. Still . . .

I grabbed it, and dressed only in my thin broadcloth and homespun skirt, leapt out of the tent and into the coldest, clearest night of my life. There was no wind, which made me think I had indeed slept for at least a little while.

I faced a man as tall as my father, but twice as broad

of shoulder, who stood silhouetted against the waning half-moon, a short, broad harp cradled in his arms. That would be the war harp, source of the ghost warriors who surrounded the tent, milky white but glowing faintly, standing in ranks as far as the eye could see. My eye, anyway. I was shorter than the shortest of them and couldn't see over their heads.

I shivered and my teeth rattled and my knees knocked, and not entirely from the bitter cold. But Yarri's light hung at my throat, and I willed light from it, and when I touched the crystal, cold white brilliance poured out and spilled over the ghosts, who stepped back, and over the warrior bard, who did not. I could see him clearly though — young and handsome, brown-eyed and sturdy, with even white teeth and a broad, satisfied grin on his face that rattled my resolve.

Not completely, though.

I swung the walking stick and hit the harp a good skillet-hard blow. The strings clanged and a few broke and snapped into the bard's face, drawing blood, and from the tent behind me I heard a startled shout.

CHAPTER 13
UNLIKELY ALLIES

In the cold moonlight, distant mountains rose up like the teeth of wolves, gnawing through the endless glossy surface of the ice-covered snow. I could imagine being skewered on one of them, being devoured by that cold, hard land.

I shouted to Doyati, "To me, old man! To me!"

I did not dare breathe his name aloud, lest the warrior bard discover the nature of my prize.

Instead, I drove the walking stick into the bard's knee, which he did not seem to be expecting, and I thought of home and Arrienda, and all that I had to find and fix to set my world right, and I called to the moon, and as the bard fell to the ice with a sharp cry, the old man crawled out of the tent with my bag in his hands, with ghost warriors hanging on to him.

What happened then happened quickly, in a grim blur and all at once.

The bard roared, "Enough!" and, still lying on his back, struck an off-key chord on his harp strings; the ghosts dragged Doyati to his feet and pulled him toward the bard; the old man tossed my kit-bag to me and shouted, "Run, Genna!"; I caught the bag and the bard grabbed my ankle and I kicked him in the head with a good sturdy farm boot. He let go of me and I lost my balance on the slippery ice and fell to the ground, and the road I had called slid underneath the bard instead of me and swallowed up him and his harp.

And the ghosts.

And the old man who had been held by the ghosts. And the tent some of them had been standing in. Or through, really.

And suddenly, there I was. Alone, flat on my back in the bitter cold, staring up at the sky, black as ink and starless. Alone.

Alone.

I had no shelter, no warm clothing. No one to help me, no one to get warm against. If I were inclined to give up and die, I was in the perfect place to do it. It would only take a few minutes, with the cold seeping up from the ice and through me like it was, and the wind starting to blow again. I'd just go to sleep in the cold, and that would be that.

But in the kit-bag, I could still feel some warmth from Yarri's heat-ball. I stuck a hand in and wrapped it around the ball, and blessed warmth flowed through me — not just through my hand, but through all of me. Clever nightlings, I thought, and rolled the ball between my hands until it was too hot to hold comfortably. But I strapped the kit-bag to my chest instead of my back, with the heat-ball up against the inside wall of the bag, and the warmth filled me up without my having to hold it. Hands free. I had a stick for a weapon. I figured if I had to fight again, I was going to need both hands.

I struggled to my feet on the slippery ice, using the old man's stick for balance. I needed another road, and quickly. The bard had Doyati and would surely take him to Letrin for the reward. My family and my village and my bargain with Letrin would all die if I did not get Doyati back.

Of course, I had no idea where he'd gone, for I had no idea what road had come when I'd called. I hoped it was one that would give the bard a hard time and the old man an easy one.

I started walking. We were both going to Arrienda, I decided — the bard and I. I might be able to arrive there first. Focused on my thoughts, I failed to brace for the black ice beneath my feet, and my feet went up and my back went down and I was lying with the wind knocked out of me before I could cry out. I got back up, and started walking and calling again, and again, just at the point where I was focusing well enough on the road I needed, my feet went out from under me. I couldn't concentrate like that. I'd never get a road if I couldn't keep my attention on calling it.

I went rummaging through the kit-bag to find something that might help.

Yarri had carried far more than I'd realized. I discovered a fine little healer's kit for minor injuries — the sorts of things I'd been trained to heal with magic, but still. The kit contained long, rolled bandages, thin, tough strips of cloth slightly sticky to the touch that would not need pins to hold them in place.

And I had a bag-pocket full of dire-worm teeth. The teeth had notched edges and were knife-sharp. I found the three biggest, each almost as long as my hand, and using one of the bandage rolls, bound the teeth to one end of the old man's walking stick. It gripped the ice just fine then.

I had to try several solutions on my boots before I found one that worked. I discovered that I could get the teeth to stay in place and grip the ice only if they were pointed downward around the toes and heels of my boots. I wound a loop of bandage cloth around the toe of the boot, all the way back to the heel, and arranged the teeth where I wanted them, and then wrapped the teeth individually, anchoring the bandages around the tops and bottoms of the boots (and around my ankle and arch to anchor the back). I had to keep stopping to warm my hands on the heat-ball.

But when I was finished, I got to my feet and I didn't fall down. I didn't even slip a little. I thought I could probably run on the ice in my boots and keep my footing. And I wished I'd had them fixed that way when I kicked the warrior bard. A bite from those teeth would have slowed him down.

I would live to get home, I told myself. I would once again wake to hear my mother, healthy and happy, calling me to help get my sibs up and moving. I would once again smell the kitchen full of her cooking, and I would stand beside her and scrub the clothes on the washboard while she wrung them out and hung them up. I would have my life back. My home. My family. My friends. My village.

With the kit-bag once again slung across my chest, the heat-ball to warm me, the walking staff to keep me steady, and my good boots biting the ice with every step, I strode off, focusing on the road I needed.

I considered what that lying cat had said — that I needed to call a road I wanted and not one that wanted me. Was that true? Or just another lie? In this case it did not matter, for to have any chance of bargaining with Letrin, I had to get home. I was *already* thinking of a road to take me to a place I wanted.

I called the roads again, once more thinking of my mama, my sibs, my friends, all the people I had to save. I thought of Letrin, too, and the stag-guarded door into Arrienda. I thought of Yarri, and of Dan. I thought of my house, the smell of Mama's pies cooling on the windowsills.

Come, I thought. Come to me, road that takes me where I want to go.

Nothing.

I walked faster and I thought harder, bringing back the smells of the season, the tartness of spring still in the air, the dark earth fresh-turned and planted, sap rising, trees in full flower perfuming the air. I thought of the pale green lace of new leaves budding out.

I remembered the voices of my friends, calling at my door to see if I had finished my chores. My mama calling me home at twilight, my papa working our small garden plot when I was tiny, and of his shoulders hunched as he dug into the soft earth and planted the luck tree that still grew by our front door. My brothers and sisters playing tag or find-me, shouting and laughing.

A glimmer caught my attention, a faint, gentle flicker at the corner of my eye.

This time, I thought, it would be the road I wanted. A road that would take me home. A road that would drop me in my village, or perhaps in front of Letrin's door.

I'd be in my own world, in any case. If I had to, I knew a boy in Hillrush who could lend me a horse to ride to Arrienda.

Or maybe I no longer did, if my moonroad vision of Catri gone and all the village of Hillrush taken away with her proved true. But if they had not taken the horses, and the horses were not dead . . .

It did not matter. I would get where I needed to be. It might be difficult, but I would not fail my people.

Still clinging to Doyati's walking stick, I stepped onto the moonroad as it slipped beneath my feet, and the flickers ran together into a tunnel black as night inside, but night lit by faint, countless stars. I couldn't catch the road's sounds. The smells, however, didn't remind me of home or Arrienda. They were redolent of barnyard stink — and the farther I fell, the thicker that barnyard stink became.

I left in darkness, but I landed on packed earth as the tip of the sun sent its first ray of light over the horizon, and for a moment all I could think was that I had barely made it. I had been fine, but now faced with the evidence of my near disaster, I grew queasy and wanted to sit down. Had that moonroad come to me an instant slower, I would have been trapped in winter until the moon slipped through its new phase and all the way to rising half — a half-month in which I would have had neither shelter nor food. I would have died.

I rose, my eyes seeing true, sun-filled daylight for the first time in what seemed like forever, and I looked around. I was at least off the moonroads and out of the Moonworld. But I was not home. The barnyard stink was stronger than it had been as I slipped between the worlds.

Yet I heard no animals.

The stink without the noise, the tiny walled-in yard before me, the even smaller house — they were familiar.

"I'm back in Peevish," I muttered. Back with the tiny old woman who had burdened us with the cat who had betrayed the lot of us. Peevish was two days' hard traveling from Arrienda, but since I was back in the right world, and since Letrin had given me until the new moon to return, I still had time to get where I needed to be. I didn't have a tent anymore. I didn't have companions. I didn't know how to get to Arrienda, and feared losing my way in the forest.

Being in the right world, though, did wonders for my mood. I felt, having managed to get myself there, that I was a girl who could manage anything.

The old woman, sending us out her front door, had told us to never come back. She knew how to get to Arrienda, however, and she *owed* me. Without her, the cat would not have come with us. Bad things might have happened, but they would have been different bad things, and Dan and Yarri would not have been led away to be betrayed.

So I opened the gate, took the single step that carried me to her low front door, and I knocked.

She didn't answer. Probably peeping out, deciding she wanted nothing to do with me.

Fine. I remembered she had a back door, too, so I walked around to the backyard.

And found out where she was.

Where it looked like she had been left for a long time.

A metal cage that reached to my shoulders, about as wide as it was tall, took up most of her tiny backyard. The old woman leaned against its thick bars, her wrists manacled to the top so that she would not be able to lie down, her arms stretched high, her legs sprawled like a tossed rag doll's.

Her head lolled to one side and her eyes were partly open. I thought she was dead.

She smelled dead. Or maybe that, too, was the yard.

But as I looked more closely, I saw her chest rise and fall, barely, while little flutters at her neck told me her heart still beat.

I crouched beside her. "Old mother, do you know where the key to the cage is? How can I get you out of here?" I spoke loudly.

She blinked once. Twice. Then her eyes rolled a little, and she looked left and right. But she did not see me.

"Old mother!" I shouted. "I'm right here."

Her gaze fixed on me. "*Shhhhhh!*" she hissed. "Taandu elixir. Green vial on the table. Hurry." Her whisper was so soft I could barely hear her. Danger, then, might still be close. Or she might be on the last edge of death.

I hurried into the tiny house. A step and I was at the table, which had been tipped on its side. Everything that had been on it lay scattered on the floor. I ended up on hands and knees, searching through shattered glass and piles and mounds of powders and dried herbs for the green vial. When I found it, I thought it a miracle that it wasn't broken; a dozen other vials of different colors were.

I picked up the vial and looked around the rest of the house. Everything that could be torn down and trampled had been. All the old woman's belongings had been destroyed. I wondered who had treated her so. I wondered why.

I carried the vial back out to her and pulled out the stopper. "This is what you need?"

Her hands fluttered in my direction, rattling her manacles. "You could raise the dead with that. Or save the near-dead."

My hand, moving toward her mouth with the elixir, stilled.

Could I use it to cure my mother? To raise my father from the dead? I did not *need* the old woman. I *could* find my own way to Arrienda if I had to. Maybe the vial held enough of the elixir in it to save everyone in Hillrush who was sick with the *saku*.

And the old woman had cursed us with the cat.

But the elixir was not mine. If I took it and left, the old woman would die. And I would be no different from the cat. Or Banris. Or Letrin. I would have betrayed someone, just as I had been betrayed. The old woman had sent the cat with us, but he was not her fault.

Or even if he was — even if she had known or suspected what he would do to us — still the question was not what sort of person she was. It was what sort of person *I* was. I could not know her heart. With difficulty and hard work, my mother had always told me, I might know my own.

I poured a drop of the elixir on her tongue, and she swallowed with tremendous difficulty.

"More," she said.

So I poured more.

The old woman began to glow. Not the way elders always say that women who are with child glow, and not the way they say children glow just before they pinch our cheeks.

Light poured through her skin as though she had swallowed the sun. Her face and body began to change. One of her feet suddenly grew enormous, half as tall as the cage. It ripped her boot to pieces, then abruptly shrank back to its normal size. Her right arm grew to three times its size, shot out of the side of the cage, broke the manacle that held her right wrist, and bent the bars in the side of the cage. Her arm turned from pale and dirt-streaked to shiny gold to the pink-almost-red of the rambling roses that run wild around our village, before returning to a normal size, and to a smooth, plump tan.

I was very glad I had not stolen the potion to give to someone I loved. It looked like she'd made some terrible mistake in making it.

But then her thin, greasy hair grew thick and white and curly. She began spitting out ruined, brown-stained teeth, and when her mouth opened, I saw new ones in their places, white and shiny and perfect. And her rheumy eyes turned a bright and lively blue.

I stared at her, stunned. She stood up, healthy and straight-backed, pushing open the top of the cage as she did. Her other hand had come free of the manacles at some point, but I didn't see when that happened.

"Look at that," she said. "Those vandals didn't lock me in after all."

She was still an old woman. But she was so very different, she might have been of another species than the filthy, wretched hag she had shed in her transformation.

She stood before me plump and lively, her face round and pretty in a grandmotherly way, her eyes full of mischief. Looking at her, I could not help but adore her. She made me want to laugh simply by smiling at me. I wanted to sit at her table eating fresh-baked pie and telling her all my secrets.

She shook her head and sighed, and told me, "You were not supposed to come back here, you know. You drag trouble behind you, and your trouble caught up with me. A wild-haired harper and a band of ghosts came chasing after you, and, in trying to find where you had gone, left me as you found me. If they're still following you, I don't want to be the skirt that catches in your door again, if you take my meaning."

We had been responsible for that?

"I'm sorry," I told her. "We never meant you harm."

"No. You didn't. Nor did I think you did. But it came like a whirlwind after you, and no doubt it will be by here again before long. You and I will be best served to get ourselves well away from here before it arrives."

I shivered when I thought of the bard, and thought of sitting in a circle with all of his dead companions, singing songs and eating with them, not knowing their nature. Having them weave spells around me until I told them what they wanted to know without ever realizing what I was doing.

She was watching me. "I have no love for them, either. And though I have no doubt something bad will come chasing your heels and run over me again to get to you, still . . . Had you not come back, who would have saved me? I would have died, I think."

She stared out into space for a moment, round arms crossed over her chest and right foot tapping.

"I owe you two favors," she said. "And though I suspect that you and I shall meet again whether we want to or not, I owe you a warning as well. Do not seek me out. Where you and I meet, trouble will always be close behind."

I could barely breathe. "Who *are* you?"

She laughed as if I'd just told her a funny story. "Oh, *that* doesn't matter. For now, I won't trouble you with my name, for it would be a burden to you. If you don't know it, you won't have to tell people we don't like things neither of us wants them to know." And she winked.

She looked at me, then, the way a bird looks at a bug. Her head tipped to one side. She frowned, took the empty vial and the stopper from my hands — I had forgotten I was holding them — and dropped the closed vial into the kitbag I carried.

"That's one," she said.

And then she reached out and pinched my arm, and I yelped. The pinch stung like a bee sting, and heat rushed through my whole body, followed by cold. Then, well, all the strangeness went away.

She said, "That's the second favor. You'll only find it

when you need it, and may not know it when you find it." Then she snapped her fingers, and quick as snuffing out a candle, she was gone.

I stood in the stinking yard, rubbing my arm where she had pinched it, staring at the spot where she had been, wondering exactly what sort of favor she thought she had done me with that pinch. Something I would find only when I needed it? How useful was a bruise going to be?

I discovered that I was glad she was gone. In her absence, I was able to realize how very frightening that transformation she made had been. No longer near her, I no longer adored her, either. Something about her made my stomach knot and made me want to run away. But she hadn't told me how I might get myself to Letrin before she disappeared, and that was the favor I would have had of her.

I heard, then, the belling of hunting hounds who had caught wind of their prey. The old woman had been right about trouble following me.

I knew their voices. But this time, I had no moonroad to spirit me away. Daylight had me. I had nowhere to run where they could not follow. But that did not mean I did not try.

I bolted away from the old woman's house toward the forest behind it, the kit-bag banging against me as I fled, my arms pumping, my booted feet crunching over twigs and dead leaves. My lungs began to burn and my side to ache. Fog caught me, first in little tendrils that curled around me, then in clouds and puffs, until a blanket of it as thick as a blizzard, and as impenetrable, surrounded me.

I had to stop running then.

I could not see my hand when I held it up and bumped my nose trying to bring it close enough. Sound carried oddly inside the fog — all the outside world was muffled. Birdsong and voices and the clangs and bangs and rattles of the men in the village at the forges and fields faded to whispers, but the racket of the hounds amplified until the sound was all around me, and in me. The sound, and the fear it caused, anchored my feet to the ground as firmly as my fog blindness. I wished then that I had Yarri's trick for going unseen. I would have hugged the nearest tree and closed my eyes until the whole nightmare went away.

The hounds grew even louder, until I could not think, I could not recall my name, or my purpose, or what was happening. I clapped my hands over my ears, but the sound still pounded in my head.

Then the noise stopped. *All* noise stopped. The fog thinned, and out of it, a horrible face pressed itself toward me — black-nosed muzzle wrinkled and lips peeled back, fangs long as my thumb bared and dripping blood-flecked foam and drool. I screamed, and the nose pressed against me. I could hear no growl, but I could feel the beast's rumbling as soon as he touched me.

The fog thinned a little more, and I saw the hound's enormous, misshapen forehead, its bulging white eyes glowing with a pale, sickly light, its wolfish ears pulled flat back against its skull. The reek of its breath brought the gorge to the back of my throat.

I shuddered but did not move or make a sound — not from any courage or sanity on my part, for I was crazed with fear, but because my body would not act on my desperate attempts to run. Which was as well, for if I had run, I think the beast would have eaten me.

I felt then the bumping of other cold, wet noses, the vibration of other silent growls, the drip of drool down my shoulders and arms and the back of my neck. They were all around me, right up against me, and though I dared not turn to look at them, I knew they surrounded me on every side.

Behind me, a woman's voice said, "I've been looking for you. We've *all* been looking for you."

The fog thinned around me. I could see the hounds in their entirety then — big as ponies, broad-shouldered, thin-waisted, long-legged, ragged, and shaggy. I would have made a meal for one of them, but for the pack I would have been nothing but a tidbit, a scrap to be ripped apart and tossed about and fought over.

The woman spoke again. "So you're the child who has led us all on such a miserable chase." As she spoke, she moved around to where I could see her.

She wore a long black cloak and, at first, that was all I could see — that and two glowing green fires inside her deep cowl.

I want to go home. I want my papa.

She tossed back the cowl of her cloak then, and in the fog-grayed daylight, her face was lovely but wrong — as if she were a woman cast by a metalsmith. Her skin was silver, polished to a brilliant sheen. Her eyes were emeralds without whites in them, her lips the red of rubies but without the dancing of light within. Yet her face was as mobile and expressive as anyone's. At that moment, her expression was one of deep disgust.

She was tall for a woman, with night-black hair, straight and shining. She bared her teeth in a feral grin, and said a word, and the enormous hounds backed up a step and sat. They pointed their heads in my direction, sniffing, and they whined and drooled.

"She's not your treat," the huntress said. "Not yet, anyway." And then to me, "You'll be coming with me to Arrienda. Unless you'd like to run again, little rabbit."

I felt my knees go weak. I could see my death in her weyrdling eyes, in the sneer that curled the corners of her mouth, in the anger that twisted her face.

"No," I said, looking from her to the waiting hounds. "I won't run."

I heard a sound then, a sound I cannot explain and can barely describe. It was deep — so deep I heard it first with the soles of my feet, before it traveled up my bones to my ears. It rang as a bell rings, but unlike the ringing of a bell, this sound did not linger. The whole world vibrated for an instant, and then, as if the earth that had spit it out swallowed it back up and snicked shut behind it; the sound was gone.

The huntress and all the dogs had turned their heads toward that sound at the same time, and the huntress began to laugh. "Very well. You'll live a little longer. The last piece of the puzzle has appeared, and if we do not hurry, we shall miss the party where it will all come together. Arrienda is yet some distance. We should get moving."

We were going to Arrienda. We were, then, almost certainly going to see Kai-Lord Letrin. The cat had said this woman would rather die than work for Letrin. But the cat had said a lot of things, and look how the rest of them had turned out.

But I wanted to go see Letrin, and I was frozen with fear, all thoughts of fight or flight gone out of me. She seemed to realize this, for though she gave a perfunctory tug at the walking stick in my hand, my rigid fingers had locked tight around it. In the end, I kept quiet when she tossed me, my bag, and my walking stick over her shoulder, and I held my breath while she whistled the dogs forward.

The next instant, we were blanketed again in impenetrable fog.

Chapter 14
The Kai-Lord

The instant after, we arrived at the stag-guarded gates of Arrienda; the silver huntress and her hounds, and me, thrown over her shoulder, inconsequential as a sack of grain she was hauling to the barn. One of the nightlings answered the door when she rapped the pommel of her hunting knife against the stone. The nightling who answered the gate said nothing about what must have been a bewildering mass of dogs, woman, and child. He simply said, "Yes?"

"I have come to make peace with Letrin."

That was not the news I would have wished from her.

The nightling guard ushered us in, and once inside, the huntress set me down. For just an instant, I caught the nightling's eye. He seemed, with raised eyebrows and the set of his shoulders, to be asking a question.

If the bard brought Doyati, then all hope might not yet

be lost for my folk. But the Doyati the nightlings hoped would arrive did not even exist. No salvation, no hero was coming for Arrienda's slaves.

I hung my head, which was his answer. He sagged, if only slightly, and he led the whole lot of us down the grand, spiraling road, through the world of twilit magic. I so wanted to flee back the way I'd come, but I did not for an instant think anyone would let me escape.

The huntress eyed me and my kit-bag and my stick, and I leaned on the stick when I walked, and made a point of limping — just a little, so that the limp seemed natural.

"You don't fool me," she said. "You won't fool Letrin. I only hope you try something with your silly stick or your little bag. My dogs haven't eaten yet today, and you would save me the trouble of finding them the sort of kicking, screaming meal they prefer."

I stopped limping and just walked.

Ahead and far below, I heard faint whispers of trumpets and cymbals and instruments I could not name, and countless voices murmuring like the first rumbles of a far-off storm. The sounds began softly and from far away, but as we moved closer to them, they swelled to fill the space around us, so loud they seemed to be crushing down on us. The roar was like a faire, but grander than any I had ever attended, being convened nearby. And when the nightling and the huntress led me through a tall arched doorway into an open field of stone, it proved to be almost exactly that.

The stone field was surrounded on all sides by a smooth, curving wall of carved stone punctuated at intervals by other doors like the one through which our procession moved. At the back, on a raised dais, several nightlings continued to sound horns and cymbals. To either side, in a semicircle of raised seats that spread out halfway down the walls, a few of the Flowers, and some of what looked to me like taandu monsters (though not the worst sort), and many tall, slender nightlings in the most exquisite of robes filed in and settled into place.

Lights appeared as if someone had brightened the sun, illuminating the vast room, and I realized I'd only seen a part of the whole. Above what I'd thought was the wall that connected to a ceiling, tier upon tier of permanent seats rose, one after another, farther than my eyes could clearly make out. And nightlings filed into those seats, too, quickly, talking, some in raised voices and some in whispers.

The ice I'd felt in my blood in the winter wilderness where the bard had stranded me came flooding back. I stood in the center of the floor, as much the entertainment, I was sure, as any dog in a dog-fighting ring. Had all of these creatures come to watch me? Could a failed agreement between a kai-lord and a child be of interest to so many? And if they had come to watch me . . . then what had they come to watch me do? Plead? Beg? Fail?

Die?

That was it — my gut knew the truth of it. They had come to watch me die, and with me, my brother, my mama and sibs, all the people of my village, and Yarri and her family, if any of those still lived.

They had come to watch the Kai-Lord Letrin mock me and punish me.

I wanted to cry. I wanted to call for my mama and have her run to me and pick me up and hold me in her arms, as she had when I was smaller, when I cut my knees in brambles or fell from a tree and lay gasping and hurting on the hard ground below.

As the truth settled over me, I bit my lip to keep from weeping. I would not give Letrin the satisfaction. Not so early in his planned spectacle anyway. I guessed he would wring tears or screams from me soon enough.

To one side of me, the huntress smiled. "You look frightened."

"If you were me, would you not be? You're going to give me to the kai-lord."

She shook her head and whispered into my ear, so softly I could barely hear her, "Give you to my worst enemy? Don't be ridiculous. You were merely the key to unlock passage to this place at this time. My plans have nothing to do with you."

Her face looked sincere, if emotionless, and I heard conviction in her voice.

I pondered the mystery of her words, and wonder began to melt my dread. Could it be?

Doyati said his mother had friends everywhere, even after her death. That she'd had spies and allies who would have fought for her, and who would fight for him.

Could the terrifying huntress and her hounds have been hunting for me to help me?

Could she have been pretending cruelty out in the open in case the kai-lord had his own audiomaerist, one who could tell him that she plotted with the nightlings against him?

I had no time to consider more, for the din stopped suddenly and, all at once, the trumpets and cymbals fell silent into a ripple of whispers and murmurs that sounded like the forest in a wind. Then drums began to pound.

Extravagantly dressed guards marched into the arena in two long rows. The Kai-Lord Letrin followed them, wearing gold and red, smiling. He smiled at his people, who seemed to fill all the space between the earth and the stars, at his court, sitting in the spaces around his throne, and finally at me.

Everyone was standing. Everyone bowed.

Except for me. I just watched him, shaking, with my stomach churning and my skin all standing up in prickles, filled with excitement and fear. I wondered when the huntress and her hounds, still and attentive around her feet, would move against him. The kai-lord's gaze met mine, and he stared for just an instant deep into my eyes, as though he could read what lay behind them. His smile grew broader.

I hoped with everything in me that he could not read what I thought. That he did not suspect the huntress.

When he sat on his throne, the drumming stopped, and everyone else sat — everyone who had a seat, that is. The huntress and I remained on our feet. I leaned on the old man's stick and tried to keep my breathing slow and steady.

No one whispered. No one moved. The vast room was filled with an air of expectation and the scents of spring flowers and sweet summer fruit. And it was filled with my anticipation and a sharp, relentless anxiety.

The kai-lord smiled at me again and said, "You're back. I've been making ready for you." Then he turned to the guards with him and said, "Bring them."

My heart stilled in my chest.

No one needed to ask who he meant. And I had no questions. Yarri and her family would be led out, whichever of them still lived. If the cat had actually delivered my brother to Letrin's hands, Dan would be dragged into the arena, too. And if Letrin's torture of Yarri had yielded results, those prisoners whose names she had given up would join her.

We heard the shuffling of feet and the clank of chains.

What I saw, though, was not what I had thought to see.

The first guard led out a group of prisoners. Mama, terrified but determined, led the procession, with chains manacled to each of her ankles and those chains running back to the man behind her.

Papa.

Alive.

My first moonroad dream had been right, and Dan had been wrong. Papa lived.

I stared at him, heart in throat, seeing him alive in a place I knew was real for the first time in two years. He was gaunt, haggard, covered with scars, wearing clothes that were falling off him. But he was alive. He looked at me and smiled, and I began to cry. He lived, and I had nothing with which to save him.

The rest of the guards brought out the people of Hillrush. All of them, grouped together by families.

The guards lined all of these people — my people — along the wall opposite the one they had come in, group by group, and locked their chains to the walls so that they could not flee.

I waited to see if more people would be brought out, but none were. Not Yarri's family and friends. No nightlings at all. All of Yarri's people, and Yarri herself, might be already dead. But I didn't see Dan, and I had to think if Letrin had him, he would have paraded him in front of me. And if Letrin did not have Dan, maybe he did not have Yarri, either.

I dared hope a little. Maybe the cat had been a friend, not an enemy. Maybe Danrith and Yarri were still safe, and somehow Yarri's name had not fallen on Letrin's ears.

The kai-lord sat tall and proud on his throne, waiting until the last chain had been locked. Then he said, "I'm surprised to see you here, Agara. And carrying your little prize, too. I had word, of course, that you were coming."

"Of course." She bowed her head slightly in his direction and said, "I weary of our squabble, Letrin. I thought perhaps you and I should revisit . . . yes, revisit . . . our previous disagreements and see if we might find a way to end them.

So I asked around, and found a proper present for you. And here I am."

He looked at me. "She would only have been a present if she'd brought Doyati."

The huntress smiled. "Oh, come now. Doyati would be quite a gift without her. And the moonroads have closed to her now, so she won't be bringing him in. She doesn't have Doyati; she has no hope of getting Doyati. But the child, you see, has value in her own right. She knows the name of one of the conspirators among your people — one who is attached to those who have been close to you for years. Who are close to you now. Do you mean to tell me that such a name would have no value to you?"

My heart sank. Whatever game the huntress played, she was no friend of mine.

He leaned forward. "How have you come by this information?"

"Did you not know she and her brother traveled with a nightling? This one —" Her hand grabbed the back of my neck and she shook me. "This one may not have known the nightling's name when you asked her, but I assure you she knows it now."

Letrin's head snapped around like a snake's, and I was

once again staring into his serpent eyes. "My spies failed to pass that information on to me," he said.

Fear flooded my veins again.

"Where yours failed, mine did not. So tell me, Letrin, can you and I perhaps find a way to be friends again? As we once were?"

"Bring young Gennadara of High House forward, first, that she and I might go over the terms of our agreement."

I wished again for Papa's sword. Or Doyati's skillet.

The huntress — Agara — took a firm grip on my arm and walked with me to the throne. She bowed again, though not deeply. I did not. I could not. My knees would buckle if I did not keep my legs straight.

Letrin said, "Gennadara of High House, I would have thought, since your life and the lives of everyone in your world rested on your success, that you would have brought me good news."

I stared up at him, praying with everything in me that he would fall dead at just that moment.

But of course he did not.

Instead, he pulled at a gold chain he wore around his neck, and lifted from inside his tunic a key that looked to me to have been cut from a single ruby. It glittered in his hand, red as blood, shot through with purple and orange and flashes of green light that moved within its core as if the key were a thing alive. "I kept my end of the bargain," he said. "I have gathered together everyone whom you bargained to save. I have brought the ruby key to you." He stroked the key with a fingertip, and the corners of his mouth twitched, as if he might laugh at any moment. "So. Where is Doyati, your end of the bargain?"

"Dying," I whispered. "He's dying." My voice grew softer; I had a hard time squeezing each word out of my mouth. "He's an old, old man . . . and he came with me . . . but then the bard stole him away."

Letrin's smile stretched across his face, like the smile of a wolf that has cornered a lamb away from its mother. "Say that more loudly, my dear," he said in a voice that carried all the way to the highest tiers of his vast theater. "Everyone needs to hear you."

He looked into my eyes, and in spite of myself, I repeated what I had said, but loudly.

"He's an old, old man, and he's dying, and he came with me — he was going to come to Arrienda with me, of his own free will — but then the warrior bard stole him away."

Silence followed my announcement.

Letrin did laugh then. "What an imaginative child you are. You could not find him, so you bring me this silly tale?"

I looked at him steadily, more angry than afraid all of a sudden. I hated when someone called me a liar.

"Think what you like," I said. "But if you have it in you to know the truth, then you'll know I speak it."

That was a challenge, and presented as such — good and loud, so everyone in the great hall could hear it — and somewhere in the *Great Book of Common Sense*, which I *clearly* have never read, I'm sure there's an entry that says: *Fourteen-year-old human girls should never challenge kai-lords.*

He stared at me, his face darkening with anger. But then he really looked at me — looked through me with his eyes gone to anthracite and his lips stretched thin — and I had the horrible feeling he was rummaging through my head.

In his eyes, I saw shock. "You truly found him." His voice stayed low — too low for any save the huntress and me to hear him.

I nodded.

He sat back in his chair, staring at nothing, seemingly lost in the news. Then he began to laugh, gently at first, and then louder and gleefully. "You truly found him! Doyati met with you and walked with you."

In the stands above, I heard indrawn breaths.

He grabbed my arm and pulled me right up to him, so that we were nose to nose. He stared into my eyes. "You have seen him. You have taken meals with him. And he is old. Old! *Dying!* It's true!"

He was by that time shouting, and his joyful voice echoed through the arena like a thousand bells.

His court behind him, underlords and ladies both, began to applaud and laugh. In the high seats the story was different.

I heard the gasps. The groans. Weeping.

This was the price of Doyati's false hope. This was what he had cost his faithful by letting them believe he would come and save them. That he *could* come and save them. Many of them had sacrificed themselves to pave the path for him, and the kai-lord would hunt them down. I saw his gaze slide upward, to the sounds of sobbing there, and I realized even those who dared to weep would suffer.

I hung my head, but his cold finger slid under my chin and lifted it up.

"The good news you brought me would almost be

enough for me to give you your bargain. The lives of your villagers. And your own life."

He stared deep into my eyes, his finger still beneath my chin, but lifting so hard I had to rise to my toes. He was looking for something — in my face, or in my thoughts — but whatever it was, he found it eventually.

He removed his finger and I almost fell to the floor. I stumbled and just barely caught myself with my hands.

I stood and looked the Kai-Lord of Arrienda in the eye, and I waited for his sentence. I had no other choice.

He was bemused. "There are no lies in you," he said, staring off at nothing. "Doyati is indeed an old man, near death, powerless. It is a stunning thing. It never occurred to me that my father's mighty brother, the blessed firstborn son, might have spawned an unremarkable child. A short-lived little nothing. A useless joke." He glanced at me, then, and chuckled softly. "By your testimony, both in word and thought, you have rendered my greatest enemy a shadow, a cipher, spindrift that I can blow away with a single breath."

His smile was gentle.

"And now I find that you know the name of a traitor. A traitor, no less, who knows traitors close to me."

I waited.

"So you and I might bargain yet. You have done me one service, though not the service we agreed upon. You may now do me another service, and for two services in the same day, perhaps you can save all those you love."

I knew what he was going to ask. I knew.

Dan had been willing to sell himself to Letrin as his slave to save Yarri and her family. But he had not sold our people to do it. It had been my job to save our people.

"Tell me the traitor's name," he said.

I wished Papa were with me then, to give me advice based on law. To tell me how the contract would work. To tell me what I should do.

As I thought of him, I realized Papa *was* there. For the first time in longer than I could bear to think about, Papa and I stood in the same place. I glanced over at him. He shook his head slightly, and his hand made a writing gesture.

I knew, then.

"We have nothing in writing, Kai-Lord."

Letrin's eyes narrowed. "We do have something in writing, child. We have the agreement you and I made, signed in your hand and mine, that you would bring me Doyati."

I nodded. "I still have until the new moon to make good on that."

"You cannot reach the moonroads."

"Perhaps I don't need them."

"I want the name of the traitor," he told me.

"You have not promised me anything if I give that name to you. You said only that *perhaps* you would spare my life and the lives of the people of Hillrush. *Perhaps* means nothing."

"*Perhaps* meant I would reconsider your case." He grabbed me by the hair and pulled me forward, and his other hand clamped down on my shoulder until I could feel my bones begin to creak. I screamed with the pain, and he said, "Tell me."

"Give me a bargain in writing!"

"Tell me."

The pain was too much. I began to cry. From along the walls, the people of Hillrush began shouting at him.

He lessened the pain on my shoulder, smiled kindly, and said, "This doesn't need to hurt. Just tell me."

I couldn't speak. Tears poured down my cheeks, and my knees wobbled. My tongue felt like a rock in my mouth.

I wanted to tell him, though. So that he wouldn't hurt me any more than he had, so that he would let my family go, I wanted to tell him.

Staring into my eyes, he said, "*Yarri?*"

Horrified, I pulled back from him.

"Yarri, eh?" He let go of me, and my legs gave way beneath me and I sagged to the floor.

"I never told you that!"

"But you wanted to." He aimed a tiny, mocking bow in my direction, and said, "And we did not even have anything in writing."

"Letrin, dearest," the huntress said, "how about *our* bargain?"

He glanced in her direction and raised an eyebrow. "In a moment, Agara."

And then he returned his attention to me.

"We had nothing in writing, and what I asked of you, you did not give me. I had to take it. You have voided our contract by not bringing Doyati, and you have refused a new offer —"

"I still have until the new moon to make good on the contract we had," I repeated.

Letrin held out his hand, empty and palm up. There was a flash of light, and a single sheet of paper lay atop his palm, and on the bottom right-hand corner, I saw my own writing. And Kai-Lord Letrin's. He flicked the contract in front of me and said, "Your writing?"

I nodded.

"Out loud, please."

"That is my signature."

He read the wording of the contract that Dan and I had read, and until the last line, it was the same, simple and direct. But then he read, "Should, at any time, either party be proven incapable of fulfilling his part of the contract, judgment will be rendered in favor of the other party."

"Stop," I said. "That line wasn't in the contract when I signed it."

"Of course it was." Letrin's voice was silky and his smile was amused. He leaned back on his throne with casual ease, stretched his long legs in front of him, and crossed them at the ankles.

"*No*," I said, getting to my feet. "It wasn't."

"Are you calling me a liar?" he asked, still all silky and relaxed.

"Yes," I said.

Evidently, no one told the kai-lord he was a liar, because Letrin shot forward like a striking snake — I hate snakes almost as much as I hate bats — and snarled, "Then produce your copy and prove your claim."

"You didn't *give* me a copy, you cheat."

"Cheat?" His voice went gravelly, and he turned to the stands of Highborn around him. "This human child offers me no proof, yet calls me a liar and a cheat. Note that, because I am both kind and forgiving, I have not yet blasted her to cinders for her impertinence."

"You *are* a liar and a cheat," I said. "And a bully."

Somehow I'd managed to miss the warning in the words "blasted her to cinders" and the double threat in the word "yet." This is proof that anger makes people stupid.

His dark eyes glittered. "When it is your word against mine that a line in a contract we both signed was there when you signed it, I assure you mine will be the word that will be believed."

Faint laughter rippled through the Highborn section of the stands, but it sounded a bit nervous. The upper sections stayed silent.

From behind me came a voice I feared I would never hear again. "I was witness to the signing of the contract," Danrith said. "I read the entire thing before Gennadara of High House in Hillrush signed it and advised her that it contained no tricky clauses. At the time, it did not contain the clause you read last."

The laughter stopped. From the stands above, I heard excited murmurs.

I turned to catch sight of my brother walking down the long, empty space between Hillrush's bound villagers on the one side, and the lines of nightling guards standing in formation on the other. He was dressed in clothing unlike any I'd ever seen before — a high-necked white tunic blazoned with a yellow sun, its rays shooting out in all directions; beneath the white tunic, a deep blue shirt, the sleeves of which were embroidered with thousands of tiny stars; and breeches of the same shade of blue, but plain except for a line of red piping sewn down the side seams. The boots, low-cut and heavily soled, laced in the front, seemed to me more suitable for warriors in battle than for a boy at the sort of fancy-dress function we were attending.

The clothing meant nothing to me, but it clearly meant something to Letrin, for he stared at Danrith in dismay.

"How dare you parade into my court dressed in that fashion?" he roared, rising half out of his seat.

Everyone stared at Letrin. *Everyone.* He looked quite the fool, red-faced and with spittle flying from his mouth, his eyes bulging and his fists clenched, shouting at a boy about his clothes.

Letrin settled back on his throne and said, "Clearly, we did not do a sufficiently thorough search of attics and basements in years past. We'll be certain to remedy that. It's been a long time since I rode the roads to view the pleasant sight of the human heads on pikes that lined them." His mouth twisted in a cruel bow, and his voice was all threat, rage damped down, and smoldering. "In the meantime, however, you, boy, cannot be a witness to the contract. You are far too young, and your signature is not upon it." He looked at his guards. "Bring the boy to me."

Two nightling guards stepped out from formation and walked swiftly to take up positions on either side of him. Each grabbed one of Dan's upper arms, and together they marched him to the dais.

When Dan and the guards stood before Letrin, the kai-lord said, "Perhaps you only found those clothes in some relative's trunk in your attic, and thought to look impressive when you came here. Or perhaps you know the meaning of what you wear, and thought to threaten me. Either way, boy, it matters not. I shall watch your clothes burn this day, with you in them." Letrin's voice was too soft for any but those of us on the dais to hear.

Dan's voice was softer, though. "I know what it means," he murmured. "Better yet, I *mean* what it means."

Letrin said, "Then I shall especially treasure the moments when you scream and beg for mercy, and when you die."

He said to the guards, "Keep him right here where I can see him." And then he turned to me.

"We've arrived at the part of this little exhibition where things will become unpleasant," he said. "For you, anyway. And them." He waved a hand toward all the people chained to the wall. "You have to choose, dear. Which family shall my guards execute first? And how shall they do it? You must decide. And lest you consider the coward's way out and tell me they should execute you first, let me eliminate that option."

"I will not pick who shall die! I still have until the new moon to bring you Doyati."

Letrin grabbed my braid again and pulled me so close to him that our noses touched. Softly, so very softly, he snarled, "You don't have any more time, because I'm going to kill you today, little girl. And since I am going to kill you today, I can prove that you will not able to bring me Doyati, tomorrow or any day after that. Thus, you are in default of your contract, and punitive measures go into effect." He loosened his grip on my hair and smiled at me, a smug smile that made me want to kick him with my boots, and in a voice aimed at the rafters, he said, "Do be quick, child, or you shall force me to torture them before killing them. A quick death is better than a slow one. Do you know that?"

I knew that. I nodded my head, just the tiniest bit.

"Good. So. Hanging, sweet Genna? Fire? Beheading? I've been told beheading is quick and painless — though not by anyone who has gone through it, of course. Or arrow-shot? An arrow in the wrong place can be terrible, though. So I do not know. But you must. Which shall it be?"

He turned me around so that I could see them all. My family. My friends. Neighbors who had known me and treated me well all my life. And Banris. Banris was there, bound with the rest of them. All of them stared back at me, and my mother pointed at herself.

But I looked at her and shook my head, and said, "If I must choose, then I choose Caer Banris of Greathaven to die first."

Banris, to my surprise, grinned at me.

And the huntress's hounds began to bark and snarl.

Chapter 15
The Cat Comes Back

The huntress, who had begun to smile at me with a smugness that bordered on glee, jerked around to stare at her animals. They were all on their feet, snarling, quivering, their noses pointed to the back of the arena, to the door Danrith had passed through.

"Down!" she snapped, and one of the enormous beasts began to lower himself to the ground again, but the others didn't. They turned their faces toward her briefly, but returned their attention to the doorway.

I stared out where they waited. Something was hissing at them. Yowling at them.

I saw a flash of brown and black and white, and a small form launched itself through that doorway, charged into the center of the dogs, leapt in an elegant arc onto the back of one of the hounds, and sank his teeth into the beast's ear.

He hung on while the yipping hound shook his head and spun in circles.

Then the cat let go and streaked off down one of the passages. And all the huntress's dogs shot after him, belling and baying in pursuit.

A cat. Four neat white feet, cloud-swirled markings, white muzzle and white belly.

Not just a cat. *The* cat.

The huntress forgot about me for the moment. She shouted after her hounds, and Letrin told her to let them go.

She ignored Letrin, let go of me, and raced after them.

I turned in time to see Letrin's expression of pure exasperation. His spectacle was turning into a circus, and it seemed the jesters were running the show. "Bring her back, her and her dogs," he shouted to his guards. "She will have no favor from me."

The majority of Letrin's elegantly dressed personal guards took off, splitting up into squads and moving in ordered lines, two abreast, down each of the exits from the arena. New guards — regular guards in plain uniforms — moved up to replace them. For a moment, no more than the blink of an eye, I was certain I saw Yarri among them. But when I looked directly at the one I thought was her, I could only see yet another nightling stranger looking back at me.

From the back of the arena, from the door through which I'd come, a rich, mellow voice said, "Well, Letrin, if Agara can't win your favor, then perhaps I can."

Letrin stood. "Are there no *guards* upon the door? Have we opened up the gates and set out a sign upon the road saying, RABBLE WELCOME?"

Everyone else stood when he stood, but I don't think he'd intended that. I don't even think he noticed. "I would have let *you* in, Tofsin, only for twice your weight in gold."

"I brought you a hundred times that sum." The bard came swinging through the room, tanned and lean and grinning, his long red hair pulled back in a tail, his harp on his back. He dragged a bloodied and staggering Doyati behind him. "I brought you a peace offering," he said. "Sorry about the cat. Little furball followed me in, and busy as I was with important matters, I didn't want to waste time chasing him back out again. Figured your people would handle it, but clearly they did not. You might want to have a word with them."

He strode toward the throne quickly, and Doyati stumbled behind him. The old man lost his footing and fell, but Tofsin the warrior bard had such a grip on him, and such strength, that he dragged Doyati forward without seeming to notice that the old man was no longer walking.

I had moved next to one side of Letrin's throne and stood looking from the bard to Letrin and back. I couldn't read their faces. They clearly didn't like each other, but they were both smiling.

"Ah. Old times. You always did bring the best presents," Letrin said. "But surely that can't be the great and mighty Doyati, the would-be kai-lord, the heir presumptive to Arrienda's throne."

"Oh, but it is. I caught him in a tussle with that girl not long before dawn on an ice field in Fargofar." He stared at me for a moment with cold eyes, and I had the pleasure of seeing the cuts on his face that the broken strings on his harp had made, and the lovely purple lump on the side of his head where I'd kicked him.

I smiled at him.

The bard added, "He said he was her prisoner."

"Did he?" Letrin said in a voice turned to gravel, and he stared at me, frowning.

If Doyati had come as my prisoner, I realized, then I would have brought him to Letrin. I would have fulfilled my deal with Letrin, and even if Doyati could not save those who had sacrificed so much to aid him, he would have still saved my people — all those people chained to the wall.

"I claimed him as my own prisoner, however," the bard said. "I found him, and I caught him fair and square. So he's mine."

"Well," Letrin said, "that's excellent, then." He looked at me once more. "Pity for you, of course. Had he come on his own in your name, your bargain with me would still have been good, and I would have honored it. But he didn't come on his own. You will pardon me for a moment while I speak with this old joke who would be kai. And then we will get to the executions." He smiled again.

Doyati said, "As rightful heir to the throne of the kaidom, I deserve a face-to-face audience with the pretender."

Letrin began to chuckle. "Old man, whatever would you do with it?" He slapped a hand on his own knee. "You're skin and bones, death on feet —"

And I realized that Letrin was leaning forward, the better to mock Doyati, and I could see the chain around his neck, the one that held the ruby key, and I was holding a good, long walking stick that, if I were quick about it, might yank that chain over Letrin's head and right into Doyati's hand.

He was saying, "And you have no rights to claim justice, since you have ignored every summons and every request I have sent in your direction asking you to appear before me so that we might discuss our conflicting claims."

It was the old man's turn to laugh. "I avoided your assassins, you mean," Doyati said, as in my head the cat's voice said, *That's a lovely idea.*

The bard said, "Shut up, old man. You have no say in your fate."

I didn't see the cat, though I looked for him. But cats are small and easily ignored.

I did see the bard's eyes bulge slightly, and I did see his hand fall away from the old man's arm with an odd, flopping motion, and it hung at his side looking . . . broken. And I saw Doyati smile.

Then Doyati took a tiny, hobbling, hunched-over step forward, and Letrin started to rise, his mouth opened to shout some order, or to make some cruel remark to the old man.

It did not matter. He did not get the chance to speak.

I stabbed at the chain with Doyati's walking stick, forgetting until I accidentally skewered the kai-lord that I had bound dire-worm teeth to the staff's business end. The sharp teeth stuck in his chest, and for an instant he didn't seem to notice. Then, of course, he grabbed at the walking stick, but Dan leapt at him, sword suddenly in hand, and speared the kai-lord's left hand to the arm of his throne. I recognized the sword. It was Papa's.

I heard shouts and screams.

And then lightning erupted from the walking stick and poured into Letrin. I could feel it vibrating with a power unlike anything I had ever felt before. It shook my hands away from it, and Doyati, with remarkable speed, grabbed his stick with both hands and hung on. "The key, Genna!" he shouted. "Grab the ruby key."

I didn't think about the consequences of touching the kai-lord while he was filled with lightning. I simply lunged forward and clutched the chain around his neck and yanked it over his head.

In the instant that I touched him, my body shook and my teeth chattered and my hair stood on end — but I wasn't hurt.

I was a bit stunned.

The kai-lord managed to wrap the fingers of his free hand around my wrist, though, and lightning filled me again. We stared at each other — his teeth were bared like an angry dog's, his eyes were wide and wild.

He was strong. His fingers ground the bones of my wrist against each other, and the pain drove me to scream, but no sound would come from my throat. I stood as one frozen, locked to the kai-lord by the eerie blue fire that bound us.

He could not take the chain and the ruby key from me without releasing my arm, but neither could I take it from him. One of his soldiers moved to his side then, and I knew the soldier would kill me and return the key to Letrin.

Then the soldier's face shimmered, and all illusion fell away, and I saw tiny Yarri holding a small sword of her own. She drove it into Letrin's right shoulder and hung on, though the lightning wrapped itself around her, and the hand that gripped me lost its power and fell limp to Letrin's lap.

Through all of this, the kai-lord bled not a single drop.

Everything happened quickly. Guards had realized something was wrong. They drew swords and started toward us, but from the stands above, countless nightling men poured over the high wall, dropped to the ground, and swarmed over any guards who looked like they were trying to help Letrin.

Freed from the lightning, I stepped back beside Doyati and handed him the chain and the ruby key.

He pressed the key into a torn place in his skin where the bard had grabbed him, then spoke to me for the first time.

"*I'm dying,*" he said. I heard his words in my head as well as in my ears. "*Save me.*"

The little magic I had could fix hurt tendons, painful joints, a bit of bleeding. I could not, though, save a man dying from being too old, too weak, too frail to crush a kai-lord with lightning from a magic staff. Not even Mama at her best could do that without taandu . . .

Taandu essence!

Men were fighting their way toward us. Big nightlings with swords and black armor — not regular guards, not Letrin's personal guards, but something more dangerous even than those. Dirtier, tougher nightlings. I did not mistake them for allies, and neither did Doyati. "Hurry!" he shouted over the uproar.

My hand was shaking. Fear rattled me about as though I stood in a high wind. But I tore through my kit-bag and brought out the vial that had saved the old woman — the vial she had said was my first gift. I was almost certain it was empty. But I had nothing else. I opened it and held the empty vial over the key, and one quivering drop formed on the lip of the vial.

Letrin could not move his arms, but he could move his head. He butted my arm with his head, and I almost dropped the vial. But I didn't, and the shaking caused a droplet to fall away from the vial.

It landed on the key pressed to Doyati's bleeding arm.

And the key began to sizzle. Doyati's skin began to sizzle, too.

Letrin screamed then — no longer orders, no longer words. He howled as a dying rabbit screams when the owl's talons pierce him. His skin began to smoke.

A second drop of elixir formed on the vial's lip. Behind me, swords clanged and nightling voices shouted in anger and pain and fury and fear. In my head, Doyati said, *Steady. Hold steady for a moment longer.*

My brother, filled with lightning, held the hilt of Papa's sword. He could not speak, but his eyes begged me to hang on.

On the other side of Letrin, from the other sword that bound him to the throne, Yarri, who had fallen to the floor beside Letrin, shouted, "Just a moment longer, Genna!" And put her hands back on the sword that pinned Letrin's shoulder.

Chaos stormed around us, but in the center of that storm, we three — my brother Dan, Yarri the nightling, and I held fast.

The second drop fell.

Landed on the key.

The key shimmered with all the colors of the rainbow, and Kai-Lord Letrin screamed, "Nooo!" and two thin lines of white light burst from his chest and shot somewhere above and behind me.

Doyati, seeming stronger if no less old, shouted, "Behold!" He grabbed Letrin's right hand with his left hand and held on. I heard, from the stands above, the countless nightlings who remained, gasps replace screams. The clattering of swords, the thudding of bodies against one another, the shouts and howls — they all died down to a near silence.

Doyati pointed his right hand at Letrin and shouted, "That which was cast for evil has been uncast for good."

Letrin wasn't looking at Doyati, and he didn't seem to be listening to him. He stared at something behind me. I turned away from Doyati and Letrin, unsure of what I would see.

In the air above the arena floor, the light that poured from Letrin's chest spun spidersilk lines around two invisible shapes, building heads and torsos, arms and legs, hands and feet of light around hollow cores, drawing a slender woman and a sturdy boy.

As the details of woman and boy became visible and the lines of light began to fill in spaces, nightlings began to call out, "Oerin!" and "Oesari!"

I turned back to Letrin, to see his face. He had acted sad and unsure when Dan and I had dressed as his wife and son. I had to know if he would show any emotion at seeing their ghosts pulled from his heart.

His mouth gaped open and his eyes stared blindly in their direction. He was no longer breathing, I realized. He was dead. And Doyati was staring at him in horror.

"Not yet, you fiend," he whispered. "You can't die yet. They aren't finished."

The lines of light that had burst with such power from the kai-lord's chest were thinning, and the spindrels that had been casting themselves to shape Oesari and Oerin slowed. Worse, Doyati was thinning and drying out in front of my eyes, his skin flaking and blowing around him in little clouds, the last of his hair falling to the floor, his face sinking in on itself until he looked like a skeleton.

I took Doyati's free hand and he screamed, "Don't touch me, or they will draw the life out of you, too."

I felt something tug inside me, pulling through me and into Doyati, and in the instant before I took my hand from him, the light trickling from Letrin's chest brightened. So I grabbed Doyati's arm again, and this time I hung on. I didn't have time to argue with myself. I didn't have time to think. I only had time to act.

I dropped the empty vial from my right hand and reached for my brother. I shouted, "Take my hand!"

Dan did. The lines of light had brightened when I took hold of Doyati, and they grew even brighter when Danrith locked his hand in mine.

"We need more people to save Oesari and Oerin," I yelled. "Everyone join hands!" My voice filled the arena all the way to the top of the vast arched dome.

"Oesari! Oerin!" the people were screaming.

A guard stripped off his silver gauntlets and took Dan's hand. A battered nightling slave who had been fighting the guard took the hand of the guard, and he in turn reached out to a well-dressed courtier. The courtier held the slave's hand, and someone reached out and took his. A chain formed, and with every hand that joined, the two lines of light grew thicker and stronger and brighter, and the bodies of Oesari and Oerin turned faster from patterns of light into living flesh. The chain of hands connected most of those in the arena, including the human captives from Hillrush, and when no one else in the arena grabbed on, a tall nightling pressed his stomach to the wall, stood on his toes, and reached up. A man on top of the wall sat on its edge, kicked off a shoe, and lowered himself until he dangled from the chest down over the wall. As the man below grabbed his foot, two nightlings above each took one of his hands. The living chain then grew twice as fast.

Power poured through me, a growing, exhilarating energy that made me feel more alive, more healthy, stronger, and more sure than I had ever felt. The light that passed through me to Doyati and from there to Oerin and Oesari was filled with love, with hope, with dreams and memories and, most of all, with joy. Two people who had been loved and adored by the Arriendans, and who had been taken from them, were coming back, and all those who added their hands to the chain had a part of that.

We could have done anything right then, I thought. We were united, all of us, rich and poor, slave and free, human and nightling, in a common cause, each of us giving a piece of our own lives — sacrifices of ourselves for this shared rescue — and gaining more from what we gave than what we had put in. In that moment we could have healed the world's sick, fed the hungry, freed the enslaved, and brought peace to the embattled.

Mother and son, still radiant with the lifelight that we fed them, floated to the ground. They were whole. Living, breathing, healthy, vital. We had won. Letrin was dead; they were alive. Those closest to them quickly clothed Oerin and Oesari in bits of their own clothes.

The chain broke then, and we all dropped hands and simply stood there for a moment, each of us breathless with the magic we had been a part of. I hugged Dan first and whispered, "You're alive."

"And you got here," he said. "With Doyati. I told them you would."

A cheer was going up around the arena, building and building, rocking us with its power and its sheer exuberance.

In that thunder of voices, Yarri slipped through the crowd to my side and hugged me as well. "You came!" she yelled in my ear. I could barely hear her. She looked from me to Danrith and back to me, and leaned up to my ear again. "We told them you would come. They didn't believe. But *we* did."

I turned back to see how Doyati was doing, to say something to him, but he was gone. In his place, and in his clothes, stood a black-haired, blue-eyed boy a year or two older than me. He had an impish smile, and though he stood in filthy, tattered, bloody rags, he wore an air of power and confidence as well.

He smiled at me as the cheering lessened a little, and over the crowd he yelled, "You saved them. You saved *me*. You saved us all."

"Doyati?" I moved a step toward him, staring at his face, looking into his eyes for something familiar. But he was too young, too happy, too handsome. He could have been anyone.

He held out his left forearm to me, though, and I looked down at it. In that instant I knew he was Doyati and no other.

Burned into the inside of his left forearm was a scar shaped like the ruby key. The rest of him was healthy, perfect, with no sign of what he had suffered and no suggestion that he had ever been an old man, near death. But that scar was bright, red, raised, puckered — terrible.

"Does it hurt?" I asked.

"It did. Until you took my hand."

I looked up at him and he smiled at me again. "You saved my life. You gave me back my life." He shook his head and laughed, bemused. "You're the one the nightlings have been looking for — they've been searching for you since the day my mother fled with me, and now they've found you. You passed all their tests, and you even managed to bring everyone together when everything was lost. And now . . ."

He looked at what was left of Letrin . . . bones and ashes in a pile of fancy robes. "And now Letrin the Pretender is dead, and the battle that we thought would consume us for years is over before it started, and you are its champion. We have found the Sunrider, and the day we find her, we no longer need her."

"I'm no champion," I said. "No sunrider, whatever that might be. I did what I needed to do to save my family and my people."

Doyati looked at me strangely. "Precisely," he said. "And then you did more." He shrugged. "But the war is over before it began, and we are free. And *you* are free, which, if you knew the predictions that had been written about the Sunrider, would make you drop to your knees and give thanks."

Then he said, "Don't go far," and from the bones of Letrin's hand took a signet ring. He put it on his right hand, then stepped onto the throne, pushing bones and silk out of the way to do so. He raised his key-scarred arm.

"I am Doyati Renewed," he said, and his voice deepened and echoed in the arena. "I am Doyati Key-Scarred, rightful kai-lord of Arrienda. And I have returned to claim my throne."

I saw nightlings creeping from the arena, a few here and a few there, with cowls pulled far over their faces and shoulders slumped. Some were courtiers, some guards, some those from the Highborn seats. Letrin loyalists, I thought.

Those who remained stood and cheered, this time shouting, "Doyati, Doyati, Doyati!"

Someone had freed my family and my neighbors from the place where they had been chained to the wall. They moved across the arena floor, and Doyati saw them coming. "Go," he said. "Be with them. But before you go home, you and I must talk."

I nodded and fled the dais, and embraced my father, no longer gaunt and haggard as he had been when he wandered away, and as he had been when I saw him on the moonroads, and chained to the wall. He was hale and happy. He seemed younger somehow. The gray, I realized, was gone from his hair, and the lines from his face. The power of all of us had saved him, I realized. He had offered what he could give, had joined hands to save the strangers, and he had been richly rewarded.

Mama was radiant, too. Not just because she was with Papa, but because her eyes were once again bright. Shining. Alert. I had Mama and Papa back. I had my whole family back — brothers and sisters, too. And my friends. Catri stood with her parents, but I waved and caught her eye, and she gave me a huge grin and our secret signal. I had my village. Everything I loved was mine again.

My family wept in one another's arms. We said those things people who were sure they would never see one another again say. Reunited, we were first stunned, then jubilant, and then, whole once again, we became ourselves.

"Can we go home?" I asked. "I'm so tired, and I want to sleep in my own house and in my own bed, with my family close by."

I had lived too much adventure, and I wanted nothing more than to be the caer's daughter and the yihanni's apprentice, the oldest sister endlessly teased by younger siblings who got away with everything, the girl who milked the cow and the goats and knitted beside Mama on long winter nights.

But . . .

Over the jubilation in the arena, over the cheers of nightlings embracing the beloved and returned wife and child of dead Letrin, over the supporters of Doyati clamoring for his attention around the dais, a harp began to play. Its notes were warlike, stirring, angry — and quickly joined by the singing of warriors. And the belling of hounds.

Chapter 16
Desperate Times

My parents, my sibs, and I huddled close.

Doyati turned a solemn face toward the far door, while the crowds quieted yet again, sensing ill had come upon us. Those on the arena floor fled.

The thinning crowds revealed the huntress returned, her dogs gathered around her, unleashed. And beside her, the warrior bard, one arm in a makeshift sling, but with the harp resting atop the sling and his good hand playing nimbly, while ghost warriors poured out of the harp and formed in ranks around him.

I had thought they were working to see Letrin dead. The huntress had said as much when she was taking me toward Letrin. When we won, when Letrin was no more, I thought she and the bard had gotten what they wanted . . . and then I had forgotten about them entirely.

But feeling the hairs rise on my arms and the back of my neck at the ghostly singing, and seeing the cold tendrils of fog forming around the dogs and the huntress, and staring into the hollow blackness where the eyes of the marching dead should have been, I knew they were not finished. And that we were not finished.

At that moment, I realized with a start that Banris the Traitor stood between the huntress and the bard, and he wore the robes of a nightling kai-lord.

Banris raised his hand, then dropped it, and the music stopped. The dogs ceased their noise, and what little other sound those of us in the arena had been making died, too.

"Doyati — mortal child — I owe you a great favor," Banris said. "You have disposed of the pretender for me, and if you are wise, mortal, you will realize how fortunate you are to have my gratitude."

"I am astounded by your . . . generosity," Doyati said. "And by your assumption that all my people and I have done, the work of a hundred years, we have done for you. And I am curious, Banris Oathbreaker. What favor will you do me?"

Banris said, "While I like not your tone, I will forgive the rashness of youth. This time. Step down from that perch you cannot hold, boy, and concede it to me peacefully, and spare yourself a slow and ugly death."

"For a short and painless one, I would guess?" Doyati asked. "You stand in *my* kaidom, half-mortal monster, surrounded by my people, and you have seen how your kind end. You should worry that I don't like *your* tone."

"Unfortunately for you," Banris said, "I brought an army. And yours seems to have run away. So I will have my wife and children." And as he said that, he looked at my parents, my sibs, and me.

He must have had the priest marry him to Mama after Danrith and I ran away that night.

Beside me, Dan quivered with rage. "You are not married to her. Papa still lives."

"Even if I did not," Papa said, his voice calmer than Dan's, but with an edge to it I had rarely ever heard, "the marriage would not be valid, because I lived while it was spoken."

I did not see our priest, but I heard his voice. "I declare the marriage of Seldihara of Far Harbor to Banris of Greathaven annulled."

Banris laughed. "I am kai-lord of Arrienda by force of arms, and what I declare as law will be law. I will have my wife and children. Now." With a gesture of his hand, the ghost warriors began marching toward my family and me.

Doyati did not move, but his voice took on the silken,

musical tones of a nightling. "This is the City of the Moon — did you know that, Banris? Even when the moon's light is thin and weak outside the gates, within our walls it holds the full power it has at its peak."

Doyati waved a hand, and colored light flew from his fingertips, spinning off in countless sparkling bubbles. I was reminded, forcibly and shockingly, of that towering statue in the wizard's quarters into which Danrith, Yarri, and I had stumbled, and from which we had fled in such a hurry. Older, Doyati would have looked like the wizard on the tapestry and much like the statue itself.

The bubbles scattered along the front line of Banris's moving warriors, floating down onto them. Wherever one landed, that ghost blinked out of existence. I could not see how they were guided, but they did not hit a living creature, and they did not miss one of the marching dead. The air filled with bubbles and emptied of ghosts.

"You had an army?" Doyati asked. "I don't see it."

Banris did not laugh.

"I see mangy curs, and an unreliable woman whose many agendas you do not know, and a harper whose fingers have forgotten how to play," Doyati added.

I looked at the huntress, whose dogs had begun snapping at the bubbles that began to brush against them, and yipping when any bare skin came into contact with the tiny floating orbs. I saw fur flying and fur falling out. They were beginning to snap at one another, too, and those around them, including their mistress.

She was occupied, too. The bubbles swarmed around her, and everywhere they touched her, she tarnished, her silver skin turning black and coarse.

On the other side of Banris, the harper fought to keep the bubbles from his silver strings, but to no avail. Several bubbles had collected on a string, and it snapped with terrifying force, adding bleeding cuts on his face and hands to those already there.

Banris looked at the chaos around him, his face growing redder.

Doyati said, "You might do well to consider that all you have heard about me might not be true. That perhaps I found it useful for Letrin to hear from an honest child that I had no magic, that I was old and dying. That perhaps the flesh I wore was simply a disguise donned to get me close to the kai-lord with a negligible guard over me." He smiled gently. "And you might do well to remember that you are a man whose entire fighting force, from fickle huntress and sacred hounds to mighty-but-dead warriors from a revered past, were beaten by bubbles. Bubbles, Banris."

"There are more roads than moonroads," Banris said. "There are more ways to immortality than this one. You will face me again on my ground, with an army that will not scatter at your feeble magic. The sun outshines the moon, and beneath its burning light, you and your inconstant kind will topple."

Then he looked at me — just at me — and said, "Sleep lightly, dear Gennadara. You alone, changed as you are, would be a sacrifice that would bring me all I desire. And I know where you live."

From beneath his kai-lord robes, Banris pulled a vial of taandu essence — but not essence of a light gold or the color of pale straw. This was as dark a brown as walnut dye. He pulled the stopper, put the vial to his lips, and drank deeply.

I heard gasps from all around the great hall. He had drunk an entire vial of night taandu essence, when drinking a single drop would have changed him beyond recognition.

An aura of immense power surrounded him, but it was an energy that shed darkness the way the sun and the moon shed light.

He began to change, to grow taller and wider, to add the bulk of massive muscles to a stretching frame. He grinned at me and his teeth grew sharper as I watched, becoming long and pointed, daggerlike and hideous. His eyes sank into deep sockets and began to gleam with their own light; his jaw jutted forward. "My servants and I *all* know where you live," he said again.

Bard and huntress looked at him with loathing, but offered no argument.

"Sweet dreams," he said, and he, the huntress, the dogs, and the bard blinked out of existence as if they had never been.

I'd seen that sort of exit once before. On that same day, even, when the old woman vanished.

I wondered what it meant.

Chapter 17
Sunrider

Yarri, Dan, and I huddled in a niche behind the throne and the stands where the Highborn had sat, and we kept our voices low. Doyati, Oesari, Oerin, my father and mother, some of the village elders, a handful of Highborn, several slaves, and a smattering of others not even Yarri could identify were having a sort of impromptu war council in the middle of the arena.

Our council was nothing like theirs.

"What happened to you?" I demanded. "I was terrified that the cat had betrayed us all, that Letrin would murder you both before I could even get here. . . ."

"We weren't here," Dan said. "The cat took both of us to . . ." He faltered and he and Yarri gave each other furtive looks.

"The tapestry room," she finished for him. "Can't talk about it."

"Where the clothes were," I said, looking at the sun-blazoned tunic Dan wore, and the sun-and-moon-patterned shift Yarri wore under my sweater. "And the . . . statue?"

I held up an arm, mimicking the pose of the terrifying wizard statue that had stood in the center of the library of magic. Both of them nodded.

"What we did — what we fought for — it isn't just about saving Mama and Papa," Dan told me. "Or killing Letrin." He sat on his knees and rocked back and forth, clearly excited. "The nightlings, Mama and Papa, and the others who were part of the conspiracy all thought it was about Letrin — the cat told us that, from everything they could figure out, Kai-Lord Letrin would declare war on humanity and attempt to erase all humans, leading the other kaidoms in a battle to destroy us down to the last child."

Yarri jumped in. "They didn't know what was going to happen. They just had a few clues, a couple of items the audiomaerist could see would be important, a few hints of how the future might run. Nothing specific. But they knew if the Sunrider could be found, then humanity might be saved, the enslaved nightlings of Arrienda freed, and perhaps even the moonroads closed."

Dan nodded. "But there were tests the Sunrider had to pass, and all the other candidates they tried —"

Exasperated, I interrupted. "Mama and Papa knew *we* were to be tried?"

Yarri said, "Of course not. They intended to overthrow Letrin, restore Doyati to the throne, and bring a real and fair peace to nightlings and dayfolk. They never planned for you to be involved."

"Oh. Well, who picked us then?" I muttered, and even in my own ears, I sounded grumpy. I'd been left out of so much, everyone else knew more than I did, and I didn't like it at all.

"*You* did," Yarri said. "When you decided to save your mother's life."

"Anyway." Dan was determined to continue. "The nightlings sought out all sorts of likely candidates, people who had good reason to take Letrin's deal to find Doyati and bring him back to Arrienda. . . ."

I interrupted again. "Why didn't Doyati just come on his own? He had the magic. He had most of Arrienda behind him."

"Fortune-tellers," Yarri said. "They told the conspirators that if Doyati tried to reclaim his throne without the Sunrider at his side, he would die, and all that the humans and enslaved nightlings had worked together for would be lost."

Right. Fortune-tellers. I didn't like the way this was shaping up.

Dan glared at me. "*Anyway,*" he said with emphasis, "all of their candidates — hunters, master craftsmen, trappers, farmers, yihannis, priests — they all failed. No matter how promising they looked, no matter how courageous or pious or honest or clever, something would trip them up, and they would end up either trying to betray Doyati or dead from some unanticipated danger."

"And Doyati was running out of time," I said, nodding, envisioning the rightful kai-lord of Arrienda sitting in that horrible mud-mound hovel, waiting year after year for the Sunrider who would travel with him and bring him to his throne.

Both Danrith and Yarri were shaking their heads. "Doyati had nearly forever," Yarri said. "He's half nightling, half dayfolk, and he inherited the powers of moon and sun, and learned how to use them at his mother's knee. He can walk freely in both worlds, and what the nightling's long life cannot offer him, the sun magic of dayfolk wizards can."

"He wasn't old and dying?" I asked.

"That was his disguise," Yarri said. "The cat said you had to believe, or Letrin would never believe."

"The problem was us, Genna," Dan said. "Humankind. We're almost gone from the world. Here in Aeiring, there are some large towns run by maraeshes, and small towns and villages run by caers, but that was because Letrin had a huge business in daylight taandu essence and needed humans to manufacture it. In most of the rest of the lands surrounding nightling kaidoms, humans have been killed off as dangerous animals. The story is the same across the seas. The cat says there are tiny pockets where humans hang on, but most of the world has been taken over by nightlings, Flowers, taandu monsters, and moonroaders who have found their way here."

"The cat told you all of this?"

"He's not *really* a cat," Dan told me, all earnest and sincere.

"You don't say."

He didn't seem to notice my sarcasm.

"So I passed all the tests —"

"There were only two," Yarri said. "That you remain steadfast in your purpose, and that you and Doyati travel together and survive to face Letrin together."

"Not so simple." I looked out from our hiding place to the powerful and the necessary who gathered around Doyati, worshipful moths before their long-awaited flame. "And in the end, not so important, either. Doyati told me there was supposed to be some long, drawn-out war between Doyati and his allies, and Letrin and his. But now Letrin is dead. So they aren't going to need me. So what happens next?"

"I don't know," Dan said.

"Me, neither." Yarri frowned in the direction of the arguing adults. "I don't think anybody knows."

The villagers of Hillrush did not go home that night. Everyone stayed on as guests of the Arriendans and were gifted with fine clothes and beautiful jewels and books and other treasures, and all stayed in Doyati's palace with Oesari and Oerin, Yarri and her family, and some of the loyalists who had been part of the plot that had restored Doyati to his throne.

We feasted in the magnificent dining hall where Letrin had given his feast for Dan and me, before he made the bargain that had set Yarri, my brother, and me on our long, terrifying journey.

This time, Dan and I got to eat the food. It tasted even better than it had smelled, better than I had imagined, and considering I had been eating beans and bitter greens that night, my imagination had been sharpened to a razor's edge. Yet I would have been happier under my family's roof, sharing with them a rasher of bacon, buttered cabbage, and morning potatoes.

My family looked like human royalty. Like the kings and queens of old, my brother said, with the authority of his ghost, who had *known* the kings and queens of old. But we all spoke in low tones, and looked around anxiously, watching doors with nervous glances that we tried not to make too obvious. The joy for Doyati's return was genuine. Still, a pall hung over the night.

Doyati sat at the head of the table, dressed in the robes of a kai-lord. They fit him well, and his people kept coming up to him and kissing his hand. But if everyone else in the room rejoiced, he did not. Every time he looked at me, I saw a sadness in his face that nearly broke my heart. I wondered if he were thinking of his mother. Perhaps of how much she would have loved to see him in his rightful place as the new kai-lord.

He had rescued his people from a tyrant. I thought she would have been proud.

But after everyone from my village, and all of Yarri's family, and all of Doyati's allies had eaten and drunk our fill from what seemed to me an endless stream of wondrous foods and drinks, Doyati rose.

"I would speak," he said.

The room hushed.

"More times than we wish to remember, those of you who wished to restore the throne to me rose up against Letrin, found a new messenger to come for me — one who fit the description of the Sunrider spelled out for us by the fortune-tellers — and prepared for the battle we would face against Letrin."

Murmurs of agreement rippled through the dining hall.

"Each time, those messengers played us false, fell for Letrin's temptations, fell under the spell of the moonroads, died, or failed in some other fashion, and proved they were not the Sunrider, and everything we fought for came to naught."

The murmurs grew louder, the nodding heads more vehement.

"This last time alone, the task fell upon the slender shoulders of a girl who did not think she was worthy of it, who did not seek personal gain, and who was not seduced by Letrin's offers of power or wealth or anything else her heart might desire."

He smiled at me again, and this time I felt my face go hot as blood rushed to my cheeks.

"She fought for us out of love — love of her family, her people, and their way of life, and even for our kind through her friend, the slave girl Yarri — and not for treasures or power. And she fought for us out of duty, the duty of the eldest child to parents and sibs, the duty of the one who can fight to those who cannot, the duty of the one who sees danger to those who wrongly believe themselves safe. Because of her love and her sense of duty, Letrin could not tempt her with his lies and could not chase her away with his threats. Nor did the unexpected dangers of the road, and she faced *many*, stop her." He paused and hung his head and stared down at his hands, and I saw his cheeks redden.

I tried not to stare at him. He was so handsome, and young again. The light on his hair made the black of it shine blue. I knew he was not for me. But I had held his hand. And he had smiled at me. I kept seeing his smile, and it made my stomach feel funny. What I knew and what my racing, skittering heart knew were two different things.

I looked away from him, realizing that I was staring, and that if I didn't stop, he might catch me, and he might know what I was thinking. I thought I would die of shame if he found out.

He said, "We have seen the power of love and duty, and we celebrate it tonight in this feast. Gennadara, Sunrider, has won us our freedom.

"But there is more now. So it is about duty and love that I wish to speak on my own behalf. And yours." He sighed as one who bore the weight of worlds upon his shoulders, and in spite of my embarrassment, I looked at him again. His eyes were closed, his expression was close to grief. "You fought to restore me to my family's throne, in the hopes that I could be the kai-lord that my grandfather had been, and my father should have had the opportunity to be.

"I am not the man my father was, the one my mother described with such devotion. I was not made to rule, or if I was, years of being both hunted and hunter in the twisted lands reached only by moonroads changed me. I have walked the moonroads my whole life, and they have shaped me . . . not always for the better."

All the little noises in the room — the sounds of chewing, the whispered comments, the rustling of napkins, and the rattling of cutlery — faded. I looked from person to person, and saw everyone around me had turned to face him. All eyes were directed at Doyati.

"I will not take the kai-lord's throne. I am not suitable for it, nor it for me. And both love and duty tug me toward the danger that comes."

Around the huge room, nightlings leapt from their chairs, protesting with words and gestures — from dropping to their knees to plead with Doyati to waving clenched fists in anger — that Doyati and none other must take the throne. That he and he alone carried the sacred kai blood.

Doyati shook his head. "I am no longer the only son or the last descendant. Behold Oesari, who was wife to my father's brother, renewed to life, healthy and young, and at her side her son, Oerin, also a firstborn son and full-blooded heir. Oerin is too young to rule alone, but he is old enough to rule with Oesari to stand for him and advise him as Mother-of-Kai. Oesari may also take a husband in order to have other children, should she choose. And because she is Mother-of-Kai, should she desire at any time to name these children full siblings of Oerin, they will be able to assume the throne if for any reason Oerin cannot." Doyati shoved his hair back from his face with a gesture of exhaustion. Or perhaps frustration. "I spoke with them before speaking with you, and made them understand the need. They have agreed that this must be done, and they have agreed to bear this burden."

Doyati said, "As acting kai-lord, I bid you all stand, as witnesses to my binding declaration."

From the back of the room, someone said, "Don't do this thing. Take your rightful place."

Doyati shook his head. As everyone stood, he raised his right hand and said, "You loved Oesari and Oerin as you loved my father. Or my mother. Or, though you had never met me, me. In favor of these, my uncle's family, both of whom those of you who are adults truly know, I relinquish my claim to the throne, both now and forever, without clause or exception, and I declare that the lawful blood of kai-lords now flows from Oesari and Oerin to their heirs, consorts, and designees. And I declare my rightful place as walker of the moonroads and guardian from afar of my people and those other peoples who wish my people well." He nodded to both nightlings and humans in the crowd. "In this, my first and last act as kai-lord, I compel you to witness and confirm what I have declared."

Ragged voices said, "We witness and confirm." I heard sobbing and hurt, angry whispers. But at the same time, I saw a line forming, and nightlings bending to kiss the hand of Oesari and to bow to young Oerin.

I was happy for Letrin's wife and child, restored to life and returned to their places.

But I shivered at Doyati's mention of trouble to come. That trouble felt to me like it had my name on it.

After the meal and Doyati's surprise, my family retired to the quarters we had been given for the night.

It was there that Doyati came, and there where he spoke first to my father, in private. Then, he and Danrith and Mama and Papa and I sat down. A fire flickered in a fireplace. We settled onto comfortable cushions, and all the while, on my parents' faces and Doyati's and my brother's, I saw the same anxiety and worry and dread I felt in my belly.

My father turned to me. "You did well, Gennadara. Neither your mother nor I have had a chance before now to tell you how proud we are of you."

"And Danrith," I said.

"We've been able to talk with him. We told him."

"Oh."

My mother said, "I'm not ready for you to grow up yet."

"I won't be old enough to attempt my trial for two more years," I said, not liking the way this was going. "And I had thought to delay it a bit."

"You and your brother passed more trials than any children in the village since . . ." My father stared down at his hands. "It doesn't matter. Danrith could waive his trial today if I chose to let him."

Danrith looked enchanted by that idea.

"I do not so choose," Papa said, and Dan's face fell.

"But then why — ?"

My father cut my question short with a shake of his head.

"Your trial is waived," he told me. "You are now given the privileges and rights of adulthood, and you are now and forevermore will be a full and voting citizen of the village of Hillrush."

I sat back and gasped. I was not ready for such a thing. I did not want marriage proposals, dowry talks, walks along the river with earnest young men or earnest old men who wished to know if I would like goats or sheep or perhaps an orchard as a wedding gift. I had watched girls older than me who had passed their trials suddenly inundated by such proposals.

I was not ready.

But my father was not done, either. "Your future will not be as we'd thought, Genna. You will not become a yihanni. We will not be entertaining proposals for your marriage from villages that need a yihanni." He closed his eyes tight, and I saw his hands knot into fists. "You will not be traveling home with us."

I stared from Papa to Mama and saw both of them blinking back tears. And I exchanged glances with Dan, who looked as if they had dropped rocks on his head.

And then I returned my gaze to Doyati, who had been silent until now.

His face was flushed, and he bit his lip. "You will be staying in Arrienda, at least for a while," he said. "Here you will receive the training in magic that the Sunrider will have to have."

"You said the nightlings no longer needed a Sunrider," I protested. "You said Letrin was dead, and the battle was over before it began."

"One of the fortune-tellers — one you know — came to me after the . . . events in the arena," he said. "She is the one who set us to looking for the Sunrider long before you were born. She said the Sunrider would be the one to unite the magics of moon and sun for the good of all, and lead the fight to throw down the immortal. We thought — even *she* thought — that the immortal she meant was Letrin."

She. The fortune-teller. The *audiomaerist.* The woman I had saved. The woman who had . . . changed.

I realized her signs had been foretelling Banris. Maybe drinking the dark taandu essence had done more than make him the monster on the outside that he'd already been on the inside. Maybe it had made him immortal — or nearly immortal — as well.

"What will I do?" I asked.

Doyati said, "We don't know. No one knows. She said you were to be taught everything of moon magic. And everything of sun magic — the Old Magic, which has been forbidden to your people since the days of kings. What you will make of that, not even she can guess."

"What if I want to go home? What if I don't want to be Sunrider?"

My father said, so softly I could barely hear him, "Banris knows where you live."

"*She* tracked the danger to you — and to all of us if you fall into his hands — and it is real," Doyati said. "We do not know how, but he could fulfill his bargain for immortality by sacrificing you alone."

So he was not yet immortal. Well, that was good to know. Sort of.

"You've changed, Genna," Mama said. "You're different."

I had lived for a few days on the moonroads and in

the nightworlds that fed from them. But I didn't feel different.

And everything I loved would be back in Hillrush, restored to the way it had been before Banris betrayed us all. My friends, my family, my life — all there.

Yet I, who had fought so hard to see it restored, dared not go home.

"Will you come visit me?" I was swallowing back tears as hard as I could.

They hugged me and held me close, and we cried together until we had no more tears to cry.

Doyati cleared his throat at last, and we all turned to look at him.

"The cat will stay with you," he told me. "And your family may stay here as long as they like and may return as often as they like." He gave me a tentative smile. "When they are not visiting, you and I will study together, for as you are Sunrider, so I am Moonspinner, or at least this is what *she* tells me. Yarri will be with us. And your friend Catri has been given dispensation from her parents to study with you as well, though you must agree to be her chaperone."

Catri was staying? "What about Danrith?" I asked. The day Dan and I set out to get taandu sap for Mama, I would have thought I would never want to spend a minute more with him than I had to.

So the moonroads *had* changed me.

"He can visit," Papa said firmly. "But he is to be the next caer of Hillrush, and he has not finished his training."

I caught a look in Dan's eye that was not the look of an obedient son. It was, instead, the look of a boy who had been on the moonroads and who had started to hear their call. I said nothing, and he said nothing, but we gave each other the smallest of nods. The future had not yet been decided for either of us, those nods said.

I said, "If I am truly an adult today, then I would like to stand and offer a *mirid* for all of us."

My father nodded and stood, and the rest of us stood, too.

I thought for a moment, needing the right words. A mirid is an important thing. It echoes in places we cannot imagine, and falls on ears we do not know.

I changed an old and well-known mirid just a little. "May we see our paths clearly, may we follow them truly, and may the roads we walk always bring us back together safely from wherever we have wandered, to wherever we dare call home."

"As said, so done," my parents both said. Doyati echoed them. Dan simply nodded.

I turned and caught Doyati watching me, a small, private smile on his face. His cheeks flushed and he averted his eyes.

The future, I thought, was not what I had been led all my life to believe it would be. But it was beginning to call to me with the same tug I felt from the moonroads.

"As said, so done," I whispered and willingly stepped onto the path that would take me toward it.

The battle between nightlings and humans continues in . . .

Turn the page for a sneak peek!

from

The Silver Door

MOON & SUN

"Genna . . ."

"Genna, we're waiting for you. . . ."

"We've missed you. . . ."

"We're waiting for you. . . ."

Soft and sweet, the voices calling me, leading me toward them. I could smell the voices, faint as spring violets, promising as apple blossoms. I could taste them like rain on the tip of my tongue. They were not friends, but waiting to be friends. We did not know one another, but we knew we wanted to.

I moved toward them, toward radiant silver light from my sad and lonely place in darkness. They were waiting, and I was going to them as quickly as I could.

The curving rain sill on the inside of the glass-and-metal doors snagged my bare toe and pitched me face forward out those doors and on to rough-cut granite.

I woke falling, and there are not many worse ways to wake — with the ground coming up fast, not knowing what's happening, not remembering where you are, with no idea how you got there, and to a bewildering sense of loss. I'd been . . . somewhere wonderful, my still-half-dreaming self insisted. Doing something amazing.

I hit the ground hard, but not as hard as I would have had my eyes still been closed, had I still been sound asleep. I managed to catch myself just enough to keep my face from slamming into the stone pavers. Barely. The shock of the crash slammed through my hands and arms and shoulders, through my back, up and down my spine, and the pain in my knees and right toe lit me up like a torch set to flames. I shrieked with the pain and the surprise.

Once. Only once. And then the hunger caught me.

A sliver of moonlight lay like an arrow shot across my outstretched arms. Moonlight. Unaware of what I was doing, I pulled myself forward and let it bathe my face, and the hunger inside of me jumped and stirred and grew. The moon, nearly full, hung overhead, and when I looked right at it, I caught my breath and my heart raced.

The moon. The moon — my beacon, my friend — shone full and fat, high in the sky, and it surrounded me with the scents of flowers that had been in my dream, and sang to me a song my heart knew. The moonroads called to me. They were in my blood, and my blood was on them; when I listened, I could hear them coming to me; I could smell them even if I could not yet see them.

The moon wanted me. It sent not-yet-friends racing in my direction. I'd missed the moon. I'd missed the roads. I simply hadn't known it.

Beneath the ground in Arrienda, there had been no moon, no moonroads, and no temptation; I had, perhaps, felt an edge of restlessness. But I had forgotten the sharp yearning, the ache to step into the wildness borne by the flickering lights and let it carry me someplace new. I had forgotten the hunger in my heart that cried out as I stood there in the darkness, bathed in silvery light.

I did not have to call the roads. In my sleep, they had found me, and needing me as much as I needed them, they were coming. Some of them — I could feel them reaching for me — some of them were as hungry as I was.

I stood, dressed only in the thin linen underdress and the underthings I slept in, bare-footed, my braid heavy between my shoulder blades, and I spread my arms to embrace the moonlight. I lifted my face and closed my eyes to better feel it against my skin.

I was lost in the hunger of the roads, lost in the nameless desire that knotted my gut and made my heart race. Lost — and glad to be lost.

And have you not yet learned that the roads which hunger for you are not the roads you want?

I jumped and shrieked at the mocking voice inside my head, and turned around in circles. And there he was.

The cat.

Gray and reddish-brown with swirling black stripes and neat white fur on chin and belly and all four paws. He sat out of the moonlight, along the top of a decorative wall, watching me with eyes that reflected bright green.

I would have thought you'd learned that lesson, he said inside my head.

The cat. At that moment, I was torn between being grateful for his presence and frustrated that he had caught me.

The moonroads called. They called, and I needed to feel them again, to step on to them, to drink in their magic. The moonroads felt like a part of me that had been ripped from me, and that I had just miraculously won back — and he was trying take them away again.

I tasted them on my skin and the tip of my tongue, I

smelled them, I felt them, I drank them.

"Everyone thinks you're dead," the cat said.

I knew this. But talking made it harder to focus on the moonroads.

"You have to step inside, Genna. The roads that want you could be the roads that long to take you to those who wish to kill you. Who tried to kill you."

"You said the moonroads aren't sun wizard magic," I said. "That the sun wizards didn't use them."

"That's right."

"A sun wizard tried to kill us," I said.

The cat laughed. He should never laugh, haughty know-it-all that he is. It makes me want to pull his whiskers out. "The sun wizards are long dead and gone."

"But the dragon smelled sun wizard magic on the note that led us to Fallowhalls and to him."

The cat tipped his head. "Come here. Show me the note."

If I went to him, I'd have to step out of the moonlight and into the shadows. I didn't want to.

I said, "The note is in the pocket of my skirt. Which is hanging beside my bed, still damp."

"You really want to step on to the moonroads wearing

nothing but your underthings? Without even shoes on your feet? You do remember some of the places the roads took you, don't you?"

I did. Lands of ice and snow. Lands of steaming, red-glowing rock. Lands with sharp grass and sharp rocks and deep mud.

Not places to wander without shoes or clothes. Not places to step into unprepared. Or alone.

I took a step toward him.

Good girl, he said softly, straight into my thoughts. *One step at a time.*

The moonroads called to him, too. And he had been walking them for a very long time. He said the call got stronger the more you walked them. I believed him.

I took another step. . . .

A NOTE FROM THE AUTHOR

I never intended to be a writer when I was a kid. I was pretty sure I was going to be a famous artist. And when I got my first guitar at the age of fifteen, I decided I'd also be a famous musician.

I actually gave both a shot, in between working at a newspaper and working at McDonald's and eventually becoming an RN. I discovered that, though I liked to draw, I didn't like to draw for money. And though I loved to sing and play guitar, I simply wasn't good enough.

Some dreams change, and some fade away when you actually try them and discover they aren't what you thought they would be, or could be.

But new dreams wait. For me, writing was a new dream. I didn't go looking for it. It found me, and it's a dream — and a reality — that has only gotten better with time.

For Genna, the narrator of the Moon & Sun stories, the lifelong dream she had of becoming a yihanni like her mother got lost when men and monsters alike told her she was the Sunrider. Now she's trying to understand her new path, and to discover if anywhere in the life of a Sunrider there's a dream that she can catch and hold . . . and make come true.

Dare to dream. Dare to chase the dreams you love.

—Holly Lisle

ABOUT THE AUTHOR

Holly Lisle has written many acclaimed novels for adults; *The Ruby Key* was her first book for children. She is also the author of *The Silver Door*. Holly lives in the Deep South with her family.